THIS WIDE NIGHT

THIS
WIDE
NIGHT

SARVAT HASIN

PENGUIN

HAMISH HAMILTON

USA | Canada | UK | Ireland | Australia
New Zealand | India | South Africa | China

Hamish Hamilton is part of the Penguin Random House group of companies
whose addresses can be found at global.penguinrandomhouse.com

Published by Penguin Random House India Pvt. Ltd
7th Floor, Infinity Tower C, DLF Cyber City,
Gurgaon 122 002, Haryana, India

First published in Hamish Hamilton by Penguin Random House India 2016

Copyright © Sarvat Hasin 2016

ISBN 9780670089284

For sale in the Indian Subcontinent only

Typeset in Adobe Caslon Pro by Manipal Digital Systems, Manipal
Printed at Thomson Press India Ltd, New Delhi

www.penguinbooksindia.com

To my grandmother
Nasrat Agha,
and to
51.7519°N, 1.2578°W

Contents

Contents

Prologue

Some strange things were happening in the house. Outside, the tides were rising and the city seemed even farther away.

Those days, I was the only one who left the island. I brought back cigars for the Captain and presents for my wife and her sisters but they sat untouched. Books and lipstick and bangles, wrapped in gold foil. Just as the dresser in our bedroom was cluttered with paints instead of make-up, still boxed up from when we packed them back in Paris. The easel bound in brown paper and string rested against the door of our bathroom. I saw the soft ghost of it in the mirror every morning when I shaved. Objects in this house had a peculiar stillness to them. Things brought back last week felt as if they'd been left here for a hundred years. Flowers rotted in their vases, fruit stank up the kitchen.

The Captain, in his lonely room down the corridor from us, had stopped making full sentences a few weeks ago. Communication was carried out through a series of hand gestures and mumbled words. He stayed in his room most of the time, with a small bell at his elbow. The leather-backed armchair he sat in came from their old house in Karachi. He had not looked so small in it then. Now, the imposing breadth of it swallowed his shoulders, his thin face and hollowed-out eyes. Now, the dull, bronze clack of the bell in the middle of the night, followed by the scurrying footsteps of a manservant to help him walk.

In the evenings when I got back from work I would sit with him. Together we read Manto and Hemingway. We worked our way through the poorly assembled shelves. I probably took more comfort in this exercise than he did. He picked out the book with the end of his cane and I read, turning the pages slowly while his unblinking eyes watched my lips. He never asked me for anything, even a hand to go to the bathroom. He chose to wait till I left the room, the quiet indignity of his helplessness trailing me like a stray dog. And so it continued, small chinks in our long chain of days.

Back in Karachi, people would ask me about him. Men whose fathers served in the war with him offered to send gifts or to come over. I would have liked to see them do it, these young moustachioed boys with whiskey and sweets under their arm coming to see the once great captain, only to find him entombed in his study, voice like a cat walking over shards of glass. I pictured their horror, the slack-jawed faces, for a full minute before I said no.

Nobody asked about the girls. Not even those boys who knew them from their school days, brothers of their friends, who fell in love with one sister or the other from a distance. They were entirely lost to the city. Dada told me he could hardly believe how much I'd changed since my marriage. You're a man now, he said as if he was wary of me.

We were all harder than we had been before. Now I knew how little we heard of the things people said about our families when our backs were turned. People talked about the trouble with the Malik family and the slow lightning that ran through them. They said it began with their mother's death, but they were wrong. It was bad luck for the Maliks from the start. Bad luck to have a houseful of daughters. Bad luck to have all that dark hair, long and loose that the djinns love so much. Bad luck for a father of all those girls.

On good days, the house was quiet. I could hear the sea singing outside our bedroom window. Since we came to the island, I had come to love the swish of water more than I ever knew how to in the city. I had not lived in Karachi for some years, and when I was a boy, beach trips were few and far in between. The vicious waves, the sand and the camels lined along the coast were never things I particularly enjoyed. In the summers most of my friends would go to beach huts, lower boats off the coast and hunt for crabs while I stayed home. Yet now, the swaying of the boat felt steady beneath my feet.

On good days it was quiet but on bad days everything else was blocked out by the sounds of the house, the girls furious in their footsteps, their voices buzzing around each other—bees trapped in a glass jar. I walked into a room and their conversations dropped to the floorboards the way heavy books do, kicking up dust. Strange to think that I was once part of their secrets. Now, they eyed me the way they would an enemy. The bright restlessness that infected their bones used to be something I saw only in their eyes, a kinship between us. There was something glorious about them, untethered and dark.

Everything that I remembered about them from before the island came to me through a haze of light. I built memories from skeletons. I thought I could find their secrets in our shared history, but I'd been wrong all along. There was nothing I could do and people had been telling me that for as long as I could remember. I would go back to my offices and shirt sleeves, to breakfasts and evenings and ordinary lives. I could not turn back time. All I wanted was to learn what had happened to the Malik sisters.

BOOK ONE

I.

They lived across the road from me for fifteen years without us ever having a conversation, something that seems impossible to me now. I'd built up the Malik sisters in my head before I really knew them. The combination of being at a boys' school and Dada's dislike for other people meant that these were the only real girls I ever saw. From the window in my bedroom, you could look through the trees and into their garden. I learned valuable things about the girls: how Maria played cards every evening with her mother, or that Ayesha always read and Bina sewed, and that the littlest, Leila, liked to draw.

I knew that their father, a navy captain whose name was on the silver plaque outside their gate, spent most of his time away from home. I saw Maria in the city sometimes, at the library or buying groceries when I stopped at the shops after school. Even their shopping was a mystery to me. I watched her pay for rosewater and talcum powder, unable to comprehend their uses. In the conversations we conducted in my head, they told me their secrets and though I watched them for years—on my way to school in the morning with their socks rolled up to their knees, backpacks sitting by them on the curb as they waited for the van—I only scratched the surface of their world.

As things went in this city, our lives first came together at a party. It was my chacha's house, a celebration for his daughter's wedding. I hated these things but I guess the bride must have been a friend of the girls because I found Ayesha in the study. Her shoes were up on the coffee table. She was curled up in one of the armchairs, reading a newspaper.

I didn't know there'd be dancing, she said when I came into the room, You can't really dance in one of these. She didn't seem particularly sorry about this. Her best sari, dark green silk and braided in silver that she had spilled Coca-Cola on at some earlier evening and was now pinned to her blouse to keep the stain out of sight. Her ankles were twisted one over the other because it was wrapped too tight about her knees, wedging them into narrow angles and restricting how she moved.

What's your excuse, she said, looking me up and down.

I usually hide in here at parties, I said, I don't know many of Amira's friends.

Am I stealing your secret place? I'll go.

Stay. I walked over to where she was sitting and pulled out a footstool from behind the desk. It's nice to have company.

She grinned. I thought, she said, The point of a place like this was to get away from company.

I waved a hand toward the long glass windows. The lights in the study were switched off but outside the gardens were strung through with lights and we were in the half dark. It was easy to watch them without being seen. This was why I always came here, even when I was smaller. I'd stuff my pockets with patties and sneak them in here, the flaky crust sticking to my trousers as I sat on the vinyl sofas and watched the guests; my own personal movie. It was why I always knew things before the rest of the family—who was going to get married or who was making more money, the rustle of secrets coming through coded body language, the way a girl put her hand on a man's wrist if she decided he would do.

My sister went to school with Amira, she told me, She's the one in the blue.

She got up and joined me by the window. We picked out her sister in the crowd, her black hair draped over her shoulders, the blue and gold of her kurta peeking through like the night sky.

She's very beautiful, I said.

Everybody says that, Ayesha said. She leaned back and tucked her shoulders against the window pane. That Maria's the pretty one, which is crazy of course because we all look sort of the same I guess—just different degrees of pretty.

She didn't say it like she was fishing for a compliment but then again, I knew nothing about girls or about compliments. She was right though—they did look very similar. From a distance they blurred, even with the years between them. In a flash it was difficult to pick them apart, but here I saw that Ayesha was a little taller than her sisters, her long collarbone jutting out differently as if maybe she and Maria had the same bones only put together differently. When I turned to face her properly she was watching me again. She bit the bottom of her lip.

It feels strange to be asking this, she said, But you're the boy from next door aren't you?

I suppose I am, I said, wondering if I should shake her hand. I'm Jimmy.

Jimmy, she said smiling all over again, You know we've always wondered about you. We used to give you new names in our head—and of course stories about what was happening to you and where you were from.

People had been telling stories about me all my life. This was not unusual, it was just how things were when your parents were dead. My mother was the real draw, the scandal behind the red curtain. Rumours about her found their way back to me always, off what little people knew of her; in these stories, she could be anything. They knew she wasn't from here and that she'd snatched up my father when he was working abroad, and from this they built their fantasies. A dancer or a woman of the night.

I dropped my head to one side and watched Ayesha shrug and move her shoulder under the tightly pinned sari. Most of these stories I had caught listening in on other people's conversations or having them played back to me on the school ground during scuffles. No one had ever sat with me this way before and told me what they were saying about me.

You know, she said leaning her head forward, We heard a rumour back then that you were half Italian.

I smiled. That's close but it isn't true.

Well you've always seemed kind of exotic, she said.

I stood there for a dumb minute, watching her mouth pull up into a grin. She had lipstick on, some of which had smeared off the right corner of her lip and eased into the curve of her cheek. Years later I would still remember that crease of pink in her dimple, when Ayesha stopped wearing make-up and later still when she stopped smiling. I wished then that I knew more about girls, enough to be charming or to even remember what an Italian accent sounded like. Instead I told her I knew the way to the kitchen and could steal us some dinner without having to brave the crowds, an idea she liked enough to follow me softly through the dark corridors.

I led her by the hand both there and back, as we could see almost nothing. She hadn't put her heels back on so I could hear the soft thud of bare feet behind me and I walked through the house as I knew it. Her skin alive against my own: foreign territory.

In the kitchen I rubbed my palm frantically against the leg of my trouser in case it was clammy, watching as she piled her plate, rooting through the biryani for legs of chicken and adding a dollop of ice cream to the side of the plate. I was impressed by her appetite, how she balanced the plate in her hand and a bottle of Coca-Cola under her elbow. Soon we were cross-legged, back on the floor of the study, saluting Chacha's cook.

So no Italian mother then, she asked.

Not even a little. Though I think it's where my parents had their honeymoon.

I would kill to live in Italy, she said, through a mouthful of sheermal.

Honestly kill?

Honestly. Kill any of those, she said pointing out the window with her fork. Well the ones I don't know and obviously not my sister.

Just for Italy.

Rome, she corrected. I'd only break an arm for one of the others. Florence or wherever. You ever been?

I considered this.

You going to kill me if I say yes? I asked.

She laughed. No.

Well yes. But only when I was very young—maybe six months or something. My parents took me everywhere. Dada says my mother would just put me in her handbag and zip off around the world. He claims she left me in a bathroom stall to go dancing, once.

It was fun to tell these stories to a girl like that, a girl whose face lit up, a street parade. Talking about my parents had a gossipy feel to it. They walked through my head, more silver screen gods than people I'd known. It wasn't that I didn't like the idea of them only that their death was bigger than our lives together had been.

Do you think it's true?

Well he never really liked my mother so it's hard to say.

Mmm, she clicked through her teeth, How old were you when they passed?

I put my shoulders up. Six maybe, I said.

Sorry, she said, We probably should have guessed that.

What?

That way I wouldn't have asked. I'm always asking the wrong things you know—Maria didn't even want to bring me with her tonight.

No?

Not even a little. Ma told her she had to or we couldn't go. She didn't want one of those boys who's always around Maria, giving her a lift home late at night. So, is it just you and your grandfather up there, she asked, switching conversations with a skill I would later come to associate solely with Ayesha.

Mmmhmm.

That's nice. I've never met my grandfathers—one of them lives up north and the other died before I was born.

Shame.

Ayesha unrolled the label off her Coke bottle, the paper sticking to the ends of her fingers. Neither of them sound like they were much fun. Is yours?

Fun? No. But then I'm not exactly the kind of grandson he hoped for.

And why is that?

I'm not very good at any of the kinds of things he wants me to be good at. School or sports, that sort of thing. I'm good at piano but he doesn't really see the point in that.

Well I want to be a writer, she said bending her neck towards me. So I guess we're both black sheep. You any good?

At what?

Playing music.

I'd be better if I practised. Dada has a tutor set up for me after school. I play cricket a few times a week just to keep him happy.

Cricket's not so bad. Where do you play?

Gymkhana.

You should come and play with us. We might just be girls but we do live just across the road—could have you home in time to practise your music.

The thought of telling my grandfather that I was going to play cricket with the Malik girls instead of my team at the gymkhana was so unlikely that I almost dropped my plate.

Somehow I don't think that'll help.

That's a shame. We'd be even numbers then—Bina doesn't like to play. Still, you should come by anyway.

Yes?

The best rumour I ever heard about you was that you've got a library. That one true?

I thought these were all stories you made up.

It's the same thing isn't it? Rumours are just stories made up by other people. Well is it true or isn't it?

We do, I admitted, Have a library. You're welcome to have a look any time.

That's very neighbourly of you, she said.

I turned my head back outside. Think they've missed either of us, I asked.

Not unless you're a better dancer than my sister.

I watched her put her plate down and fold back the newspaper, slotting everything she'd moved in the room back into place like a person who was used to hiding. The room seemed lighter with her in it, with the glitter of her glass bangles as she stood on tiptoe to replace a book from his shelf. I'd been in this room a hundred times and never had the guts to move a paperweight across the desk, let alone borrow my uncle's books or blow dust from the picture on his table of Jackie Kennedy on a camel from when she visited the city, even though it was a picture my father was famous for having taken. Ayesha seemed to ease into places, a gift I would envy for as long as we knew each other.

It was only later that evening, when we crept out of our mutual hiding place, that she introduced me to her sister. I felt my tongue wind back on itself, dumb all of a sudden. I offered them a ride home and Ayesha dropped her eyelashes at me in mock flirtation and said, Well I suppose we are going the same way.

Maria shook her head. You don't have to do that, she said.

Ayesha laughed, This way we don't have to wait for one of your admirers to. They always look at me like they'd rather run me over than have me in the backseat. And then they linger for ages afterwards hoping to catch a minute with you outside the house.

Don't pay attention to her, Maria said and they followed me out to the car, wrapping shawls about their elbows. Strange to think I'd left the house that evening not knowing either of them, not even wanting to go to the party—Dada was sick and he'd put me in a suit and shoved me out of the door so I could represent the family. The whole way there I'd thought about how I'd rather be at home and the whole way back I was willing the driver to go slower, to stretch out this time in their company.

They deconstructed the night, plucking through the list of who'd shown up and locking down the potential spats of their friends. They spoke in the quiet, secondhand language that all families have, phrases cobbled to new meanings, almost forgetting I was in the front seat, though the Malik sisters never began a conversation from the beginning, they stepped in halfway through the story and expected you to catch up.

Isn't it strange, Ayesha said, as we slowly circled into the street we lived on, That we've lived across from each other almost our whole lives and never properly met?

I expected them to slip out of my life after that. It wasn't as if our families would have encouraged a friendship. Dada was always pushing me to get out more, to spend more time with the boys from school—these were the sons and grandsons of people he worked with, of people who gone to school with my father, and I liked them fine but I was a private sort of kid and mostly they thought I was weird. He wanted friends for me, but the four neighbourhood girls wouldn't have been his first choice.

Ash and I were about the same age and though we didn't go to the same school I saw her often at the library or the bookshops near my school. We ran into each other enough that the awkwardness wore off, even for me. Ayesha started asking me to take her places; to Sunday bazaar, or to school when her van was late or stuck in the rains. I wasn't used to girls asking me to take them anywhere. She'd show up at the door with her bag slung over one shoulder and smile brightly, without embarrassment, which I liked.

Out of the party clothes and shoes, she was a different person. She didn't dress like other girls. I knew her to wear her father's old kurtas often, flat shoes and her long, black hair always messy. She'd braid it down one shoulder for school, but on the weekends it was wild. At the school gates, I saw other girls with their salon-style waves, how they'd fuss over it and preen, exchanging glossy magazines as they waited for their cars, and understood the distance between her and them. She stood by herself, one leg propped up against a wall and a paperback flipped open against her wrist.

She even came over to the house one afternoon to borrow some books, on her own—which Dada would have been scandalized by but it was a Sunday, and he was out to lunch at the press club and the cook was on holiday. She pulled them off the shelves and piled them on the floor, settling there to sift through them.

When I'm older, she said, I want a library just like this one. Only I'll put the books in glass bookcases so they don't spoil. Not just the ones I write, but all my books.

Are you planning on writing many, I asked.

Only as many as I need to, she said.

I'd only asked to tease her a little, but her face scrunched up. I didn't know anyone our age who could be this serious. The boys at school never thought past the weekend, and here she was blueprinting a home for her future, fitting in glass bookcases. There was nothing in Ayesha's house of dreams but a book case and a desk, a study littered with the spoils of travel. The rest of the rooms remained unfinished, a life unburdened by men or children.

Need to for what?

I don't know how many I've got inside me, she said, They're always buzzing, J. I've got a head full of bees.

Sounds painful, I said.

Maybe I'll write one about you, she said, tilting her head to one side, All the best books are about orphans and only children. You're storybook gold.

She expected the same of me, of everyone around her: single-mindedness, ambition to match. She wanted to know what I had planned not just for the next year of university but the rest of my life. Conversation I was unused to having. When I told her Dada planned to have me follow him into the export business, a family trade since they had came to this country, she was surprised.

I don't even know what that means, Ash said flatly, And if I'm honest I can't really see you behind a desk.

Don't let Dada hear you say that.

What would you do, she asked, If you could do anything at all?

I don't know. Maybe I'd play the piano.

I was lying on my back on one of Dada's sofas and the long fingers of afternoon light stretched through the net curtains to line my stomach. I felt more relaxed than I usually did when I was in Dada's space, even though if he came home to find Ayesha on the floor he'd be angrier than he would be by a few misplaced books. The only context in which it would have been alright to have her over is if her mother or her sisters were with her. The two of us alone in the library was unthinkable.

Well, she said, pursing her lips together. You should at least try.

I liked the way she said it, the preciseness with which she put her words together. I trusted her lack of politeness, and our friendship grew thickly. By the end of the month I had told her more of my life than anyone before.

The truth was not so glamorous; under the shroud of mystery I didn't know that much. My father travelled all the time and was forever settling in new cities, making homes in little apartments for a few weeks. He made some money from his photography but mostly he blew through what my grandfather gave him. When that stopped, he began calling his brother. My uncle said he called him from Spain once, asking if he could wire him some money so he could put it on a bullfight. Six months later he sent home photos of himself in a matador jacket, squinting into the sun, and my uncle could never be sure if he'd been in the fight himself or not. The long and short of it was that no one should have been surprised when he came home with a wife they'd never heard of, a pretty French girl with little English and no Urdu at all. She wasn't a dancer or a cocktail waitress or any of the other things that the rumours insinuated. She was just a girl, only eighteen and barely out of school. They were both of them too young to be married but the money was gone and my father had to come home. So he brought her back, a French wife to shock his father with, and six months later, there was a little boy.

It's hard to imagine they were devoted parents but I had fond memories of them, blurry as if we'd spent all my childhood underwater. I remembered my mother's hair floating over me as she bent to kiss my cheek, the flush of her perfume and her long scarves brushing my face. My father was only his smile, the curve of white teeth under the black moustache, though all my life it would be stories of him that I would inherit. His books, his old ties, his records, his friends. People expected me to be bolder for being his son, birthing him back with every anecdote, while year after year my mother faded into the wallpaper, pressed behind the paintings.

Of course what Ash really wanted to hear about was my travels. I'd been to New York, to parts of Europe that were postcard images on her bedroom wall and settings for her favourite books. It didn't matter that I'd been too young to take any of it in, she wanted to know whatever it was I could remember. Though it was harder with Ayesha around. The mere mention of these places would make her face light up. You could see all the workings with Ash on her face—all the bright spots in her mind.

Abba is always away, she told me, He used to send us postcards from foreign countries but when I was twelve or something I started crying every time they came. Ma thought it was because I missed him but really I think I was just jealous. Anyway he stopped, and now he just brings us gifts and writes the occasional letters so I stuck the old ones up on my walls instead, with the messages turned in.

I could picture Ash's bedroom if I tried. I imagined from her clothes and from the way she sat down at a table, books spreading out beneath her, that she was probably messy. There would be clothes and scarves everywhere and maybe stacks of her writing secretly bound and hidden under her bed.

How come you never travel with him? I asked.

At school there were always boys whose fathers were in the army or air force or navy passing through. They would be there for a month or so and then somewhere else right after. Their wives were warrior women, strapping children and households to their backs and leaving the next day. It seemed like a good way to see the world. I'd pretended for a week at school that my father had been a pilot, but the truth snuck out eventually.

Ash sighed as if the knowledge of this was an old wound. Ma wanted us to stay here. She says an education divided into cities isn't proper learning. Besides I don't think she really wanted to be in a different city every other year. Ma's a creature of habit really. Even Karachi still feels foreign to her.

This too grew to make sense to me. The swoosh of her mother's voice and the lightness that carried her still seemed otherworldly to me. I saw flashes of it in the girls but nothing complete, nothing quite so planetary. She seemed to sit in between worlds, unreal. A daughter who hankered after trains and planes as much as Ash did must have been so strange to her.

But travelling was all she ever wanted to do. Ash, who was bad at school but good at reading, was the same kind of dreamer Dada always accused me of being. She was never lazy about it, though. Most weekends she spent with the Captain's aunt, Khalajaan. She ran her errands and read to her and gave her company in exchange for a small allowance. And, even more importantly, the promise that Khalajaan would eventually tour Europe and take Ayesha with her.

On lazier Sundays, Khalajaan would nap and Ash got to organize the books in her study. It was far from the proper library she longed for but I liked hearing Ash talk about her work there—she was a good storyteller as not many people are. She could talk me through my maths class and I'd probably have paid attention to that too.

Those early days of our friendship were what I would look to for the rest of my life: the world two people create when they are first beginning to know each other. Still, it got to look suspicious when we were wandering around town that way. Ash didn't give a damn what anyone thought but when Maria asked if there was a reason she was hiding me, she flared up.

You better come to the house, she said. Just to show there's nothing private.

I'd dreamed up that drive many times. On Eid and other holidays, Dada sent over food or sweets but the cook took those and I would watch the silver pots make their progression from my bedroom window.

Most mothers wouldn't have let their daughter be friends with a boy they didn't even know but Mehrunissa wasn't most mothers. Most mothers wouldn't have let Ayesha dress the way she did, with her man's clothes and loose hair. They might not have encouraged their daughters to play in the sun or told them to rough around less. Mehrunissa said she was raising modern young women to live in a modern young world.

None of the girls were home when I got there. On Thursday afternoons they helped out at a free school near where we lived. Maria was finishing up at the convent then and taught English and history, and Ash marked papers. The younger two helped where they could: Bina minded the children still waiting on the verandah for their mothers and Leila wandered about the place, charming the art tutor.

When Mehrunissa said she'd heard much about me, I felt the floor shift under my feet. In her little sitting room, with its artificial flowers and sweet-smelling candles, we drank tea and waited for the girls to get home. The practice of conversing easily with grown-ups had not yet found me. With most of my grandfather's friends and the extended family, I kept to single syllables and hoped I was cultivating an air of mystery.

I twitched in my seat and reminded myself why I was there: for Ash, who switched out the colours in my days. I thought of her elbow, hanging in the window of my car as she leaned against it and waited for me at the store earlier that week. Ash, who sometimes wrote in her notebook even as I was speaking, who made fun of my comic books and who despite herself loved Emily Brontë, a secret I only uncovered when I found a shredded paperback in their bathroom, *AM* dented into the back. It was the first house I'd ever been in with books in every room. Even in a room with no shelves, there were books under cups or hidden behind pots; Barbara Cartland novels tucked in the slots of the swings. Books in other houses were rare, precious thing, tucked out of reach or behind walls of glass, leather-bound and glossy. These tangible tattered things with dog-eared pages and tea stains were remarkable. I shifted my cup of tea on its coaster, knocking over a mystery novel that Mehrunissa kept beside her sewing.

How is Amira, Mehrunissa asked me. I've heard it was a lovely wedding. She's a very beautiful girl.

I think she's happy. They're moving to Lahore soon I think.

It always seems so unfair to me when girls have to move for their marriages—just uproot their whole lives and go, she said.

Yes, I said. I was trying to concentrate on the china cup between my fingers, balanced on one knee. Out of the corner of my eye, I saw a slither of black fur. The cat slipped through the door and wound itself around my ankles.

You're not scared of them are you?

I don't think I'd ever been in a room with a cat before. My grandfather has a dislike of them. I remembered wanting one quite desperately when I was younger. He'd said he had nothing against the animals but would rather they stayed out of his way entirely.

Does she have a name, I asked, gingerly scratching behind her ears.

Kiran. Mehrunissa glanced upward. Ridiculous name for an animal but the girls insisted.

Have you had her long?

Since Leila was born, she said. The girls begged for a pet—my husband never had animals growing up but I always did. We lived in a house near the mountains, by a lake, and the place was a menagerie.

Your parents didn't mind?

She flicked a wrist in the air. They were just like we were, she said. My father's library had these long windows that blew open in the summertime and there were always birds on the bookshelves, branches bending into the house. You see they knew something very important— animals are more than creatures for our amusement.

As she spoke, I could see it building in my head their house by the lake and its walls of red brick. Its colonial breadth melting into the dark of the forest. They lived in the mountains; I'd heard of those secret towns where the rest of the world drifts away. How funny to think that she married a man from the city, a war-man with shrapnel in his wrist. I would keep the song of her voice for the rest of my life—the doughy sleepiness of my listening, fixed on her words as she drifted me out on to that lake with her.

Her sister who raised the lion cub, feeding it from her mouth the way birds feed their babies. The time her father rescued an eagle from the side of the road and nursed it back to life. The very first animal they ever had—the dog that saved Mehrunissa from drowning in the lake. She had gone for a swim on her own—and I could see so clearly the little nymph she must have been, reflected back at me in pictures of her daughters as children, blinking all around us in the middle of the night following a terrible argument with her eldest sister. She was caught in the middle of a rainstorm and sure she was going to die, the flux of water pulling at her lungs. But she did not, and animals had lived in the house ever since. She had pneumonia for five days and the dog slept in her bed, something unheard of in most homes.

I was the youngest of five, she said. She talked without looking at me, and still without letting me feel alone. I loved my sisters but those animals were my friends. In a way raising animals isn't so different from raising children. I had a dream when I was thirteen that the kittens were crying in the garden and I ran out of bed to look for them. And there, in between the eucalyptus trees, I saw the faces of all my daughters. That was still seven years before Maria was born, but I knew that morning that I was going to be a mother.

Do you always see things before they happen?

She shook her head.

There are no rules about this sort of thing Jimmy. I wouldn't trust anyone who told you there were—these things come and go from you like smoke. Anyone who says they can harness it is lying because they want something from you. She smiled. Don't tell the girls I said that. One of my cousins reads tarot cards for a living and they're all a little fascinated with her.

Kiran was on my knee by the time the girls came home. It was dark then and they sat around the table in a circle, all falling scarves and trailing kurtas, draping themselves over the chairs and sofas like crumpling ragdolls. Ayesha placed herself on the arm of her mother's chair and stole her cup of tea.

J! she said, I'd forgotten all about you.

That's not very flattering, I said.

That you were meant to come here, that's all.

Ayesha, her mother said, grabbing her wrist. What have you done?

She lifted her elbow to look at the bruise stamped on to the back of her forearm. I must have hit it in a door or something. It's a lovely colour.

She was always very proud of her bruises and scabs and she got them often, a byproduct of living as she did: rough and fast and always falling out of things and into rooms. They are like war wounds, she would say, and Maria would snort and roll her eyes.

My shoulder jerked up when Maria put a hand on it, asking if I wanted another cup of tea. I was not used to being touched.

I should go home, I said, Thank you.

You won't stay for dinner? Ash put up both her eyebrows.

Dada will be waiting for me, I said though I made no move to leave. They were still so strange to me, these girls. The younger two especially were only bright flashes in my mind. I didn't leave right away, watching them move about me. They didn't seem to mind having me there, amid their bustle. I sat with my now cold cup of tea while they ran errands, prepared their meal. Ayesha unpiled her books on to the dining room table and Bina brushed out the cat's long black hair. They moved around me like I wasn't there. I'd thought it would be hard with Bina and Leila—of course I knew a little about them from the years I'd spent watching the girls and also from Ash. I was nervous of people, especially smaller ones but they weren't nervous of me.

Leila looked up at me, blinking. Her darkly curtained eyes were the quickest of them all. She narrowed them at me, at the worn leather of my shoes, the buttons of my shirt like she was cataloguing everything. She asked if I would sit for her painting. Her pictures were populated with people, showed Sohni and Mahiwal across their river.

So you like to tell stories, I said. Like your sisters.

The smear of paint that was the girl's head made me think of all their hair, the long silky masses, and whether or not their mother's ever came down from her tightly wound bun.

No. Nothing like that.

No, nothing like that is right. Ash ruffled the top of her sister's head. Leila's stories are more like fibs.

I do not tell fibs!

Yes, you do. Last week you said Miss Munawar gave you no homework for English but I saw Farhan earlier this afternoon and he had homework.

Leila pouted. She said I didn't have to do it.

And why's that?

It's none of your business.

Maria or I could always ask her ourselves, you know. Or Ma could—

Ash!

Why didn't you have any homework then?

I told her it was Abba's birthday and that I was sad he was so far away.

Abba's birthday is in March, child.

I know.

Ash rolled up her eyes. You're going to get caught one of these days and don't expect me to drag you out of your messes.

Don't tell Maria, she begged.

I'll see what I can do.

She winked at me over Leila's shoulder. It was only a small thing but it stuck to me the rest of the evening.

Before I left, they took me up to the roof of their house, Ash's favourite place ever and past the narrow stretch between us I could see into my bedroom window, the desk with its pens and mess of paper in plain view. All those years I had watched them, they could see me too.

II.

By the time Maria decided to join St Patrick's, I was spending most of my time with the girls. Over the past few months, I'd only been sleeping at home. The rest of the time I lived in two worlds: school and the Malik house. I took my dinner there as many nights a week as I could without feeling guilty about leaving Dada to his own company or that I was overstaying my welcome, but even this began to matter less. I started by going over on Mondays after cricket so I could pick Ayesha up from the library near the gymkhana and soon I was there most evenings. It was easy to say yes to their invitations, even for me. They made me set the table and never made a fuss about me. I was just another voice blending into the spikes and gaps in their conversations, the kind of which I'd never had before. At home, we only spoke to communicate something.

These were my last few terms at St Patrick's and already people were keen to talk about what would come afterwards. Ayesha and I spent hours building up the years ahead, turning them into everything our lives weren't, everything we wanted them to be. It seemed then like we would soon have the reins to our own worlds and it seemed so close, so tied to the bitter, frantic edge of the finishing of school—even as the plans other people had laid out for us waited like quicksand.

We'd sit in cane chairs in the garden and talk about what we wanted to do and in these conversations the world belonged to us. Leila built her houses in gold. She wanted a rich husband, a studio of her own. I want a wardrobe the size of Marie Antoinette's, she would say. Decadence was the only thing she took away from history lessons. She was a tiny Cleopatra, Nur Jehan, a queen in miniature. Our laughter couldn't touch her.

You know, I think all I want in five years is for Papa to be home safe, Bina said. She was sitting with her knees poking out on either end of the cane chair, her kurta puddled like a hammock and the cat's small black body curled into it. Bina's wishes were never for herself.

Are you sure you don't want a rich husband to match Leila's? I asked.

I don't think I want to be married, she said.

Ever?

She shook her head. I'd have to leave Ma and Kiran and all my things. I'd much rather just stay here.

Ash pulled at pages of her notebook and said she didn't want to think about it. We all knew what she wanted and knew also that journalism school abroad was unlikely to be possible. Recent letters from their father suggested he would prefer a more conventional education. *My mother*, he'd written, *went to Kinnaird College. I think you could be happy there Ayesha*. Kinnaird might have been across the country, but that wasn't far enough for Ash. I found it difficult to place her in the future at all; a house with a husband and children didn't seem right for her. I could never see Ayesha living as other people do.

I was hoping to kill the conversation before it got to me, but Maria told us then that she'd got a new job and she'd be starting in two weeks. The future was closer for her than the rest of us. She'd been at the convent for a year now, teaching once in a while but spending most of her time as an assistant.

Where is it? Leila asked, a natural doubt colouring her voice.

Bina got up and put an arm around her, winding herself on to her chair. We're so proud of you, she said.

Maria smiled and looked at me. It's at your school actually Jimmy.

Pats? They never hire women.

I know, she said looking pleased and the comfortable smugness suited her—it made her look shiny and solid. I'm working for your history professor. He took interviews and seemed very positive about it all.

It was brilliant and I told her so. The history professor was famously hard, and he must have seen something in her to take her on at a boys' school.

You won't find it embarrassing to have me around? she asked.

Not even a little. The boys will all fall in love with you and maybe it'll make them like me more if they know we're friends.

Ash raised an eyebrow and said she didn't think it worked that way, but Maria's smile cracked her face.

You will definitely be lovelier than any teacher I've ever had at the school Maria.

And what does that matter, J? Ash elbowed me lightly, her bone grazing the dip between my ribs. She'll probably be the cleverest.

That's quite enough compliments for now—I need to stay close to the ground so it doesn't hurt when I'm knocked down by teenage boys, said Maria.

It was stranger than I expected to see her in school. I guess I'd never really thought about the girls outside that little house, that they might exist in the wider world. When I was anywhere other than the house with them it felt like we were moving in a bubble, a tiny fraction of the city cordoned off just for us.

Maria wore the classroom with the awkwardness of someone new to it, and it dimmed her loveliness. She'd always been for me the ideal of beauty, she and her sisters merging to form what I considered woman. She pulled light around her, air switching when she entered the room, and I thought the boys would see this, would see her as I did.

Here everything about her seemed scattered. I noticed for the first time that her kurtas were the wrong length, hanging inches lower than most women wore them, below the knee and how her shalwars, which ended narrowly at her ankles, were the wrong shape. Even her hair—too long and nothing to do with it but to braid it down her back—wasn't right, following her up and down the grey corridors. In her schoolteacher's clothes,

Maria was a different woman from the one I knew. She was not shy but the spitfire speed of her conversation was gone. Here she paused between sentences. When we walked out of school at the end of the day, Maria did not look that much younger than some of the mothers, the ones picking up their little children of three or four years. These women, with their lipsticked mouths and coiffed hair, were a different species.

Maria was good at what she did. More than clever, she was firm with us. History had never been something I enjoyed but I worked a lot harder with her around. I didn't want to do badly in front of her. Our relationship was already constricted by new rules. I offered to drive her to school but she said it would look bad, like she was going to play favourites. In the classroom, she hardly ever looked straight at me, only to shoot me a look of disappointment when I got a question wrong. I remember her once finding me passing notes in class and fixing on me an expression so hopeless that I could not sleep for the next two nights. Her hold over me was complete, but it grew to be that way with all the boys.

She was the first woman known to us in this way. We were not used to women who were not our mothers or sisters or ayahs. We watched her with awe, a freakish creature in our midst. It drove us to do better, to earn her respect. They didn't fall in love with her as suddenly as I'd predicted, but it happened all the same. The trick was not in her words, but the way she spoke them. She was not lightning but slow honey, womanliness pouring into the classroom, making us all sit up a little straighter.

The history professor was a traveller. We'd heard that he'd lived all over the world before coming back to Pakistan. He worked at the university most days and only seemed to be doing this job as a favour to the headmaster. It seemed like centuries past to us but he'd been at school here once and felt a certain kinship. He came in a few days a week to give us lectures, but it was Maria who ran the classroom day to day—she who set our assignments and marked our papers.

He's a strange one isn't he? I said, over dinner once. Mr Amir? We've heard all sorts of sordid things about him. I winked over the plates at Leila, whose eyes rounded as they always did when gossip was about.

What sort of sordid things?

I think, Maria put down her fork, He's brilliant.

They say he has a baby somewhere in Germany. Just upped and left when a job opened up here and didn't even think of marrying the mother.

Is that true J? Ash asked me, leaning forward in interest.

Don't be ridiculous Ayesha.

Maria, who never raised her voice, was looking down steadily at the table. We saw the streak of colour paint her throat and all turned to watch her.

Jimmy you shouldn't gossip, Mehrunissa said, settling things. It's beneath you.

But it wasn't. The saga of Mr Amir and Maria was generated almost wholly on the machinery of such gossip. You might not think it of a boy's school but St Patrick's was seeded with this kind of talk. Nothing ever happened to us, and so the content of our days was filled with the lives of other people.

Mr Amir was nothing like the men we wanted to be, with his rolled-up shirt sleeves and messy dark hair, his glasses—there was something about him that fell short of the hero mark, despite the supposed intrigue of his past. We all wanted to be pilots or cricketers. The trouble in East Pakistan was already starting, and tensions with India were running high. So we all wanted to be fighter pilots—saviours, martyrs, kings. The glory of the written word escaped us entirely. Even Ash's ambitions did nothing to change my own view of the field of academics, of journalism, of novels. Such endeavours were tangled up in our young boy brains . They were good enough for girls, for Maria, for Ash, but I and my team of men had more important work to do.

At any rate, he was too much a part of the school to really be a hero. We liked him well enough, but missed Maria's gentler way on the days he took our classes. His manner was brisk and unforgiving. He would stroll up and down between our desks, firing questions with a speed that chased sweat down our spines the whole time.

Maria stayed always aware that the position would have been happily snapped up by any of the graduate students at the university. They would often drive Mr Amir to school in their Jaguars, bring him foreign newspapers and take him out to meals to curry his favour.

She stayed long hours at the library, drew up lesson plans with unparalleled attention and preciseness. The class she assisted with was European history but she spent hours at the library doing research in the professor's chosen field: refugees lost in the Partition. Even then it was a tricky part of our history to be involved with, still so little known. Most historians were focusing on the grand narratives, and it still seemed too soon to be picking these things apart. In the interview she had expressed an affinity for his line of work. He had encouraged her to study, said he would teach her the way he did the rest of the students.

What we didn't know then was that she had taken him up on his offer, studying privately for a masters in history under his tutelage. At the end of each week, she'd take her lesson plans into his office but also papers of her own. He held all his students to exacting standards but he was even harsher on her than the rest of us. He would read them in front of her, his red pen ticking in one hand. Maria spent Thursday evenings locked up in the bedroom she shared with Ash, with a book jarring the door so that no one could enter. Those tutoring sessions focused her as nothing had before. Maria was used to a more low-key ambition, falling somewhere between the firebrands of her family and the laidback Bina—but suddenly she was a weapon. All her weeks led up to those afternoons. The school would clear for Friday afternoon prayers and the two of them would sit in the jammy heat of the classroom, the ceiling fan rocking above them, monstrously loud in their silence. I would wait in the corridors for them to finish so I could give Maria a ride home as I always did on Fridays when the van left without her, listening to the radio and trying to play back flowery ballads with my fingers, using the wide handle of my thermos as a set of imaginary keys.

The lessons began to bleed into evenings so Maria wouldn't return home till dinner. I started going home with the rest of the class. He would drive her back afterwards, coasting through the city in twilight with an unbearable slowness. The moon and the sun both in the sky and Maria coming up the drive, mouth pale and skin bright. When she finally confessed the lessons to their mother I saw a kind of relief flutter over her face, all those missing hours finally accounted for. Mehrunissa was too pragmatic to get mad about some lessons. She offered her congratulations instead, cryptic and even reluctant. I hope you get exactly what you want out of this, she said.

The rest of us watched our teacups. There was something naked in Maria's face that embarrassed us all, the coolness stripped from her. I could feel Ash twitching beside me, her feet jerking along with the songs on the radio as she scribbled into her notebook. The girls always brought their work to tea, books or drawings or sewing. They never wasted their afternoons and because I didn't want to seem lazy in front of them, I started bringing my homework with me. It usually fell by the wayside because it was always much easier to be caught up in whatever they were doing. I helped the younger girls with their maths sometimes—I was not especially good at it but I was two years ahead of Bina and more patient than her sisters. I even posed sometimes for Leila's drawings. She used her sisters for all her models even for the men in them, but with me around that became unnecessary. I spent hours holding still while she watched me, her small face screwed up carefully.

This afternoon, it was just the five of us in the room. Our hands on the table, working typewriters or pens and pages, and Maria alone in it all, tuned up and buzzing.

The way love lit her from inside. Finally the electricity of her that I had always sensed was on the surface. The boys, already warm to her, were struck all over again. My mistress, when she tread on the skies, on the tops of our heads. She could barely stand to be in the same room as him any more, breaking into shivers when he walked past the corridor.

It made us love him more. We sensed something noble, some solid manhood in him that made him worthy of her devotion. The boys were now a pack of hungry eyes, stuck to Maria all the time, but I watched him. He moved with heavy feet now, walking through water, a spellbound man.

He kept an account of each encounter. Years later I would find his journal, an imperfect record of their love affair. A thin catalogue of her body, his weak words barely holding up the glory of her—he spoke of her as parts, never the whole. Thickly separated eyelashes, smudging the tops of her cheeks. Her lips parted in a groan, the soft sum of her thighs.

What they spoke about in those hours in between went unwritten. We are left to imagine this, the stuttering rides in his car, her long fingers trembling as she smoked his cigarettes, rolled the windows up and down. A foreign restlessness infected her bones. She moved like she was someone other than herself. His accounts were also sparse on the subject of how things finally started up between them, what it was that broke the delicious tension—was it Maria who went to him or he who asked her in? Did they fall together in the growing dark, moving like creatures in one of Ayesha's plays?

It was the talk of lovemaking that baffled me most. Boys at school had circulated pictures for years now. I stared at the postcard-sized porn, like artefacts in a museum, the cold hard fact of how bodies collided. I understood the logistics of sex, why people wanted it, how it made them go out of their minds with lust, how people could stare at each other across crowded rooms, parties, classrooms, weddings—and thought of those postcard positions with something hazy and dark, wolf-like want. What seemed complicated was how they got there—what words went between the looks and the actions.

I imagined Maria's long grey kurta, buttoned all the way down to the floor. How she must have taken each button apart with trembling fingers. How the canvas of her skin must have been unveiled slowly, how the hot room would have grown bright and moon-ish as the lights went up. Their industrial glow on her breasts, her pillowy stomach, the snag of hair below.

Maria in his office, the woman-teacher trembling like a girl. We know she knew of his past, the rumours that circled him like crows over a corpse and how the truth of it must be buried there and still she chose him, chose this—the implication of that—

Her fingers catching his wrist, wrapping around the bone there like a snake. He would have touched her face to say no, once, maybe even twice, but she kissed him, something that used to exist only in the movies. There was no place in the dark office for what happened between them. Outside, wind whipped through empty school corridors and whistled through the half-open windows. Maria left her clothes on cement floor, gave her freezing body into his hands. Fear turned her skin cold, statued it blue. The fluorescent lights above them, pale and flickering, the business-like briskness of his voice dissolving as he moved to turn them off—but she wanted to see everything. The smear of her palms against the desk, her quivering spine as she put herself in his hands. It was the surrender that mattered more than anything. What giving her body must have meant, I could never understand that in a thousand years. It was never the same for men, and Maria, she was never like other women.

The lovemaking affected the girls too, even more powerfully than it did us at school. Unspoken, but the change seemed to switch through them all. They were a house lit up for feast days. They were a circle of birthday candles. In its early stages, the affair swung Maria away from her sisters; now, it wound them closer back together. As it happened to her, it happened to all of them. Now, when I went to the house, there was always slow jazz playing, the games and the work abandoned for more languid activities. Even Ash put away her typewriter to read more than she usually did, her head in Bina's lap while the other girls stitched or drew.

For the first time in my history with the girls, I felt outside of what was happening to them, this invisible net of sisterhood. The slick happiness of their smiles and how they took more sugar in their tea, drank it thick and milky.

If he hurts you, I'll kill him, I said.

We were outside the school, waiting for my car to come pick us up. Usually she would have refused my offer for a lift but it was expected to rain and anyway, she had been much gentler lately, less likely to stick to those rules.

I put my hands into my pockets as I said it and screwed my eyes up to the sky, with its blackening clouds clustered together.

Maria laughed. You're very sweet Jimmy.

I mean it.

And I did. I don't know what I could possibly have done to that man, older, squarer. I had not yet reached the years where I would try and build up my body. I only knew how I felt, and said it anyway.

III.

It never occurred to me that this alchemic change in the girls could have come about without their knowledge of the situation. Two Sundays after I thought the affair had started—from the point, at least, that Maria had come blushing into class and Mr Amir's hazy-eyed mistake with the dates of the Crimean War prompted rumours to pass through our classroom like a forest fire—I spoke to Ash about the situation.

Maria and Mr Amir? she said, Don't be ridiculous.

Ash, I said carefully, It's pretty common knowledge at school that he's fond of her.

Well of course he is. She's brilliant, isn't she? That doesn't mean anything.

I wasn't trying to insult her.

Why is it that when a woman does something brilliant, you can't just see it for what it is—there has to be something else there to explain it.

I'm not saying that's why she got the job. No one's saying that.

She turned to stone beside me and said, Not yet at any rate. Not directly.

Let's not argue about this.

I'm not arguing.

I was only saying they've grown fond of each other. You ought to be pleased for her.

I'm pleased that she's working, Ash said, pulling herself up. We were laid down on the floor of their attic, the wooden boards flat against our bellies and she slithered up now, to cross her ankles and glare imperiously down at me.

I'm pleased to see her so happy but no, I don't believe there's any more to it.

Alright.

She would have told me if there was, she said.

I lifted my shoulders and edged myself up off the floor.

You know best, I said, We won't speak of it any more.

I watched her fold herself into a ball and pull out her typewriter. The keys clicking furiously informed me that our conversation was done and I could leave when I wanted.

I started wondering if maybe I'd misunderstood. We knew nothing for sure and could so easily have been caught up in something of our own fevered imagining. We were all more than a little in love with her ourselves and these were the shiniest people in the school. Maybe we'd only put them together in our head because the laws of the movies told us that they must come together. I watched for some invisible sign of our overstepping when Maria came home that night. Colour high in her face and her fingers leaves in the wind, she shut the door behind her. Beside me, I felt Ash quiver and the game was up.

In their bedroom, the two of them finally alone. Ash, always full of words, could not bring herself to that question.

There's nothing you want to talk to me about? she asked.

Maria was taking off her earrings while her sister shifted in the mirror.

What do you mean?

Is there something going between you and that man?

His name's Amir as you well know.

Ayesha sat down on the edge of the bed, her back carefully turned to Maria.

Well is there?

Don't be childish Ash. And anyway what do you know about it?

Everyone's talking about it.

Oh everyone—you mean Jimmy.

No I don't mean Jimmy.

Don't tell me you care about what people will say, she laughed. Let them talk.

I can't believe this is a joke to you.

He's a good man, Maria said.

She poured her earrings and necklace into the enamel box on her dresser. Their voices now were harsh whispers, new anger stretching the bounds of secrecy.

And are you going to marry him?

You sound like Khalajaan, Maria said.

They slept on separate corners of their bed that night, and somehow by the morning, the news of their fight had trickled through the house. They didn't argue like this often. Ash lost her temper all the time but Maria was always too patient to be drawn into it, and it was usually Leila who got caught up in these squabbles. The force of it shook through the house, descended upon the women like a monsoon.

When I next showed up at the house it was Bina who let me in.

They've not made up yet, she whispered, leading me into the sitting room. Ma's up there now, trying to get them to talk. Maria's not spoken to any of us all morning. I don't think I've ever seen her like this before. She's usually so—it's not her way.

It was the weekend. I always came over after my lessons. Most of the time Ash would already be in the garden, and we'd spend the evening out there while everybody else went about their weekend business indoors. Sundays as days off was not a concept that existed in the Malik household. They had none of the languor of the other people I knew. They didn't rest well, always about on their feet, always moving, shifting, working. We'd sit on the swing in the back garden. I'd read her stories and she'd sit there watching me, chewing at the ends of her nails till I finished.

When I went in she was at the dining table and the swollen red eyes surprised me. I'd never seen Ash cry and a country where this was possible seemed distant to me. Her feet were folded up beneath her on the chair.

I'm sorry I didn't believe you, she said without looking up at me.

It was enough to send me all the way through the floor.

Don't Ash. I shouldn't have said anything.

She fussed as she gathered up her books and pens and told me not to be a martyr.

We all had to find out eventually.

You think she'll speak to me?

Her pen rolled off the table and she scrambled down to get it, saying, Your guess is as good as mine, as she went off.

I got up the stairs before I realized this was a part of the house I'd never been in. We went up to the roof so often and I was always in the dining room and the kitchen but I'd never been in any of the bedrooms before, only glancing at them through half-shut doors and guessing what was behind them. I stood on the landing and called her name.

I'm sorry, I said when she came to the door. It was the sort of apology that stuck in my throat not because I didn't mean it but because I had trouble making it sound like I did.

What for?

I shouldn't have said anything to Ash.

She lifted her arms behind her head, gathering her hair up into a knot. It made her face look smaller, drawn over the wide bones of her skull. Anger didn't suit her.

Don't worry about it, she said, It's not as if I told you not to say anything.

I still didn't fully know what it was I had said, what secrets had been unlocked, but I could feel them spilling through the house. The fight was between Maria and Ayesha but now that it was out it would burn through them all. To my mind, she was lucky in a way to have this fight—something to centre the conflict while the rest of them came to grips with what was happening.

She put an arm behind her head, pulling all her hair into a knot. It was going to come out anyway, she said, I just thought I'd have more time.

I twitched in the doorway, letting my legs work around each other.

Maria turned her head back to me, looking at me properly this time. It was nice to have something, you know—away from everyone else, she said as if she hoped I'd understand that.

Is your mother very angry?

Maria looked up at me. Why would she be angry?

I went quiet because I could not figure out what I had been thinking. The slippery-bodied knowledge that I carried in my head, of heated skin, of stolen afternoons—that could not, after all, be what they knew. I was not even sure that I knew it. That dizziness sat in me while I tried to explain that Mr Amir was not the sort of man Mrs Malik might have chosen for her daughter.

She frowned. Who knows if it will come to anything yet, she said. At any rate, I think she's glad we're meeting men—that I am. Most of my friends are married by now and she doesn't like to say—she doesn't want to be one of those mothers—but I know she's worried.

I could only think of Maria dancing at my cousin's wedding, how men had flocked to her then, packs of them swaying about her.

I don't know what happens, she said as if she'd forgotten I was still there, I always think I have them until I don't.

What do you mean?

Only that the initial attraction is so easy. Men are such simple creatures. It's the whole world beyond that that I feel lost in, she said, I don't suppose this is the sort of thing I should be talking to you about, anyway.

I don't imagine I'd be much help.

Maria laughed. Everybody plays this game from time to time Jimmy—you'd better start learning.

Then she reached over and pressed her fingers over the top of my head and the firmness of her hand felt good there, as if I could trust her to hold my skull together.

Won't you two make up? I asked.

Eventually. I'm not in any particular hurry. I love Ash but she can be so—

I know.

She's exhausting is what I mean.

I did know what she meant. Ayesha was exacting. I found being in her life was a mixed reward. Only the other week, we had argued over dropping my piano lessons down to every other week. My grades were bad and Dada thought I should be spending more time with my studies. He'd cut down the hours I was allowed to play, and Ash was furious I hadn't fought this.

You have to stand up to him J, she said, If you care about your music at all you have to practise.

It's not like I'm stopping altogether. And anyway how many boys do you know who play piano Ash?

That's not the point. How on earth do you expect to be a first-rate musician if you don't practise every day?

You don't write every day.

Yes I do.

Even on the days you work for Khalajaan?

I write less but I still do it. She screwed up her nose. And anyway that's different.

Different how?

I have to work for her—you're just coasting along on this dream your grandfather has built you that you don't even want.

It was the voice she said it with, flat and unreservedly right that made me angry.

It's not as simple as you think.

We left it there, but I hadn't missed the way she looked at me. It didn't feel good to have someone you admired be disappointed in you. I think she must have thought it would spur me into some kind of action but it only made me lazy and lonely instead. I spent a couple of days up on the roof instead of at the Maliks. I read comic books and ate day-old samosas that I'd stuffed into my pockets from not having anyone to share them with. If Dada noticed that I was around the house more, he didn't say anything. He may not have encouraged my single-minded friendship with a houseful of girls but he didn't want me to be lonely.

I even went to cricket that Sunday. The boys drove me around afterwards, drove up to a shisha place in Zamzama. It was funny and weary that night, watching the smoke rings float up in the low-ceilinged room, the collected drawl shifting in and then out of my consciousness. It was impossible to sit up on those sofas, their slanting bones made to pull you in with your feet on the table. We tracked in mud and sweat all over their rugs.

They watched me like they couldn't figure out why I was there, trying to get the measure of me.

You got a girlfriend, then? Munir asked me.

He was the captain of the team. He was the kind of boy built to live inside one of Leila's paintings, all hard and tall.

No.

No? You're always hanging around with those girls and not one of them is your girlfriend?

I choked on the smoke. No, not even close.

You must have thought about it. I mean, come on, I've never got a good look at any of them but if they all look like her then, well. Yasir put his lips together and whistled.

I wanted to say something then but Yasir, his skinny throat and pimpled cheeks, was swaying in front of me.

I was breathing heavily through my nose. My brain was loose, rattling around up there. I put my hands on the table to find them clenched into fists. Even unpicking my fingers was difficult. I held on to the table and focused squarely on Munir.

Something in the pipe? I rasped.

He shrugged.

I had been around the boys just enough to know that they considered weed and all other substances fair game. The kind of boys who wouldn't touch alcohol because of god but had no trouble scrambling their senses with anything else they could get their hands on. I went along with Munir sometimes, to the slow swinging roads behind Empress Market where everything looked busy and dark. We'd sit on charpais and eat gol gappas without talking. When the other boys were there, they would talk about people I didn't know, their fathers' friends at the club or the girls they knew. I could switch to the background the way I was used to, a space where nothing was expected of me and I never had to talk. It was an easy way to kill evenings. These were boys who walked through their lives without worrying too much about tomorrow, and in the back seat of Munir's car I was almost one of them.

The Malik sisters together on the bed, knees touching and the gap below the door blocked with pillows and piles of rustling newspapers to trap sound. Below in the low evening sun, their mother and Khalajaan had tea spread on the table and the girls knew it would last long enough for them to keep their confidences.

What was it like?

Maria laughed, the sound high-pitched.

Where should I start?

Did he kiss you? Leila asked. Oh please tell me he kissed you.

I wouldn't want to think about that, Ash said over her shoulder. She sat with her back to them, a book on her knees. She wrinkled up her nose. Not with his face all scruffy and beardy—doesn't it get in the way?

Don't pretend you're too good for this discussion Ash. We're all curious.

Can't you get him to shave?

I haven't asked, she said flatly, And to tell you the truth—here is where her voice went low and hesitant—I rather like it.

The squeal that followed could have been any of them.

Amira said it hurt—Leila started.

Leila! Don't tell me you asked her, Maria said.

Well who else was I supposed to ask? She was my friend, too, you know.

If she was, why weren't you invited to the wedding?

Anyway, she didn't mind.

I can't believe you asked her.

You're not answering the question.

Oh. Oh well—

Ash rolled her eyes. She snapped shut her book.

Don't be shy, darling. We can all tell you're dying to talk about him.

I am not.

Well it's the least we can get out of it—a little education.

Don't be disgusting, said Maria, but she was smiling.

When they laughed all together, it shook the chandeliers. Their knowledge of men was scattered. Ash, who was the most worldly of them all, had learned what she knew of men from her books. Women carry mysteries under their clothes and men carry histories.

Their knowledge of the machinery of love can't have been that different from our own, but the instructions were different for girls. Married friends proved to be of little help. Those who were pleased with their husbands only smiled knowingly, and instructed the girls to wait their turn. The others, with lemony smiles, were fond of dampening expectations. But neither approach was really enough to quench a real curiosity like that of the Malik girls, a four-fold desire to know more. The veil of delicacy made these things seem distant, something that happened in stories and off-screen in the movies.

In the later days, both Mehrunissa and the Captain seemed fond enough of Amir, so I never really knew how much she found out. They folded him into the family with a warmth particular to them. But, to my mind, she never really lost the coolness with which she treated him in the early days. All mothers are lionesses after all. For all her mildness there was a steel to the woman and Amir was the wolf in this story; she could not let him win.

Already Maria's association with him was dripping into the world outside the school. She never saw anybody else, and her little band of friends circled wider apart from her until there were no more invitations, no weddings or parties for her to go to.

Maria, glowing in her own little world, did not notice or care but Mehrunissa, so keenly tuned into all their lives, would have noticed it all. That flickering in her daughter, trailing up the steps and singing in the kitchen, up to her elbows in soapy water. Caught up in some net of uncertainty.

To her mother, that net must have been a prison.

IV.

Eventually the world will swing forward, the clicking out of time subsides even for lovers. It was clear to me that they could not stay as they were forever. When Amir invited Ash and I to go to the movies with them I thought maybe I knew something of what was happening. He looked too big for his car, a paper man folded into his seat, pushing his rounded glasses farther up his nose. He pulled at his collar the whole way there, talking fast enough to jumble his sentences and not notice how quiet we began to get in the back. He took us to the drive-in cinema at Hill Park, which was a novelty. Most of the time we went to Bambino or Rex and spent so long in line that we had no time for drinks or popcorn. Amir had even booked tickets earlier that day, a grown-up gesture that astounded us.

It was one of those broad, historical epics that go on for hours and the close-knit agony of it itched through me. I was never very good at sitting still in a crowd. Even concerts were a strain. I held myself very still now, Ash's knees humming beside me, the familiar shudder of her when she was nervous.

Having a good night? I whispered, leaning over in the interval. Her face twitched as the lights went up.

It's fine, she said.

I elbowed her, Be nice.

I don't see why you care, she mumbled. Ash, who should have been pleased with the movie, who had not been able to see *Ben Hur* when they finally showed it at Capri a few years ago because Bina wanted to come too but violence upset her and there was no one else to go with. This blood and dust creation, bursting gold on the screen, should have been a treat.

Would anyone like some coffee? Amir asked, standing up. He folded out of the seat he'd been cramped into, a different man from the one who'd stood in front of our classroom.

We shook our heads but Maria got up to join him. Their bodies, as they walked away, swayed towards each other. He put a hand on her wrist and she turned her face up, sunflowered and bright.

I wish he wouldn't touch her like that in public.

You wish he wouldn't touch her at all.

Jimmy.

Why are you so against this Ash?

I don't think he's good enough for her is why. Do you? Besides, she's too young to be getting mixed up with someone already.

I sighed. This was an untruth that there was no point discussing. She knew as well as I did that most of Maria's friends were already married, only a very few of them holding on to their jobs in the process and even fewer still who kept working without a husband. She was an exception to every rule, even in our circles.

You don't like Mr Amir?

I have no opinion on him.

He's a good teacher.

A good teacher, J, she said, Is not the same thing as a good man. I'd think you'd know that.

There was a tightness in her voice as she said it that seemed alien to me. I stood up and put my hands in my pockets, paced about a bit. My feet were stinging, old dress shoes too tight around my toes. I bounced up and down a little on my heels to get the blood flowing.

You're making me dizzy, she said flatly.

Would you rather I went home?

You wouldn't dare.

I sat back down and we waited in silence for the pair to return. I watched them for the rest of the movie, their dark heads bent together. Maria's hair trussed up along one shoulder, swinging when she moved to speak to him. I watched the switch of laughter in their long necks, his eyes craned so he was only half looking at the screen. The strangeness of them. Marriages I was used to never touched or looked or spoke like this. I thought about my uncle and his wife up in Lahore, how I'd never seen them hold hands even.

We walked back to the car from the canteen. The lights from the billboards flashed over her face, illuminating her in measures—the drag of her eyebrows, the crook of her tipped jaw. The painting on the lobby card—a different film, something glossier with a girl turning her hip in a pink sari—seemed to wink at me. I put my hands into my pockets as Ash and I walked ahead, something spooky about the parking lot with the people cleared out and nothing behind us but the clack of Maria's heels in the distance.

Do you know what it would be like with Amir if I were her brother instead of a sister?

She swung her hand in a hook and then wiggled out her fingers in front of the light so they glowed against the dark of the leaves.

He'd be scared of me then, don't you think. With my father gone he'd have to ask me permission. I wouldn't be someone just to be stepped over.

I caught her wrist and tapped my fingers against the bone. You're still scary to me, I said.

A few days before the cinema, Mr Amir asked me to tea. After the bell rang for lunch, he took my elbow. He was supervising one of our reading sessions and my head was still wrapped up in books.

Are you on the cricket team, Jamal? he asked.

I considered my books, the red ink all over the margins. I was bad at cricket, something that never failed to surprise people. People had been mistaking my height for sports ability for years now. It was only my grandfather's fondness for the game that kept me going to practice.

Technically, yes.

So technically you must be going to practice on Sunday?

I was meant to. Practice took place in a field just outside the city, a plot of barren land belonging to one of the boys' fathers. It was near the National Stadium. The boys would often stay on at one of the dhabas nearby and smoke shisha till the night matches started.

I skipped it most of the time. I even dressed for the game and then went somewhere else instead, just next door if I was feeling bold or I'd take the car and park somewhere to read.

I'm not really, I'm on the team but I've not been playing much lately.

Would you mind having tea with me instead?

I said yes right away, because it would give me somewhere to go and because I was curious.

When he picked me up, I was in my whites. I looked down, embarrassed as I got into the front seat. I told Dada that one of my friends was driving would have me back home in time for my lesson but he didn't ask any questions.

He drove out towards the edges of the town, the hot steam of tea and salt air. We sat down, suddenly shy with each other, and for some time, the conversation went slowly around topics like school and books. He tapped out one cigarette after the other, the chai growing cold between us.

His shirtsleeves were rolled up, glasses tucked into the front pocket. It was the first time I'd ever seen him outside of school.

You're very close to the girls, aren't you? he asked and neither of us needed any clarification.

I shrugged and said, I live near them.

He nodded. The knot of his eyebrows looked very still.

I've a mind to marry Maria. I've—well I've quite decided I want to.

That's good, I said, astonished. I had no idea it was something to be considered. Men and women married, it was the way things went.

I wonder, he said, What do you think she'll say?

Maria's fond of you.

Fondness is not the same as love.

I had my hands on the table next to my tea and I laced them together. I could see their faces leaning together in my head, the soft stage lights cutting them out of the dark.

I suppose you think me rather weak and romantic for even taking that into consideration.

Not at all, I said, though of course he was right. Privately I thought he was quite mad. I wasn't used to people speaking like love had anything to do with it. It made me shift around in my cane chair as if I didn't know what he was going to say next.

He shook another couple of cigarettes out of the pack and nodded towards them. My fingers hovered over one before snapping back, sensing a trap of some sort. I didn't want to commit myself to whatever this was.

Let me be clear, Jamal. It's not that I don't want—to ask Maria to marry me. It is only that I can't be certain she'll accept.

I suppose you'll have to ask and find out.

His fingers fumbled with the match.

Surely you understand, Jamal. She has to marry me.

I shrugged.

Then I guess she will. That's your answer.

He threw his hands up. I finally reached for that cigarette, holding it in my mouth while he waited for the words to find him.

I—Maria Malik is not the kind of woman I want to marry unless she wants me.

I would think, I said, That no one would want to be married to someone who didn't want them.

Good point, he amended. But Maria—she's not like other girls.

All men think that when they're in love. Without thinking. It was the sort of thing Dada would have said.

He laughed.

Do you know anything about the father?

I've never met him.

Captain Malik had been away for the whole time I had known the girls. There were letters and cards on their birthdays. Any of my own memories of him were just sketches from across the road, indistinct and shadowed.

His mouth twitched. I gather he's not around much.

He hasn't been for some years. I know he writes to the girls.

Already I liked Amir better than I had when I sat down, but this line of talk made me uncomfortable. I never spoke about the girls at school though the boys were always curious, and it still felt disloyal here.

Amir nodded then, and moved to shake my hand. It's good of you to speak with me like this.

Maybe I could have told him more. Of Captain Malik I knew only that he was a man who loved his daughters. He wrote to them every month. Photographs showed he once had a beard, that he was on familiar terms with the cat, his bookshelves packed with more literature than most military men would read. But these were not the kinds of things Amir was asking about.

I knew that he met his wife when she was travelling to the city for her sister's wedding. She was only seventeen then, and his parents already interested in some other girl for his attentions. They found each other at a party and by the end of the evening, he'd made up his mind. It was a quick courtship. They were married within the year, a winter wedding with her dowry sent down from the north. Mostly his family in attendance because hers did not really approve and because it was so fast, only three months in the making. He built the house with his father and it was only after Leila was born that his trips away began to grow longer and further flung.

Even if there was nothing holding me back, I don't know what I might have said to Amir. Captain Malik was just fiction in my head, only a handful of facts corralled together.

We drove back after the theatre in silence. Amir and Maria in the front, both of them still as the car skidded into the driveway. I was not surprised when Amir asked to come in.

I'd like to see your mother, he said. If that's alright.

Ayesha slipped straight out of the car and into the house. I could see her light her way up from floor to floor through the windows. She must have stopped outside the living room, feet sly and quiet on the slick marble floors. Her shoes in her hands. She would have waited there with her head tilted slightly forward, the same lip twitch I usually saw when I dropped her off at Khalajaan's for the day, before marching straight up.

When the three of us got inside, Mehrunissa was at the table. She had taken off her make-up for the evening, looking even younger in the half light. She lifted her glasses off her face and watched us.

Amir apologized for having come alone. Properly, he said, I should have brought my parents but they passed away some years ago. He spread his hands here, the fingers angling over his knees. I'm afraid I've not got any close family in the city.

I'm sorry to hear that. Her voice lighter and further away than usual, echoing down from a mountaintop.

I want to marry your daughter.

We all felt it, a sigh uncoiling through us all. By the door, I uncurled my fists and wondered if I should really be there. Too late now to leave without breaking the thread of the moment.

I assume, he started again, You'll want to wait till you've spoken to Captain saab—

Mehrunissa shook her head. Assume nothing of the sort. My daughters have the freedom to marry who they choose.

Maria in the corner, her head bowed. I had the awful thought that she was crying till she lifted her face.

I need some time to think, she said. I can't just say yes.

White-knuckled and stuck to his chair, he nodded.

Her lower lip sucked up between her teeth. I had never seen her nervous before.

Maria, said her mother. The name slow and drawn out, with something bitter and resigned mixed through.

I need time.

Alright, he said, You have time. And he released the arms of his chair. I watched him unfold himself and walk to the door. They said goodbye without touching and Maria disappeared into the dark stairwell.

Left alone at the table, her mother pressed the tips of her fingers to her temples.

No one lived as these girls did, no other mother would have allowed these freedoms. But even this freedom was not boundless. There were things you could live in the world without and things you could not. This was not a city for hiding sins or secrets. Khalajaan, who disapproved of the whole thing, blamed Mehrunissa entirely. This is what happens, she said, When you give your girls too much freedom. They run wild like animals.

Mehrunissa poured out the tea, her fingers stiff with worry. Every night she was counting prayer beads.

We'll be happy with whatever decision Maria makes, she said, and hid her hands under the table to hide the shaking but this did not stop Khalajaan. It was another two cups of tea—You do not want your daughter to be a blemish on our lineage—before she had said all she'd come to say.

Sometimes it was hard to remember that Khalajaan had a husband once too, that they had travelled the world together and it was in his memory that she wanted to see Europe again and his memory that kept her from doing it. He'd died ten years ago and left her without children. She must have been a different woman then. Maria told me that there were pictures of her wedding and she was almost lovely. Lovely not the way the Malik women were with their willow-tree bodies and rivers of hair, but the way all young brides are, flushed with pride.

For three days Maria saw no one. There was nothing to be done, nothing at all that could coax her out of the room. At school, there was a certain emptiness in the hall that could only have been her absence. Aside from that, things went on as usual. Amir took his own classes. The boys bristled under his impatience, crowding around me at lunch to ask when Maria would be back.

At the house it was different, the whole turned inside out. Mehrunissa frozen at the table every day, her pencil poised over the crossword, unmoving. The girls spent most of their time upstairs in their rooms, a part of the house quartered off to me. I saw them only in flashes, leaving or entering the living room. They carried up trays of tea and toast to Maria. These came back down with still full cups and crumbs, though I knew she'd eaten nothing. I could see her rubbing the toast between her fingers till it came apart on the plate.

On the second day, Bina came to sit with me, half-moons smudged under her eyes from no sleep. She rubbed at them with little fists while I poured out the tea.

Do you think she'll tell him soon?

Of course. She isn't making him wait to be cruel. She just needs time.

Oh.

It is this way sometimes, she said, biting the end of her thumb. With Maria and with us all.

With you all?

She took up her tea and looked out the window. It was early winter, the thin sunlight piercing through the curtains. I went there straight after school, unable to meet Amir's eye as he sat in his car in the parking lot, smoking cigarettes, a paperback folded open but untouched on his dashboard.

I watched her squint up at the sky and then back down at me.

When Papa asked Ma to marry him, she didn't say yes right away.

No?

She waited for days for the answer to come to her. She didn't want to leave, you see—her family would be so far away. She has never found it easy to be apart from them. She did everything she could to find the right answer. There was a woman in the city she knew who read tarot cards so she went to her, another one who took answers from scripture—she took almost a week to make up her mind.

I must have looked surprised because she leaned over and squeezed my fingers.

Maria's just in a tight spot.

But it's not the same. She's not even going very far away. She wouldn't even have to leave the city.

Bina shook her head as if I didn't understand.

That's not the problem. It wouldn't be the same.

Why not?

She'd never be able to come back.

That's ridiculous. She'd be able to visit all the time.

I felt her fingers flutter gently, coaxing against my wrist.

Yes but she'd never be home with us again—this wouldn't be her home any more.

And I understood that I was not in that us, that it was something I would always be on the outside of. I would never be part of what they meant when they spoke about this kind of love. And soon, it seemed, neither would Maria.

I was there when she finally came down the stairs, her silent vigil at an end. We had only just finished tea, the remnants of the table not yet cleared, Ayesha kicking her feet beside me.

She sat with us and picked over Leila's homework as if nothing at all was happening. When the doorbell rang, she told us she'd invited Amir over without even looking up from the page. We couldn't tell what she would say. The still measure of her shoulders remained, even as Bina let him into the room and the rest of us snapped to attention, straightening collars and sleeves, tidying ourselves up for the moment.

When she finally stood and told him yes, I could feel the shiver in the room. The house releasing the breath held from the night he'd asked. The shake of its bones as Amir stepped in and the settling of a new order. Maria was getting married.

V.

Baat paki was just the beginning. The celebrations were small, bright and sweet. Boxes of mithai wrapped in tinfoil sent out to the houses around us. Dada, who was fond of the girls by now, invited them and Amir over for dinner. He meant to take an interest in the couple even though the date of the wedding was not yet set. She refused to be married till her father got home.

Being engaged suited Maria. To see them together now, I could hardly think there had been a time when they might not have ended up like this—Amir was led by her in all things. It was easy to forget that only weeks before we had all swung in the balance of her uncertainty.

Maria swanned about town with him now, loving the newness of how they could go places together and eat in restaurants, and how he could walk through the front door instead of dropping her off at the bottom of the driveway. They'd arrive together at teatime carrying paper bags of greasy samosas and chaat, Amir smoking outside in the garden and trying to make conversation with Ayesha. We waved them off as they went to see his friends, the other writers and journalists and teachers who looked like they never slept or shaved or showered and talked in a different, more loaded language. Maria could take her place there now. She had a world outside of ours. This was impossible.

It's all happening so fast, Bina said, as she gathered up the things they'd left behind—a half-empty cup of chai with a cigarette butt floating in it, and chocolate wrappers curled under the saucer.

Well that's what happens when you're in love I guess, Leila said. She was leaning back, with her elbows on the marble patio. Everything else must seem so quiet, she said.

Ash snorted, snapped a biscuit in half. Don't let what's happening to Maria make you all loopy about love Leila, she said.

What will we call him, she asked, When they're married?

Bhai I suppose, Ayesha said, drawing the words through her teeth. We can't just call him Amir.

Bhai. Leila tried it on her tongue.

Come to think of it, I'm not sure you should really be calling Jimmy by his first name. He's so much older than you—maybe you should call him bhai too. Or Jimmy Bhai.

I won't, Leila said flatly, That's ridiculous. We've known him so long already. And no offence to you Jimmy, but he isn't my brother.

Hush beta, Ash said, swatting Leila on the shoulder. That's no way to make the boy feel like part of the family.

Their car was still in the driveway while we talked. Maria unwrapping the last globe of chocolate with her fingers and bringing it to her mouth. He was tapping his fingers against the dashboard and singing to her, head bopping as he did so and not stopping even when she screwed up the wrapper and lobbed it neatly at his head. The car skittering back into the road and taking them places none of us on that patio knew anything about.

In the year leading up to the wedding, everything changed. Ayesha and I both in our last years of school, that strange time where everything gets chucked up in the air. The whole hot summer had gone like this. Nothing else had really happened, so all our time had gone in plotting other people's futures.

I spent the last week before school opened sitting in front of my window, wishing the time would move slower. It was monsoon season, coming down so hard that even the steps between my house and the Maliks seemed impossibly far. The warm trap of my bedroom, the smell of rain and the thick curtain of it in the back garden reminded me of the time before I'd known the Malik sisters, how I'd spent most days back then. My voice growing thick, hollow from not speaking at all. I was dreading school enough to wish for the rain to go on forever, as long as it could hold it off.

It was funny because I got a lot better at school before I got worse. This was where Amir came in, things shifting and even thawing between us. I called him by his first name openly now and we'd sit together at the long dining table with my school work. He was always sucking the tip of a pen into his mouth, helping me where he could.

It's not enough to be clever, Jamal, he would say tapping the side of my head. You can't expect them to look into your brain and see everything you've got up there. You have to show them.

His presence in our lives seemed to bring both Mehrunissa and my grandfather a certain relief, as if they'd long suspected that the girls and I could use a male presence in our lives. He was the kind of man you'd want on your side in a fight, with a sort of sensible hardness to him. It was difficult to imagine I'd ever been so wary of him, so unwilling to let him in. It wasn't only that he was young and easy to talk to. We all respected him now, even Ayesha. That initial coldness between us, the time it took for it to ease, slowed me down that year. More of Amir could have kept me from sinking but as it was, I flung through those months like a wrecking ball. I hadn't recognized the affection that lay behind his manner—his frustration with me when he thought I wasn't living up to my potential. Every essay and exam felt outside of me, a small series of reflections that I cast out into the world like a net to see what I could catch.

The idea of all this nothing—the essays, exam scores, letters from teachers—leading to a place at university seemed impossible. I had the idea that no matter how the rest of the year turned out, my grandfather would probably find something for me to do. I was not alone in this, there was a group of us at school set up in similar ways. Boys I'd never really got on with before but that last year, we drew together. We were a band apart from the people taking it seriously, joined only by indifference. They were wary of me at first. Over the years, I'd been a weird presence at the school, never friendly or overly hostile. Now, I leapt into it with an energy I'd not felt before. Piling into their cars after school, skipping tuition and music lesson and dinners with the girls in favour of chasing around the city with people I barely understood or liked.

Everybody ignored it for a while—either not knowing what to say or wary of prodding me when I was finally doing what was expected of me: being one of the boys. Even Ash, who'd never had any problem saying exactly what she thought, held off.

Only Amir pulled me aside.

You're not really thinking about this, Jamal. About your future, he said, after I missed the dinner party that Dada and Mehrunissa planned for my birthday, showing up at the house past ten o'clock, still buzzed. The food was cold, the party almost over. I wanted to go straight to bed and sleep till the punishment of the next day, already drowning out the cold tones of Grandfather's voice, but Amir dragged me out to the lawn with a bottle of Pepsi, sitting me down on the stone steps and looking at me like I'd let him down.

I slid down on the cool grass, rocking back till the heels of my hands sank into the soil. I felt good there, rooted and calm. These days I was used to my clothes and the inside of my mouth reeking a bit, like tobacco and the sourness of mornings, like other people.

You're not like everybody else you know, Amir said. He dropped to the ground, next to me. I think you deserve better than to drown into the crowd.

I shrugged a little. Everyone's part of it eventually, I said. I may as well get a head start.

Even the girls?

The girls are different.

The words croaked through me, mouth dry and fuzzy. I drank down the Pepsi and didn't look straight at Amir.

Why? Because they work harder than you do? They're not cleverer, you know. And this is your grand rebellion? Life is bigger than this year Jimmy, he said, But you're not going to prove that by throwing it away.

My silence, sulky and sudden just then, was something I would be ashamed of in the morning. I held the stock stillness of my pose till he sighed softly and walked away. I knew I should have said something—maybe a promise to try harder and be better as he got up and left but I couldn't find the words. Him standing by the door, brushing the dirt off his trousers and looking straight away from me.

It was the year, also, that Ayesha thought she would finally leave the country. Khalajaan's much fabled trip around Europe was starting to take on firmer shape—next summer, she promised, and Ayesha could hardly think about anything else. Her walls were papered over with maps. Over every city, she scribbled names of the writers who lived there, the ones she loved and the most important ones.

Everybody wanted to go abroad. We all watched the movies and worshipped the cities with blue skies and buildings that all looked like hotels and people walking around with umbrellas. Still, it was different for Ash. It seemed to grow in her that year, her eyes flicking off into the distance. Heartsick for something she barely knew.

I don't care for Dickens, she explained flicking out his name with a flourish, But I can't ignore him.

Funny because I didn't know what in the world I'd do if she left, if Ayesha was ever further than a few minutes from me but I understood it all the same. Everything about her seemed too large for that small house, the room she shared with her sister. Ayesha, in her trousers and rolled-up shirtsleeves, could exist in any city in the world for me. There was nothing for her here, and over time, I think it was something we both knew.

I took her to get her passport. It was October, and sweltering still. Dada knew someone who worked in the office so we skipped the lines of people waiting outside and slid in quickly.

The day before she was due to have her picture taken, Ash cut off all her hair. No one could believe she had done it. She came down to dinner one evening, with most of it shorn off. She had done it herself, she told them, standing up in the bathtub so she could stare right into the mirror. There was a patch in the back that was uneven, the ends making an upside-down U, but for the most part the hair sat curly and close, snug around her scalp. It made her look so different from the rest of them, so starkly her own self. Never again would the four of them sit on that low, wide swing in the garden, their dark, identical ropes of hair swinging down their backs.

Her sisters missed it most. Even their mother, usually her champion in all things, only put a hand on the top of Ash's shorn head, with nothing to say. Maria tried combing out what was left, trying frantically to smooth out the spikes and towers of it, but gave up eventually.

It's no use, she said. You'll just have to cover it up or something. Wear a scarf.

Now, sitting behind Ayesha in the car, I could see the nape of her neck, the way the hair feathered down from the base of her skull, the forgotten city of her skin carving out to spine.

It changed everything about her face, the lines hard where they used to be soft. Bringing her into sharp focus, her serious eyes impossible to avoid. Her mouth tipped up in a smile when she caught me looking at her. Cheer up, J, she whispered, They'll get over it eventually.

I mourned it more silently, never forgetting the wild strands, how they caught in the frames of her aviators, or how she would spread it out with her fingers like a net. A few last long hairs were picked off the elbow of my sweater, a few weeks later. I had been finding them everywhere—in the buttonholes at my cuffs, stuck through the pages of books or wrapped around my pens. Leila's little face crumpled when she saw them, spreading them out on the table in the sunlight, their broken ends stuck out in fiery points.

She shook her head. Ash'll never be pretty again, she said.

In the photographer's shop with the big lights pouring into her face, she looked terrifying. I leaned back against the wall and watched her perch on that chair, not nervous or fidgety for once, just still in the light. The room smelled of hair oil and hot tea, and Ayesha squared her shoulders, a familiar movement that would normally shift the curtain of her hair off her shoulders down her back.

Smile! said the photographer.

Ayesha bared her teeth like a weapon.

There was nothing about that time that seemed still, all orders of things shifting slightly from where they were before. I watched the girls, the way they fluttered to the end of the year and how they managed to reign in the loose energy they felt. Even Maria—the whole of that time mapped out to her wedding and she still went about the world doing things that were normal and natural. I could barely get out of bed in those days without thinking about the end of the year. By the time January rolled around, I'd almost stopped trying at all. I'd wake up in the middle of the night, nausea hitting me like a punch in the gut because I'd remembered suddenly that I'd learned nothing for weeks, that there were piles of notes and textbooks to be memorized if I was going to turn things around, if I was going to get out of this at all. I lay there thinking about things, making empty resolutions and plans to spend the whole weekend with my head in the books, wrote up plans for learning and revising, till I fell into a nervous, twitching sleep.

And then the morning would come and all that resolution was gone. I stayed in bed, unmoving till noon and then crawled down the stairs to drink tea on the front lawn, smoking a cigarette and reading. It's funny because I read a lot that year, more than I think maybe ever before and later—schoolwork sent me straight into the arms of novels. I finally found my grandfather's study, a tall room filled with bookshelves, as fascinating as Ayesha did. We sat there often, in the armchairs by the window. Every once in a while, her leg would swing against mine and I felt then that maybe things were going to be okay.

For his part, Dada developed an affection for the Malik family without my really noticing it. They came around on Eid, the girls lining up on the sofa, and he was soft with them in a way he'd never been with me. I guess he finally stopped thinking of them as something that was distracting me—it was hard not to admire the girls when you met them. I found myself constantly following the way they spoke, wishing I had the same manner. All of them, even Leila, carried a kind of confidence that seemed to me something wholly grown-up.

He spoke with Maria about Amir, about the Captain and his return at the end of the year.

It was in an act of uncharacteristic generosity that he offered to host an engagement party for the couple, six months after they'd decided to marry. It was winter, a month of soft weather in the city. Everybody got married in December or in January, soaking up the lull of the cooler days. I think he thought Maria should enjoy some of the privileges of being a bride while she waited on her father but it came off strangely. Most of the people who came were Dada's friends. Neither Amir nor Maria had the large families that generally swirled around occasions like this one. There weren't many of Maria's friends. The way the whole business with Amir had played out was bound to distance them from people, but for her this was especially pronounced. She never complained about it. Not then or even later when all the girls whose weddings she'd danced at chose not to show up at her own.

From the Captain's side there was only Khalajaan but when I asked about their mother's family, Ayesha only shook her head. She tugged at one earlobe, a tic she'd picked up lately without her braid to pull on.

I don't think so, she said. Ma says they might make it down for the wedding but we're not very close.

Didn't you ever visit?

We went a few times when I was younger. Leila was only a little baby then, she said. I loved it, it always seemed quiet up there and peaceful, and the rooms all had these wide, open windows so it felt like you were always in the sky. I used to hide in my aunt's bathtub with pillows and a pile of books. I don't know what happened, but we just stopped going.

Doesn't your mother miss them?

You know I think it only makes her sad to go up there for a little while, she said. I asked her why once and she said it wasn't the same.

What do you mean?

She was a guest in her own house. After all those years it seemed like too much. She had been dreaming of the tall trees, the mountains, the cabin her parents went on holidays. She wanted to drink Kashmiri chai and have people tell her stories. It wasn't the same to be just a visitor, you know?

I could understand that. I'd felt like a visitor almost all my life.

I went to see Amir at his flat, the day before the party. He lived off Zamzama, locked up five flights of stairs. The staircase stained with spits of paan and graffiti and the whole way up I could smell the butchers across the road, raw meat and smoke. I'd never been anywhere like this before. Everything seemed bright through his blinds and farther away, the city was just a mess of flickering lights and from his single sideways window I blinked down at the dizzying fright of it. Inside, the flat had a spareness I liked, the smell of coffee and tobacco and old books. He rolled us a pair of cigarettes and pointed to the shelf of books he thought might help me.

We sat by the window in little cane chairs. He was much calmer than I expected, but here in his apartment it felt oddly formal between us.

I've been looking at houses, he said, in a flat voice I'd never heard him use before. For myself and Maria when we're married—

Oh.

I can't really expect her to live here.

I like it here, I said. The paint was peeling and the apartment stank of the street below but there was a sturdiness to it, a square quality that made me think of Amir. The room fit around him like he'd laid the bricks himself.

Amir laughed. It's fine for me Jimmy, but I don't think it's really the place for a woman.

I felt the panic uncurl from my spine when he called me Jimmy; he'd been so on edge all afternoon, stiff in a way he hadn't been for a long time.

Maria won't mind, I said, and this was more than hero-worship. The kind of women who care about that sort of thing don't tend to marry teachers.

I want to give her the best, he said, carefully. And I'd hoped to do this without dragging you into it but—

What's wrong?

He got up, hands fidgeting in his pockets.

I want to ask your grandfather for a loan. It's not the manly thing to do I know, I should work harder and wait. But Captain Malik is back in four months and we can't wait, we've got to do it straight away. She won't do it unless he's here and if we wait, we could be hanging on him to come back for another six years, you see?

I nodded. He wanted me to say something, I could tell. He leaned back against the window.

Well, he started. Do you think he'll say yes?

I put up my hands. I don't know, Amir.

Of course. Of course. I'm sorry for asking, I feel ridiculous.

I'm sorry.

Don't be stupid Jimmy. I'm the idiot—trying to get a child to do my dirty work for me. Never mind.

Is everything okay?

He smoked quickly and nervously. I could see the space between his knuckles where the sky flattened against the rooftops, an uncertain blue.

Yes. I don't want you to worry.

I could talk to him if you like, I offered, even though I had no idea how on earth to bring up such a thing.

No. Please don't think that's what I wanted you to—I only thought you might know if he was likely to say yes.

Okay.

I mean it Jimmy. Don't mention it to him. It's bad enough I have to ask without me trying to worm my way through his grandson.

I nodded again. Everything about this conversation made me want it to be over. I poked through my bags, fishing the books back out and putting them on the small coffee table for something to do with my hands.

I'll speak to him after the party. He gave me a tight smile. You're not going to worry about any of this, are you Jimmy?

I put the whole thing out of my mind until the next afternoon when I went to get Amir for the party. Dada had Amir's suit ironed in the house so he wouldn't crumple it driving over. I took up a drink, in case he was nervous. His fingers twitched like spider legs as he tried to sort out the cuffs of his shirt so I picked out the cufflinks myself, the dull gold clink of them in my hands as I steadied his wrists against the table. Downstairs, the sitar player was starting up the music. It filled the still empty house and Amir's forehead rumpled into little creases.

Dada likes you, you know, I told him.

What?

He does. He thinks you're a good influence on me, I said. It was easy to talk about this with my eyes on his wrists, curling them in white cotton and fastening it there. This whole party, all of it—it's as much for you as it is for Maria. He thinks being around you is going to teach me how to be a man.

The splitting open of his face as he laughed, I spilled the last cufflink through my fingers, and it clanged, battered, to the floor.

I don't know if your grandfather is on the wisest track there beta, he said, picking it up and dropping it in my open palm. But I'm willing to be flattered.

Don't worry, I grinned. I've got no intention of trying to be like you.

I'm sure he'll appreciate that in the long run. I can't imagine a man like your grandfather being very happy with a history teacher for a grandson.

There was still that stiff tightness in his face. I wanted to sit him down and tell him not to worry, the way he'd said to me the day before. But it was time to go down now.

VI.

The return of Captain Malik vibrated in the air. I'd been walking up that driveway for years and the day he came home, it felt like the architecture had widened, the rooms skittered in their foundations to make room for him. For weeks, the girls had talked of nothing else. The mixture of excitement and nervousness shaped everything they did, from housework to how they dressed.

Ayesha started brushing out her hair, longer at last, and wearing the clothes Mehrunissa bought her instead of old shirts. She scowled when I teased her about them.

I want to make a good impression, she said, Maybe when I'm old enough he'll take me with him.

Why don't you just ask?

It's easy for you to say. Boys just to have to ask for things and it happens but it's all more complicated when you're a girl. People expect certain things of you, she said, sighing and stretching out her legs in the grass. She was even wearing a dupatta over her shoulders, the ends of it frayed from where she'd caught it underfoot. You think maybe my relationship with my father would be better if I'd been born a boy? You know Ma told me they'd have called me Raja if I was a boy. Can you imagine? You have to be so good-looking to be a boy called Raja.

I'm sure you'd make a very handsome boy, I told her and she whacked me with her dupatta.

He was standing in the window when I came in and he was smaller than I'd expected, but I found myself unable to sit down. I dragged down the bottom of my shirt and fussed with my collar.

So you're the young Jamal I've heard to so much about, he said, and I remembered then that Napoleon had been five feet five inches.

He put his hands in his pockets and looked up at me so that I felt each of my seventeen years down to my toes.

How is your grandfather?

Very well, sir.

You look, he said slowly, walking around to the desk, Very much like him. Less like your father, I think.

I nodded, and his eyebrows went up.

Everyone says so, sir.

I was sorry to hear about your father, he said. A pipe burning in one hand though I'd not even noticed it till then. He was not much like others his age. I suppose he was wild, but very clever all the same.

No one ever talked about my father, avoiding him as if the memory was still a sore wound. I cleared my throat. Everyone says so, sir.

Well then chhotay saab, he said, sinking into his chair, Tell me about yourself. So, you've met this man of Maria's then?

Mr Amir teaches me history at the school.

I think I heard something about that. Good school, Patrick's. Is he a good man?

Yes sir. And a very good teacher.

The Captain gestured for me to sit down and my eyes flicked up around the room as I did. I'd never been in the study before. It stood between the living room and drawing room but without the Captain in the house, it was always locked, like Bluebeard's den. It was not so different from the kind of studies my grandfather or uncles might keep or the kind of place I might imagine Amir growing old in but settings like that—all that leather and wood— always made me uncomfortable—feeling out of place.

I hear Amir's spoken to your grandfather about a loan.

Yes, sir. I shifted in my chair. I didn't have anything really to be nervous about—I now knew nothing about the whole matter, having dropped it entirely when Amir asked me to. Still, somehow, discussing it with the Captain felt disloyal.

And he has agreed to lend him the money?

I don't know.

Well, he said, leaning back in his chair, I'd rather he didn't.

Sir?

I don't want this man going into marriage with my daughter with debt on his back. Maria deserves the best.

I wondered how he'd heard about it at all. It didn't seem like the kind of information Amir would have freely divulged.

I want you to speak to your grandfather, he said.

Dada and I don't speak about business too much.

The Captain raised his eyebrows. The old man's not grooming you to take over? he asked.

I've not got much of a head for maths.

Business has nothing to do with arithmetic. I'd think your grandfather would have taught you that.

I didn't ask what a navy man might know of business, didn't question it either when he closed his lips tight and said, I will find somewhere for them to live myself.

He sat so still as he looked at me, a kind of harshness to his face that made my hands sweat. I believed then that he could pull a house from the sea and put it beside his own, shaping an empty plot of land with the sheer force of his mind.

Most women weep on their wedding day, tears streaking through their make-up as they are handed into cars with their husbands, their family gathered around for the rukhsati—saying goodbye to their families with kajal running down their cheeks. Even I'd been to enough weddings to know the memory of my cousins being bundled into cars, tiny balls of shivering red and gold—but Maria's eye were clear and bright from her first qabool hai. We stood in tight circles around her and when she hugged me, I felt the loud drum of her heart thumping against my chest. She leapt out of the hall and into the car. There was none of the pageantry that people expected, only her naked happiness.

We watched the headlights vanish into the dark road. Dada was putting them up in a hotel for the night. When I turned to go back into the hall, my suit jacket draped over one elbow, I saw Ash standing in the doorway. The lamps lit up behind her head so everything was on fire, the red tent, the bright flowers in her hair. She was trying not to cry, I realized. Her lips pressed close together.

Are you alright?

She held a wrist up to her mouth and didn't look at me. There was a garland of roses and jasmine around her hand, and I could see the wires inside it pressing into the side of her cheek, streaking it lipstick red when she lowered her arm. Still dry-eyed, but she nodded and looked up at me. Everything is changing, she said, Nothing stays the same.

I'm still here, I said.

She untwisted the flowers, plucking them off her fingers and on to the ground. She stared down at the scatter.

Let's go get some tea, I said. There's nothing left to do here.

We sat in the empty hall while people fitted into cars and drove away, the wedding deconstructing around us as the plates were cleared, the buffet table packed away, the once white tablecloths whisked away, stained.

I would always remember the blue curtains of their little house, how all the windows looked out to the sea. It suited Maria, that small house, because it fit around her and her new husband, snug and soft. For all her beauty, I would never have put her in a palace. She belonged there with the flowers and trees of this place, the small armchair by her window with her books and lesson plans and sewing. If it wasn't dark, I would walk the five minutes to see her. Following the smell of their house through the row of cottages—not the stink of burning candles but something light and sweet that just seemed to hang in the air.

Amir after his wedding was a changed man. The stiffness he carried in the weeks leading up the wedding vanished altogether. Everything about his body seemed to move better, as if his limbs had been taken apart and sealed back on properly.

They honeymooned on French Beach. Soon there were photographs of the two of them in the sand, joining the family archives. My favourite was of Maria on a horse, striding over the sands, her black striping through the sky. Her smile was one of warrior queens. The albums came out. One of her parents on their wedding day, her father tucked into a suit and her mother ageless. Ones of the girls all together, Maria at six and sixteen. Maria holding a baby that was either Ash or Bina. Even I made an appearance; a picture from the party my grandfather threw I stood between all the sisters, the camera catching me in a distant moment. I was staring into the middle distance but around me, the girls were laughing. Ayesha had her hand on my forearm and only just looked up in time so you could see the flick of her long eyelashes, disconcertingly coy. I would never get used to the way she looked in that picture, girlish and soft, as if the camera took her out of focus.

Just like at the wedding, Amir's family was nowhere to be seen. There was nothing in the house or in his conversation to prove that they'd existed. He seemed to just appear, a sum of all the stories people told about him, eating toast in the front room of that little house and telling me I had to spell better.

Have you not got any pictures of them from before they died? Ayesha asked.

Amir shook his head. They were lost along the way. My parents left almost everything behind when they came over during the Partition—what pictures they had on them were lost to the fire. The trains we came through on were burned.

Her eyes went wide.

That would make a great story, she said.

Maria frowned. I can't believe you said that.

Obviously I'm not going to use it. I was only saying that it's interesting.

Across the room, Amir shrugged and folded one ankle over his knee. You can use anything you like Ayesha. Only if you let me read it, though.

Thank you.

I'd love to read something of yours. I know I'm just a history teacher but maybe I can offer some insight.

Ash looked upwards. I think I'm alright.

She could be secretive about the writing sometimes but then there were days when it was all she ever talked about. The conversation around it was vague and I never had any hope of discovering what it was she was writing about or what it was that made her angry. It was the writing that controlled the weather on Ayesha's face, blue skies when it went well and monsoon storms when it went badly. She flicked between extremes faster than anyone I knew.

Even on the bad days, I never knew what to expect. There were times when she would lean her head on my shoulder and sigh Jimmy, till I took her out for tea and we walked the length of the beach unspeaking. Other times, she wouldn't come down to see me, even as I stood at the bottom of the stairs. There was no way to predict it, no possibility of peering into the citadel of her head.

What does it feel like, I asked, watching her fingers twitch over the typewriter.

She didn't look up from the page. It feels like opening up my oesophagus, she said, And trying to reconstruct dinner, she said.

Slippery?

Ash laughed.

Impossible.

These were not the only stories Ash had told. In a way, slapping together pretty lies was in her nature. There were separate rivers of deep practicality and nonsense in her and when they ran together she stormed. The most frequent victim of her stories was Leila, a little liar herself. Ash once told me that when she was little she would write spells into her notebooks, garbled messes of words she couldn't put a meaning to. She convinced Leila that these were family secrets, handed down by her aunts, and Leila too little to remember much of them swallowed this like a charm. Her braids would swing on either side of her head as she rocked back and forth, learning Ayesha's spells with more grim determination than she would ever apply to a lesson at school. When, years later, at sixteen, Ash coolly revealed that the whole thing had been a sham it shattered Leila's face. She was too old to be angry about it then, but she never forgave it. Ayesha had crushed jasmine in her hair and spread dirt across her palms, had made her say words that stuck in the hollow of her throat, little Leila repeating them with the same sincerity she kept for scripture, her index finger dragging along the page of the holy book when the maulvi came on Friday afternoons to teach the girls to read Arabic. Leila, who used these words to bring her grades in school when she did not study, to win the love of the beautiful boy who brought their vegetables every week, to give her the winning ticket to the school's prize draw (a locket of real silver as her unclaimed prize). And then every time they didn't work, the soft cut of Ayesha's voice saying she must not have said the words right, she must not have believed strongly enough.

A children's game. Say the words wrong, Ash said, and they can mean the opposite. This was what the maulvi said when he taught her to read: Arabic is a complicated language, he explained as he circled an agate ring around his finger, Get the words wrong and you could be summoning the devil instead of god.

It had made so much sense that the rules should be the same.

On her two-week honeymoon, Maria wrote letters to her sisters from the beach. It was only a few hours away but she wrote them every day. The hut was Dada's and it was his car that Mehrunissa sent out every other day, taking the newlyweds baskets of food. When Maria sent them back, she packed in her notes.

In a way, the marriage was not the event it might have been to other families. The long engagement meant that Amir was familiar to us all. But it didn't change the fact that now the girls only saw him as the man taking their sister away.

The other side of those letters was gloomy. They spent those weeks packing up Maria's things and setting up her new home.

It's the first time any of us have ever been away, Bina told me, as she sorted through the bookshelves and extracted Maria's. We've never even been on holiday without each other.

The house shrank without her, tightening around the family. There are some people who leave the room and you stop thinking about them right away. None of the Malik sisters were like that. Their absence took up room, a seat at the table. We lived those two weeks on her letters, which were short and friendly, as if coming from a great distance. She talked about how the ring felt clammy around her finger, constricting the skin, snake-like. After the first two days, she had taken to wearing it on a chain around her throat.

I thought about the chain she usually wore, a string of silver knotted together at the back. The soft gold wedding ring, swinging around her neck. Amir was the luckiest man I knew.

In the hut, they lived and breathed alone. Outside, there was nothing but the sea. Out of season for tourists. She walked out in her nightdress at noon to sink her toes in the sand, trailing back up the porch with gritty feet. She sat next to him and lifted them up, one after the other. Her hair netted over her shoulders, shifting all at once when she moved it off her neck.

You look like you belong there, he said.

It was not till Saturday that the families came in, filling the huts around them. It was then too that men dragged their camels and horses along the beach, the glittering capes, charging for rides.

They walked up and past them, not touching but leaning comfortably against each other, fingers brushing as the wind swayed their long bodies like grass. In the early months, they could barely look at each other in a crowded room. She'd never held his hand before or touched his shoulder in a world outside their own. Their eyes learned a kind of visual Morse code, certain numbers of blinks for yes and no.

Here they learned about beds, about springy mattress and how sheets could get caught beneath them. The slip and slide of pillows. They learned breakfast preferences, how Amir drank his tea standing up, and usually by a window with a cigarette in one hand. She watched the narrow pane of his back against the light, looking at his skin without fear of discovery. They learned the measure of each other's breathing, the switch between the body being awake and asleep. The smell of her mouth in the morning, sour close to his own, and how her legs swung over the side of the bed as she slept as if rocking out of a boat.

On the Sunday they were meant to come back, they took one last walk along the length of their strip of sea. It was early enough in the morning to still be emptied out, quiet as the end of the world.

We could swim out to sea, she said, And never come back.

He could have lived with her anywhere, even among the waves and crabs, but he said nothing, instead only letting his hand touch the curve of her hip, and led her to the car. They drove in silence, watching the shore recede to city. People packing markets and shrines, the whole way home lined with warm bodies, the crush of blood and bone shoving into their world.

She spent one last night in her parents' house then, as Amir packed up his bachelor flat, loaded records into boxes and put away his posters. In her old bed, her sister breathing heavy beside her, she did not even try to sleep.

VII.

When the end of the year ticked around it took us all by surprise. The fever of the wedding had burned through all our lives. I'd forgotten about the exams, the execution date of results. I finished school with marks that even I thought were beneath me—shocked to find myself caring. I'd playacted at indifference for so long that part of me must have thought it would just sink under my skin and become part of my bones. Instead I sat in the office where my teacher told me I'd failed almost everything but history and maths, and felt the world shift beneath my feet. It was worse than even I'd known to expect. I knew before he said it: I'd dug myself into a dead end. Even Dada's connections couldn't get me a place at university with these grades.

I drove home on my own, nerves shot to pieces. I turned circles around our block, revving up the engine at each corner to drown out my brain.

Ayesha stood, watching me, from the end of the drive. I didn't want to go in so she waited till I'd exhausted myself.

Results? she asked.

I nodded. I could feel my back break out in little rivers of sweat, crawling down my spine.

You want to come in for a cup of tea?

I shook my head. My tongue was a furry beast in my mouth, unusable.

What if I snuck you in the back so you wouldn't have to see anybody?

I stuck my hand out through the window and squeezed hers. She waited while I parked the car, unusually still, and led me past the driveway and sat me down by the tree before disappearing into the kitchen. She came back with a cup of tea and sat down next to me.

Maybe I should get you water instead, she said, quietly watching my face.

I'm fine.

Are you going to tell me what it is? she asked, tapping her nails against the thin china handle.

Slowly, the breath stopping at all the embarrassed pulse points on my throat, I did.

Oh J.

Don't.

Have you told your grandfather?

Does it look like I have?

You want me to tell him for you?

I couldn't do that. It would have softened the blow—Dada loved Ayesha and anything filtered through her would be better than whatever came straight from me—but he'd think even less of me for it, later.

No, it's fine. I don't think I can let you stick your neck out for this one.

Well you'd better go quick. She checked her watch. Maria and Amir are coming around for tea. I'm guessing you won't want to see them straight away.

My stomach leapt and crashed again. I'd not even thought of Amir, of how I would face him. I thought of all the hours he'd spent, head bent towards mine with a pen behind one ear. I gulped some of the tea and walked around to the house. I wanted to do it quickly and then go up to my room and disappear into the fortress of my bed where nothing and no one else existed.

I think they all thought it would change me, kick some kind of spirit back into me. If all I needed was proof that I wasn't invincible, maybe I could still reach all the things they'd hoped for me.

I was taking a year out—the grown-ups had convened to come to that decision but really, it was the only option—and at the end of it, I would take some of the exams again. Only the ones I absolutely needed.

Only the Captain almost seemed to think it was funny. He shook his head when he heard. I didn't think it was possible to fail everything, he said. I didn't correct him. My middling grades in history and maths wouldn't have saved the situation. Don't they have some kind of system to prevent that?

His wife turned sharply from him and raised both her eyebrows upwards.

The topic of conversation at Dada's house or at the Maliks' never strayed far from my future. They suggested I find something to occupy myself with, something to keep me busy but I never really did get into anything. Even music seemed like a good use of my time to Dada now, better than the sight of me lying sprawled across my bed till the sun was low and red in the sky. I spent most of my time around the house, reading or eating. I only ever played the piano at night any more, without lessons, so I kept at it on my own, loudly and into the late hours, keeping the servants awake with my hammering.

He cut off my money so I had no way of getting anywhere, no gas or cigarettes. I was housebound. The first few weeks were bad. I could feel time trickle through me, slow and deliberate. I didn't think I would ever get out of it.

Munir came around a few times and offered to take me out. He was one of those people I thought I could stand to be around, out of the boys from school, but more importantly, he always had money to burn—more careless with it than generous, precisely. He lived close enough to my house that it was no effort for him to drive past and get me when he went out. I would wait by the front gate when he came later in the evenings, so Dada wouldn't hear the honk of his car or the wheels on the driveway. It was okay as distractions went though it meant I was always stranded wherever we went, waiting for him to decide when to leave.

The poker games started around October. At this point I'd been a rat in the cage for two months.

They started playing in the dhabas, groups of them rolling out of their jeeps and descending on the street-side cafes. Cross-legged on the charpais, smoking cigarettes and eating nothing. I never had any money so I just watched, smoking somebody else's cigarettes on the side and watching them sweat over the cards.

Eventually they started hiking up the stakes. More money made the games more intense. There were a few brawls, nothing serious and then one day a boy with pockets full of winnings was held up at gun point on his way home. The next week, two of them fought in the street. The owner got wary then, and he said we could come around whenever we wanted but we couldn't play any more. You're bad for business, he told us. And we must have looked out of place. This was the kind of place where people got their breakfast before work or took their wives to look out at the sea. We didn't fit.

Chutiya, Yasir said, holding up a piece of cotton to his nose to stop the bleed. Where are we supposed to go?

I'm trying to think, Munir said.

The club? Gymkhana?

In the rearview mirror, Munir looked at him as if he'd grown horns. Are you retarded, he asked, You want to play poker where our fathers get lunch?

I know a place, I found myself saying.

The first night Dada had the cook send us tea. I think he must have been relieved that I was bringing friends home—both that they existed and that I was no longer disappearing in the middle of the night. Most parents might have come down, made small talk with the boys. They may even have known some of them from my days at school or through their parents. But Dada hated small talk. It suited him fine just knowing I was in the house and less likely to end up in some kind of trouble.

It started off okay. The boys would come around in the evenings, after finishing whatever it was they did, college or work or cricket. These were the ones who had stayed in the city, a crowd of friends thinned down from school. They didn't like not being able to smoke in the house, having to take their cigarettes and joints into the bathroom, or how Dada stocked his liquor cabinet so meticulously that it was impossible to take anything and not have it noticed. The house was quiet as a church too, not the sort of place that lent itself to raised voices or the kind of shoving around they'd got away with in the dhabas. Still, this gave everything a terseness that hadn't existed before—the silent rooms, the overhead lights, the spare room and cups of rapidly cooling tea. It looked like something out of a mob movie. We played around an old ping-pong table.

It set up a tighter atmosphere, one where it was a lot easier for people to get carried away. Things didn't progress the way they did at the dhaba. There was no slow run of cars alongside, no hum of vendors and beggars and other people's voices. In the room, it was just them and me sitting quietly in the corner. I fit in well, supervising and making a bit of money from being the host. However closely I kept an eye on them, I couldn't stop them from hiking up the stakes and I'm not sure I wanted to—it meant more cash for me. I wasn't just doing it for the cut I got. But now that I finally had the money to leave the house, I never did.

It was December before it occurred to me that maybe I should be doing something to regulate the room. At that point, there had already been a few serious incidents. One when Rehan was accused of cheating, getting so worked up that he went around to the other kid's house the next day, his father's thugs in tow, threatening to blow kneecaps. There was enough old blood there that it calmed down quickly, but something about it still put me on edge. How we must have looked to anyone outside of our circle: boys playing at grown-ups, Ash would have called us. Their fathers, who gambled themselves, and mothers who played a little would have rapped each of their boys on the wrist and that was all. These were the days before prohibition, before the casino closed and before the city tightened for everyone. A clutch of seventeen-year-old boys trapped in a small room with a bottle of stolen whiskey and someone who failed maths and accounting keeping the books, we were the picture of what this city would turn to in the future, in the years stretching too far ahead for us to see.

There was a reason the boys and I fell into the pit so quickly. There was nothing else to do to distract us from ourselves, from whichever quick spirit was shouting at us to rebel. We were not yet old enough to tell apart our impulses from our actual desires. All around us, the country was speeding into something and people more grounded than us were trying to push it away and build walls against the waves. We were setting fires just to see what they'd kill.

The whole of that year was one long summer, months simmering and bleeding into each other. I never knew what day it was, and always slept till noon. There were weeks where I hardly saw the girls or Dada. Maria was on leave from St Patrick's, working on her masters. Ayesha spent most of that year at Khalajaan's, writing in her spare time. Amir and I had drifted apart at this point. It wasn't that he gave up on me, I just stopped answering his calls until we only saw each other when the whole family gathered. He'd stopped trying to nudge me either way when it came to my life. By then it was only Captain Malik who persisted even. Making speeches about the military on his last night in town. His mangled loyalty meant he could rail against the war but never let anyone else do the same.

It was Ayesha I missed most of all. All our long afternoons together gone, the hours we spent doing nothing at all. Sometimes I went to see her before the games and asked if she wanted to come over, but the answer was always no.

Why don't you come over for breakfast, she asked, You can drive me to Khalajaan's after?

I did try once. Still tired and sore from the night before, still smelling of tobacco. They watched me as I sat down at the table, wary in a way they hadn't been even when I was new to them. Halfway through, I got up to use the bathroom and splashed cold water on my face. Above the sink, I could see just my eyes hanging in the mirror. Beneath them were stains of disordered sleep colouring the bottoms of my eyes.

When I came back out, the table had been cleared and the only thing left was my morning coffee. I finished it alone at the dining table, while she gathered up her things. I was glad they were all gone.

The harsh yellow of the morning filled the car. It lit up the curve of her head.

You know, I said, touching the top of Ayesha's hair with my hand, You've got some brown in there. I've never noticed before.

Only in the sun.

It's always sunny around here.

No more than the other girls, she said swatting me away. Leila keeps threatening to dye hers when she's older.

Oh?

Golden.

That would drive your mother crazy.

She keeps saying she wouldn't care, Ash laughed. As if it'll somehow convince Leila it isn't worth it.

She's going to see right through that, I said, steering up the hill Khalajaan lived on. The car swerved a little and I saw her lean forward and grasp the dashboard with her fingers. It made me think of the days we worked together, watching her fingers fly across the typewriter while I played the piano. She would hum a little while I practised and I like the sound of the keys chiming in with that of my music. I thought we sounded wonderful together, better than any record.

I can imagine Leila blonde actually, I said, pulling up outside the house, A bit like—what's the name of your aunt?

One of the Captain's cousins lived in Clifton. She read fortunes for actors and politicians.

Mrs Firoz, Ash rolled her eyes as she said it, Oh Leila would love that.

Very bohemian, I said.

Mrs Firoz once told Leila she had the second sight and for a long time after that Leila carried a crystal with her everywhere, studying its rotations to see into our hidden futures. She even went to Sunday bazaar with me and Ash once, hoping to find a pack of tarot cards. I wished for some of Leila's sight now, if only it could help me out of this conversation and the deathly grip of Ayesha's pauses.

Look J, she said. This was nice.

Khalajaan's swans clucked about the lawn. I watched them with half an eye, Ash doing up her lipstick in the mirror. She pursed her mouth in an O the way Maria taught her.

I miss you, she said slowly, Or more like—I miss the way things used to be.

Everything in me tightened when she said this, screws turning on some imaginary board.

I guess you like being one of the boys, she said, putting the lipstick back. I switched off the ignition and was glad for my sunglasses. It was difficult to not look at her when she watched you like this. All the girls had the same round eyes as their mother, the clear brown that went soft and light in the sun like the melting of gold. Of them all, only Ayesha had a way of fixing them on you, unsmiling, however. After all, she had none of the girlishness of her sisters.

It caught me up all the time when I was in school, finding myself confessing things to her just off that look, though those moments were rare. We'd always been better as partners in crime.

That's not it, I managed.

No? She blinked twice, her lovely black eyelashes dusting the tops of her cheeks. She wore confusion rarely and loosely, always taken aback. Her clever eyes blanking out.

Let's not talk about this now, I said nodding towards the house.

No.

You're late, I said, softly and then, on impulse brushed the top of her hair again.

It's only that I worry about you, you know.

Doesn't everyone?

She rolled her eyes at me impatiently.

Anyway, she said. I've got to go.

She lingered again at the car door, said: Come again soon J, before finally shutting it and disappearing into the house.

I thought then that it was difficult as it had ever been to have things I could not tell her, this person so close to me. I stayed there for a bit outside Khalajaan's, the dying cigarette in one hand. When I took off my sunglasses, I caught a quick glimpse of my sunken eyes in the rearview mirror, and turned away.

It was a warm Monday in February when Taimur did it. I was still in bed and I heard the phone ringing in the other room but didn't move. No one I knew ever called me at home, it always rang for Dada or sometimes on Fridays it was our cook's wife, calling from the village to hear his voice.

I lay still under the covers. The evening before I took Ayesha to Sunday bazaar and we walked around for so long that the soles of my feet were sore in the morning. I heard a clearing of throats in the hallway and a pause before Dada said my name. He sounded so far away, so old and quiet as I got out of bed and slipped across the marble floor towards him.

Who is it, I asked, but he just handed over the receiver, watching as I brought it up to my ear.

Jimmy, thank god you're there. Munir's voice was as thin as nails against chalk boards. It's Taimur, he's done it—the bhenchod's finally—

What are you talking about?

He threw himself over Kalapul this morning.

The bridge cutting the centre of the city, arching over the commercial district. I felt my stomach slide up the cavity of my torso and then bang back down.

What?

You know the money he lost last week—they're saying that's what made him do it. Jimmy, you've got to get rid of everything, the books, the room—clear it all out.

I slid down the wall and fitted myself, cross-legged, beneath the table. Dada was still next to me, standing.

There wasn't much I knew about Taimur. He'd been a scholarship kid at Pats. He'd got into every university in the city and some abroad but didn't have the money yet to go. He'd been working part-time as a mechanic to make up the tuition, spending the rest of his days interning for someone's father—I think maybe it was Rehan's, but I couldn't be sure. We'd never really spoken.

When I handed him the ticket of what he'd owed, his face blanched bone dry. He looked at me the way felons do on their last days as free men. Men like ticking clocks. I heard stories about boys in Lahore who'd blown out their brains because they'd played too hard and lost too much. I'd never thought something like that could have happened here, not in my grandfather's living room, not drinking tea out of his china cups, unwrapping samosas from greasy paper with the boys I'd gone to school with.

VIII.

Nobody asked me about it directly. Not Dada or Ash or even Amir.

There was no way for them not to find out. Even if Ash hadn't walked in as I was unsticking a Jack of Spades from the bottom of my foot, perched on the ping-pong table, rifling through receipts with a bucket beneath me, kerosene and a lighter to one side. It was the largest scandal to rock the city for days. A boy like Taimur may have slipped under people's consciousness even with the connection to Pats but he was more than that; he'd worked the whole year at one of the most important law firms in the city. He'd been seen too much to be forgotten. There were newspaper articles speculating about the waste of his brilliance and his wondrous youth, rumours of a heartbroken lover in Maleer—all the props for a grand tragedy.

I was terrified every day that his father would come find me. I sat at the dining table, rod straight. I took out the textbooks for all the exams I was meant to give in a month, finally dusting them off from where they'd sat in the cupboard for months, but it was too late. I'd missed my shot. The words blurred together on the page. The line of communication between Dada and myself, always spare and wanting, was now gone entirely. We sat through every meal in silence. Half the time, he could barely look at me. I had expected an awful argument, the screaming, the punishments. It never came. Instead, the silence between us hung around my neck like a noose.

It was the time, too, for the city to fall apart. We could feel the seams coming undone even before the military came in. These were the years that would be written down in history as bloodstained and dirty but it didn't happen all at once, instead it crept slowly upon us. People shot through the streets like lightning to get home. No one at the Maliks' ever went out any more, spending time in the house instead. I'd never wanted to be there less. I thought of all the years of freedom I'd wasted at the dinner table and they were eating out of me now, every evening as we continued to playact at normalcy. Over dinner we hummed the conversations of ordinary people, at last. We still talked about what was in the newspapers, about Leila's drawings and what the girls in Bina's class said or wore. The things that mattered stayed off the table.

The way tensions rose in our house and in the city, the way the whole country seemed to teem with a dull thickening heat—the days before monsoon storms. By the time war broke out, we were almost relieved. It gave the feeling a name; something that couldn't be quantified when it was just curfews and military men stationed outside schools or people sent back past the border. Everyone had family in the East who were selling their businesses and moving back. We heard about distant relatives with abandoned tea plantations, families who lost children on the way over, but this was when the dam broke, the hush-hush business of whole families fleeing in the night, smuggled across the continent in only the clothes on their backs, with just the jewelry in their pockets.

I was reading in the garden when it happened. Ayesha climbed over the wall between our houses, something she'd not done since she was twelve and we barely knew each other. When she flipped over on to the grass, I laughed after a long time—it was like time was turning back, like the world with Ash in it was coming back to me. Instead she drew herself up, her doomstruck face staring up at me.

What's wrong?

Papa's been called back.

It was a few weeks before the country would officially be at war but the Captain had news that things were getting bad. We sat together in chairs on the verandah, a radio buzzing between us. We stopped pretending, and soon stopped speaking altogether. Most nights after that day were spent listening to the news or reading the papers or packing away Captain Malik's things. Dada only nodded when he heard, said he thought the Captain would have left after the elections, the riots growing red, but I didn't know about any of that. I'd been hosting card games while the country was going up in flames and now here we were, on the cusp of war, and I could nod along to everything people said because I knew less than anyone there.

There was something still about the Captain, sat in his study while the rest of the house milled about him. He just kept reading, kept drinking pots of tea. His daughters and wife grew alternately pale and pinked, their skin switching colour as the panic in their bodies rose and crashed in waves.

He was not the first person to keep a cool head at the prospect of war; he'd been a navy man since he was as old as I was now. It was the stoniness in how he handled his family that caught me. I saw in this flashes of Ayesha's own consumption when she was writing, but harder. It was clear that he loved them, that he wanted them to be safe and wanted even to come back to them soon. But their distress only burst against him, never making it past the walls—no reaction in him, for example, when Mehrunissa left the dinner table the night before he was due to leave, her eyes sea-like. He stayed still while the white ghost of his wife's figure moved over the lawns, hands still dripping with food, mouth working thoughtfully over a bite. For years afterwards, this was the image I held of him—his shoulders as wide as the chair, how he held up his chin to the ceiling and didn't move.

We only found that Amir was leaving with him a few weeks before the fact. I never learned if there was any grand announcement. Bina told me about it when I brought over some of my father's old coats to see if the Captain wanted them.

She spread them out on the sofa.

They look too small for Pa, she said, But maybe Amir can use them.

In this city? I laughed. It wasn't yet noon and already the heat had plastered my shirt to my skin.

No. You haven't heard? Amir's leaving with him. He said he'd travel with Papa and look out for him.

There was something about the fact that no one had told me—not Amir himself, not Maria, not Ash—that filled every bone in my body with a dull ache. This was a new world and I was outside of it.

When is he leaving?

The same time as Papa, of course. It's two weeks now I think. She lifted her little shoulders and shrugged, Maria's beside herself, I can't imagine what she'll do. All alone in that little house.

I couldn't either. Maria wasn't built to live alone. I think maybe few people are but none of these girls, none of these girls who'd never been lonely in their life. The way she and Amir moved to each other at the end of the day, what just seven hours apart could do to the lights in their faces. I couldn't imagine what a longer, firmer separation would cause.

We drove to Kemari in three cars. Their suitcases on our knees and Ash's legs were live wires against mine. It was still bright when they boarded the ship, the dockyard full of families. Our goodbyes seemed solemn in comparison to the sobbing wives hung around the necks of their husbands, children wound around knees.

The Captain shook my hand. It was the first time I saw the years in his face, the lines softening where before they had been steel. Who was I saying goodbye to? A man who most days couldn't put his tongue around my name, who called me Jamal still with a stiff humour—even Jamal saab when he wanted to make me feel especially young and silly. Amir put his hand on my shoulder.

Take care of them, he said.

I squared my shoulders and swallowed. When he embraced me I felt his weight leaning all the way into me before he straightened and detached, then shuffled over to his wife, the whole scene silent enough that I could hear only the moving water behind them and the crinkle in his starched shalwar.

We stood at the shore watching them go. I think Maria would have stayed until it was out of sight entirely, but Dada put an arm around her shoulders and dragged her away from the gathering dark. I'd never seen him touch anybody before, let alone a woman. We filed back into the car, mechanical as schoolchildren pouring into class. The whole way home was silent, only the sound of the azan in our ears, pulling us back into the belly of the city and away from the docks.

Something seemed to click after that. I gave up smoking, I walked over to the Malik house every day—when Munir called, I asked Dada to say I wasn't home. I was building new limbs. It wasn't enough just to keep going. I set up residence at the dining table in the girls' house again. I took work for the exams I was meant to take over to them. I asked Maria for help and looked her straight in the eye when I did.

I still flinched when they touched me—Mehrunissa's hand on my shoulder when she asked me if I wanted more tea, a slight shiver going down my back when Ayesha leaned over me and the bones of her elbows cracked against mine. I got better at hiding the signs. I'd grown three inches that year, taller at that point than anyone else, even Dada, even Amir. The space between my shoulders and head was more room to hide the shaking. My spine jiggling every time I drove over Kalapul or switched on the radio or lay in the bath and remembered that the rest of my body was still there.

Still, it seemed to happen quickly. Everything before the war seemed to have moved slowly, honey sliding across the floor; now, we lived at a higher speed. One day, Taimur's father called at the house and the next, Dada was telling me to pack my bags.

Even then, the shouting I prepared for never came. He put his head in his hands and said without looking at me that he'd never thought it would come to this.

What did he say?

Dada stared at a spot on the wall behind me.

He told me what I already knew. That there is nothing about being a parent that is easy.

Dada cleared his throat.

I'm not sending you away. This country is falling apart and Jimmy, he said softly, You have made more messes than either of us know how to clean up. Taimur's father is not the kind of man to hunt you down but you and I both know it would be easier if you left.

He was sending me to London. Somehow, I'd managed to swing through the exams. Amir would still be disappointed with the grades, I would never do as well as he might hope for me. But it was good enough for university and Dada booked my tickets almost immediately. There wasn't much of a gap between the decision and execution. It seemed impossible to think that I'd just said goodbye to Amir only to be leaving myself. My promises to look after things back home were falling hollow.

And it was strange to leave a country in wartime. Patriotism streaked through, boys who had never cared for anything before but their cars read the news and followed politicians and ran into the streets for blood. The streets were lit, people hanging outside post offices for news from their families in the East. Every night on the television, there were boosting messages of victory but no letters, no telegrams came through. We were fed a single story, the narrative of which would come crumbling down eventually but hadn't begun the slide yet—though I would already be gone by the time that happened.

Ayesha was furious with me. With my inability to appreciate what was handed over. She never hid what she felt. The jealousy spiked in her voice. How she glared at me for not caring or wanting it even.

How can you be such a fool? she asked me. How can you possibly want to stay?

This was only a week before I was leaving. We were in the garden again and the cracks in our lives, my booked tickets, shot through my veins.

Maybe I don't want to go so far away from you.

Oh god J, she snapped. She was cracking open peanuts with her fingers, her kurta spread out between her knees to catch the shells. There's so much in the world that's bigger than other people.

Well maybe you should come with me.

Her mouth curled at me, sour. Don't be ridiculous, she said. How could I possibly come with you?

You could, I said. There was a high pulse slamming in my throat, making the words come slow and measured. We could get married and then you'd have to come with me. You could come to London and I wouldn't have to be alone and you wouldn't—

I could hear both our breaths drop at the same time. She sat up, tightening herself like a warrior. She must have seen I was serious because she looked as if the sun had just dropped in the garden beside us.

What on earth are you talking about?

Well maybe not married but an engagement of sorts then. Baat paki—everyone already thinks we're going to marry someday we could just speed it up a little and then maybe you could—

You think I care what other people think? You want me to marry you because most people already think I'm going to?

No that's not—I want you to marry me. There's no one else in the world I could imagine being with.

You don't know any other girls, she said flatly.

Don't be ridiculous.

She gripped the sides of the wicker chair and drew in her breath through clenched teeth. Jimmy, if this is a joke, she said, You're getting sliced.

I stared down at her and her body went to butter, the shoulders slipping down. When she stood, the peanut shells spilled out of her lap and rained on to the grass.

You know I can't, she said.

Why not? Honestly why can't we? What's stopping us?

She didn't tell me that we were too young to be thinking about it or that it was a stupid thing to say. She just shook her head and said, I don't think we'd get along that way.

When I left the Malik house that day, walking over to my house in the last hour of light, I felt exactly the

way I did when I'd first met them. That night, after the
party, driving Maria and Ayesha home, granted a glance
into their lives and then leaving it, I thought then how
possible it was for it all to end there. I couldn't be sure I
would ever see them again, I couldn't even really be sure
that they were real. Back in my bedroom, with everything
I owned either packed into boxes or covered with dust
sheets, I felt the wave of that first feeling again.

Lights passing through me. The ship leaving the
shore.

BOOK TWO

BOOK TWO

I.

And what did he remember of that year, his first away from home?

Well, most of the time he slipped through the city like a ghost. Novels had not prepared him for anything about London—not the cold of his flat (padding through in two jumpers and long socks all of January) or the long, winding streets that seemed to lead into each other so he was always lost, always ending up halfway across the city from where he needed to be, too nervous of his tongue to hail a cab or ask for directions. There were mornings where he'd be at classes two hours early because he'd just never gone to sleep, stayed up all night with a bottle of wine to keep warm, staring at a map of the city on the wall, trying desperately to make sense of it.

After the first few months, the novelty of living on his own began to wear off. He missed the kitchen of the Malik house, and eating his meal while looking at another person; not just staring at his plate, watching a cold collection of canned meats disappear. The phone calls from his grandfather were infrequent—one every two weeks at first, to check that he was still alive, and later, even more scattered. They exchanged telegrams that betrayed nothing—BUSINESS GOOD STOP WEATHER COLD—but in the end, these interactions were not very different from how their conversations had played out in the same house. A KEEP WARM from Dada had stunned him with the quiet intimacy it suggested. He could hear his voice, the slow and heavy weight of it, more clearly there than he ever did over the phone, where the static cut them off every other second, a constant reminder of the wide oceans between them.

In February, he got his first letter but it was not the one he'd wanted.

Dear Jimmy,

We talk about you every day and sometimes it is even funny how much we miss you. Mostly it seems to me as if no one has changed since you left. Life here goes on as you might expect. It is quiet here without Amir. Have you heard from him at all? He writes letters but I can't make sense of any of them. He tells me about my father and how much he misses me but makes no mention of coming home. He asks me if I'm comfortable and I want to know if he thought about that at all before he signed up, but no he thinks it's so noble to run into something like this. He thinks he's protecting Papa protecting me. Well good for him.

I've taken over his old class can you believe it. I keep expecting to see you in the classroom, sat at the back with your notebooks all splashed over with ink and that weird hazy look in your eyes. You know you have a way of disappearing in a room, my friend? The only other person I know who does this is my sister. And speaking of Ash, what's this business with you and her? She won't tell me but I know something's up and not just because there's not a single English stamped letter in the house. She misses you though you know she'd never say. When I think of the pair of you arguing like this even when you're on separate continents, well I just want to scream. Stubborn but you always have been.

Write to me if you won't write to her. Ma's worried you're getting thin over there or falling into bad habits or both. Let me assure her that you're no more a degenerate than you used to be.

Maria

He read it twice, and then put it in his coat pocket and left it there. Writing back would mean talking about Ayesha, and he could not even think about her without needing a drink. It was the weekend. If he started drinking now, he would stay indoors till Monday with a few bottles and the record player left by old tenants. He walked over to the windows and cracked them open, not caring that the air was thin and crisp outside, liable to choke his lungs. Two months in, the flat still felt like it didn't quite belong to him. The bookshelves stacked with Proust and Dickens, the yellow curtains and the wallpaper patterned with lilies. He slept on the couch some nights because the long windows of the living room let the moon into the room. The narrow, low-ceilinged bedroom felt like a coffin.

He put the glass down on the window sill, the sun burning bright in the low, brown circle. He took the letter out again and sealed it back up. His window looked over the back of someone else's garden, badly kept and overgrown. It was now almost a quarter of a year since he'd seen Ayesha. The longest they had ever been without speaking to each other, by far.

They had not even properly said goodbye. The last time he'd seen her was at a farewell dinner and Ash was somewhere else, that sea-deep look in her eyes that Maria had described in her letter. She was wearing an old shirt, grey and wide at the sleeves. Pushing back her short hair with one hand, mouth tugged up at one side.

He undid the front of his trousers and lit a cigarette. It had been a few days since he'd last let himself think of her—of course she had slipped in and out of his mind, but he had not allowed the thought to linger. He pulled at himself with both hands, the cigarette balanced in his teeth. Her bony elbows on either side of her plate, leaning forward for the tea so that her shirt parted at the throat, loosening to fall back from her collarbone. Her mouth curling into a little pout when she caught him looking at her, flushed. By then it had been a week already since the incident, since she had stopped meeting his eyes entirely.

Outside, the light was thin and fading. He finished in an old napkin that did not belong to him. He pulled the curtains, emptied his drink and went straight to bed.

His leaving had torn something in both of them—the emptiness Maria spoke of in her letters gaped wider every day. Ayesha did not grow used to his absence, instead it wore more stubbornly every day. The deafening quiet of the city slowly cleaned out of people.

What stretched before her were only days. If Jimmy could have seen her, he would not have known what to say. The fire flushed out of her, instead, a laziness more his own, simmering slowly up and then down. The second Sunday after the last day of school, she pulled out everything in her closet and began finally to stitch up her hems—the kurtas had been shorter for two years now; Ma and Maria had been begging her to take them up to fit the fashion, to buy new clothes, anything. What she had was boundless energy and nowhere to put it. What she had was a world pulled from books and movies and a city she only knew through houses and bookshops and school, nothing learned of its streets or secrets.

Her fingers bitten and her brain numbed from three hours sat by the television, where two women were discussing whether a doctor was handsome enough to marry. Her mother humming in the next room, the cat purring at her feet. She felt it coil around her legs, drag the thread from her fingers.

I can't keep on like this, she said.

Keep on like what?

This strange nothing. I need something to do.

Well put in more hours at the school.

It's not enough. The other day I was jealous of Bina's biology homework. I hate biology.

Her mother lowered her glasses and looked her over. Maybe you should go talk about it with Maria.

I would but I can't drive.

Her first adventure of the year: learning how to drive in her father's old car. Her instructor spat paan out of the window every few minutes, and pushed yellowing fingernails into her hand when she took a turn too sharply (and she always took a turn too sharply).

He's a soap-opera villain, her mother said, I keep thinking he's going to bury you in a ditch somewhere.

But he was the only person she ever spoke to who wasn't related to her these days, even if these were only stilted and pretending exchanges, where he asked her about her father.

He was a mechanic now, though he hadn't always fixed cars. In the years her father still lived in Karachi and still drove cars in Karachi, Mr Khan worked on movie sets and they all went to see them. He and her father had gone to school together. His voice garbled through the full mouth, the chewing paan streaking red along his lip.

I've known your father since he was only a little boy, he said, as people always did. And I remember you when you were little too—sitting in the back, with your sisters. You only came up to my knee then, he said, slapping the navy cotton where it gathered halfway down his leg.

And this was how it went in this city, of course; their butchers and carpenters and tailors had all known them forever. A place crawling with people and still it seemed like no one ever met anyone new, anyone who hadn't already known them all their life. She had never met anyone she didn't already know all her life.

Still, it did not change how it felt to be skating over the badly kept roads and the back streets, drifting over bridges and watching the cement blocks of apartments blur beside her.

It was August and too hot to breathe some days, and the car had no air conditioning, just a busted-up fan on the dashboard and a flattened-up copy of *Jung* that her teacher used to fan himself. She invited him in for tea and he said yes, sitting on the patio with one leg crossed and using his newspaper to swat flies off his ankles.

She's a good girl, he told her mother. But maybe she drives too fast.

Too fast? The thread of motherly concern working through her mother's voice, the wail of dying sailors strung through the word. Ayesha pricked that spot of worry more than the rest of her daughters, more than anyone else could in a lifetime—even with a husband in the forces and a family near the border.

No no, bajji. Don't worry about it. I won't let her go too fast. He winked at Ash. I only meant—mostly the girls I teach they drive very slow. They have the fear in their hearts. She does not.

Ayesha's never been afraid of anything.

Clever girl and she can drive her own car now—you should get her married before she gets into too much trouble, bajji.

Her mother smiled. I'm not ready to let go of her yet. My eldest has only just left the house Khan saab, I can't be expected to do without both of them all at once.

When this war is over I'll find her a husband, he promised. All the good boys are doing their duty right now.

Mehrunissa looked away then, her eyes flat and unblinking.

We know all about duty in this the family, sir. You don't need to tell us.

But the city was still full of boys. And now she was more aware of them than ever. They spilled out of restaurants and coffee shops, somehow still living the life they had before, boys who had been going to school with Jimmy and somehow untouched by all the wreckage around them. There would always be boys like that, boys who got airlifted out of a crisis and put in London to weather it out.

When he wrote back, his reply was short and uninteresting. The letter had to fit certain parameters of acceptable information. There was too much he was not ready yet to give away or admit, not to all those people waiting back at home. That this city was ready to chuck him back into the sea, and let him swim back to their shores.

It was difficult, here, to remember that he spoke English. People were not unfriendly, just largely indifferent, but he was conscious every day of how thick the words sounded in his mouth, how many times he needed to repeat things. Conscious also of how young he was and how little he knew and all this consciousness was what stopped him from learning, from propelling his life forward.

In London he was relearning the art of loneliness. Something barely remembered from his younger years, and now burnt up to something bigger.

Leaving did not prove to be the escape it had seemed back in Karachi, when Jimmy was heartsick and looking for a way out, a way to buy time away from whatever future he was meant to step into. Instead this is what he was drowning in, his days marked down to a desk in one of those offices, pushing numbers and wearing suits. He was stuck walking to classes in the morning and thinking more of the past than he did of the present.

The books he bought for university seemed to be written in some secret code that the whole class but him understood. Maybe someone like Jimmy had never made friends easily and maybe he would never grow into a more social skin, but in this new city the breaks were much harder. He was living he thought in a version of the world watered down just for him. The concept of conversations was lost on him, slowly at first and then all at once. Trapped in elevators and classrooms with people whose first names he never remembered, he found himself coughing till he reached his floor. His hands shook when the doorbell rang. If the corner of his eye found a familiar head on the street, he would walk as far as three streets in the opposite direction to avoid contact. The lack of company bled his world to grey. Lately, he went to movies for the conversation and because he hoped it would be loud enough there in the talk of other people to sink his thoughts.

Even here he found himself remembering trips to cinemas back home, Capri or Bambino, and how all six of them would pile into the car, the four girls squashed in the backseat, their limbs wound together like jalebi, and Leila always complaining about being in the middle. When Amir and Maria got married, they could take two cars and Amir would even buy tickets for the first show so they could be the first to see it. Jimmy would sit next to Bina because he alone was patient enough to explain the plot to her when she lost track of it, but sometimes he'd have Ayesha to the other side of him—and her face in the glowing dark was wonderful to him. They would watch the epics, stories from the

Bible dipped in colour and armour, and the whole time he was aware of having her breathing beside him in the trapped closeness of the dark. Here, he swapped out the history for harder movies, things that Munir and the boys always went to see back home: pictures with guns and moustaches and men in suits. And still he could not escape.

If there were a pill he could have taken to make himself forget he would have done so but nothing of the sort existed. The boundaries between knowing the girls and not grew indistinct. They were always just across the road, two short walls and a garden away. He heard the story, so many times, of how Ayesha climbed to the top of the roof when she was younger, using the trees that grew close to his own window.

How once up there, she found it impossible to get down. The door leading to the attic was locked. Too scared to scream for her sisters in case her mother heard, she stayed up there for what seemed like hours. The girls and Mehrunissa circled the garden at teatime, calling her name. She huddled silently against the drain pipe and after dusk, tried crawling down the branch that got her up there in the first place, only to crash on the balcony and break her wrist.

He had not been there when she was taken to the doctor, steely mouthed, arm as stiff as a drawing board. Not written on her cast or watched as her mother cleaned her cuts every night with alcohol and water. The girls held parties in her bed, Leila drawing pictures over and over of the girl falling out of the tree, until one was just right.

But the picture in his mind of little Ash, folded against the narrow wall of the roof or her arms stretched out to grab the branch with the tips of her fingers was so clear in his mind that he could not always be sure where he was and he wasn't.

He remembered so little of his life before the Malik girls. Even when the specifics returned, they did not seem real. Plays acted out in a different life, the world turning to colour when the girls entered his life. Summers and winters blur together. There must have been people then—people other than himself and Dada in that house. There were even times when he caved out of his natural state of isolation at school and went around Munir's house or to the beach with some of the people from his class. Holidays in other cities. He spent a summer in Lahore with his uncle and aunt, once.

Dada sent him to Lahore for the summer a few years ago and he kicked about for six weeks there in his uncle's office, sharing a tight, air-conditioned room with a much older boy from the university, not doing much other than reading and drinking pints of cold Pepsi. He remembered nothing about the work, only the smell of sweat in the small room, and how he'd sneak down to the reception room and call Ash.

The spitting hot summer streets and going home in the afternoon to find his aunt laid on the sofa with a cold cloth on her head, the radio still going in the background. She was the only member of the family he actually liked, completely devoid of the cloying maternal attention that most of his female relatives slathered him in. She made sure his shirts were ironed in the morning and let him borrow her books (even the dirty ones with the heavily lined spines, flipping open to certain passages easily). Other than that, she kept out of his way. Dinners were quiet, often just him at the table with his uncle and aunt wafting in and out from various social engagements. Once, wandering home at midnight, tipsy and loose-footed, smelling like champagne and perfume. Both of them in an odd burst of affection kissed the top of his head before tripping up to their bedrooms.

He'd not wanted to be there that summer, had wanted to stay in Karachi and sleep till twelve and drive up and down along the sea with Ayesha or listen to records in their attic. Any other year and he would have loved a summer, a whole stretch of weeks not under his grandfather's thumb, but that year missing her filled his mind.

He'd thought (at the time) Lahore was lonely, too hot, too far away from anyone he knew. It all seemed different now.

II.

The second letter came in April, postmarked on his birthday.

Dear Jimmy,

We all wrote you letters but we're sending them out slowly. We want you to have one every couple of weeks though I guess they'll be too late to be birthday letters. They will all be very different I'm sure. Ash will ask about the city and Leila will want to know what art you've seen. Bina has been knitting you a scarf. Don't tell her I told you. It's vile of course but you must wear it every day or you'll break her heart. She'll know if you don't, she always does. She's sending it over with Munir. His mother visited your grandfather last week, and we hear he's going to be in England in the spring. Don't let him get you in trouble, that boy hasn't changed a lick since school. I keep seeing him in the dhabas. He's been after Nighat still but she thinks he has a girl in Lyari and won't have him till he gives her up. I don't think they'll ever make a match of it which is just as well.

You said being in London made you feel like the world was bigger, and to be honest, you being in London makes me feel the same. I know Papa and Amir have been floating all over the place, but I don't think about them in quite the same way. I remember what it was like when they were here but I can't picture them on their ships, their caps and their cheeks scratchy from not shaving. I have no idea what your apartment really looks like but I can build it in my head. I can build you in my head. You in a suit and tie, a proper little sahib. Somehow I don't believe you'll ever come back.

But of course, you may have some of us with you soon. I mean, Khalajaan's got to take that trip sometime, doesn't she? She keeps talking about it still, and Ayesha is getting itchy. I catch her taking the passport out from the locker and staring at it.

Write to her. It's the last time I'm going to say it, and do it soon, will you Jimmy. She needs it and she'd never ask herself.

Maria

On Eid-al-Adha, a telegram from Dada—SENT MONEY FOR GOAT STOP EID MUBARAK—he was glad not to be in the city then. He thought again of Lahore; Bakra Eid had been in the summer that year, and his uncle had taken him up for the sacrifice. They'd been at the farmhouse for the week.

The hill in the heat, his uncle's hand on his shoulder after, saying softly that he had always wanted to do this with a son.

He didn't do it himself, though, it was the gatekeeper at the farmhouse who slit the calf's throat and his son who held down the body. He thought of Abraham and felt his own throat tighten, wishing he could blink the whole scene away.

When they drove back to the city two days later, it still smelled of blood, rotting carcasses not quite cleared away. Back home, the two of them on the swing in the back garden, he told Ash that he'd done it himself.

Did you actually, she said. Her voice flat, eyes behind sunglasses.

Of course. Chacha wanted me to, you know—every man does. He said it made him feel like I was his son.

God J. That's great for you.

Then she got up and went inside. They didn't talk much for the rest of the week. Mehrunissa and her daughters were particularly sensitive about the slaughters. They never participated, had not done so even on the rare holidays when Captain Malik was home. On Eid, theirs was the only house with no goats or cows lined up outside—another thing among many that set them apart from everyone else he knew, another thing about them that people thought was strange.

But this year the Maliks were let off the hook. The whole country boiling up to war—who could think of Eid, of festivals and food? What happened to a city when it stood at the start of a war?

Something like nowhere else in the world. Karachi was both a new world and the end of days.

It was in December that the slender choke of irony tightened around their throats. They had parted with their husbands and sent them off to fight a war on a distant border and now the monster was at their door, no one there to protect them. Leila would wake up in the middle of the night from wild fantasies of her father swooping in on a boat and warding off the enemy with a large gun. Where was Captain Malik during Operation Trident? Who could pull Leila from her dreams of the city caving inwards—I have the sight, she murmured as Bina rubbed her hair and hugged her slowly back to sleep. We're not safe here.

In the end she was only half right. Yes, they were under attack, no, they were not safe—but the war passed and in the new year they were still alive.

This is how it happened during the Partition, Mehrunissa told them. There was no telling what would keep you alive. It was like there was a blanket of protection over some houses, some invisible spell and the night would pass and in the morning, some houses would have death hanging over them and another's life.

Every morning was new then, and holy. Splitting open their days with tea and toast by the radio, the whole family crammed around its song, every soul in the city hinged to one thread. People talk about next lives, but in times such as those you lived seven lives a week.

By then, Maria had moved back in with her family. She did not last long in the house by the sea on her own. Everything in her skin felt as if it was going to waste. Her husband had left her rotting in their bed. The decay crept up inside her, with the smell of old flowers. The gutters upended outside their street, meals unconsciously prepared for two that went bad in the kitchen sink.

Admitting the loneliness had not been easy. For weeks, she brought Mehrunissa stories about crime in the city, hoping she would be asked to return home. Hoping she would fold.

It never happened. A month after her husband left for the war, Maria showed up at the door with a bag of her things. She unpacked in her room quietly, while Ash watched her from the bed through the triangle of her knees. She fit back into her old room—her old life—with a complicated ease. Her new womanly things felt out of place in the old bedroom. Lace nightgowns, perfumed scarves and the last of his clothes that still smelled like him.

The move soothed her nerves. In the twin bed next to her sister, she could nest for hours. Though the woman who had returned was not Maria the wife or Maria the virgin, but a stranger. For the first time in her life, idleness found her. With Amir gone, her compulsion to learn slowly bled away and Maria who had loved to teach and study now spent her days listless and unmoving. The house worked around her, the machine women turning cogs in their collected lives, and amidst all the bustle Maria was still.

For twelve months she waited for him, double the time they'd ever spent together. Penelope at least had children to occupy her.

In her new world, breakfast could last all day. She'd sit there by the paper without reading, just awake in her chair. The room filling and clearing around her, and

Maria still there in the evenings when the rest of them fluttered back home. She took up her letters then, the only thing she kept at with any regularity. She wrote to her husband every day and her father every week, and in between, the steady hammer of her letters to Jimmy, her tongue clicking over her lower lip as she spelt out the words in her mouth first. She took up Ayesha's typewriter sometimes, liking the clean hard lines of it. It hid the shaking of her hands, the occasional tear.

She tried to seduce him back to her. In the few days of their marriage, she never had to be that way with Amir. There were no tugs of war as she had seen in other marriages. They moved together. They slipped around each other, no knocks in the pattern of their life.

I miss your warmth around me, she wrote. Her pen bolder than her tongue. Her mother told her never to put down anything in writing that she might later regret. The secrets of their life could not go here, not that early classroom heat. She remembered, in her bedroom, Ash snoring three feet away, how he slipped the straps off her shoulders. The room would spin and burn. His fingers on the inside of her thigh. His mouth on the back of her neck.

She would not tell him here that she loved him. She worried that if she did, he might not come back.

It was Ash who walked the news into the house. It came on a Tuesday morning, while she was sitting on the lawn, her feet up on the cane chairs and the newspaper draped across her knees. They were still bringing in the post and it was early enough for her to still be carrying the sleep in her eyes, furiously blinked out when they told her: Amir was missing. Missing in a wartime such as this could only mean one thing.

They're sending your father home, beti, the messenger continued, patting her arm in a gesture mixed with consolation and indifference.

They sent a general. So many people had died, those who were in the business of handing out bad news grew skins thick enough to bounce cricket balls off. What this seasoned man saw on Ash's face was clean surprise, the fresh shock of someone who has never met death before. It worked over her mouth with curiosity, as the click-click of problems now to be solved: how would she tell her sister, when would they find the body, who would bring him home.

She put her tea down on the grass.

Would you like to come inside?

No beti, he said. Give your mother my salaams and tell her I will come and visit when your father is home.

He stepped into his car, the large, black beast of it disappearing up their driveway, a vanished envoy of bad news. He had put this in her hands and she turned it over, this message she could not fathom how to deliver.

She was always a bad keeper of messages, never good at social translations or the distribution of stories. Once, only three years ago, one of Maria's friends called and Ash picked up the phone. Tell her I'm out, Maria had mouthed from the top of the stairs, and Ash had parroted dutifully into the phone: She says she's out, with the casualness of a baby. Maria had been angry for days.

This was a considerably larger burden to deposit. She picked up the cat and her books, and moved towards the house when she felt a dampness spreading down her elbow. She looked up and there it was, the skinny crow that had just shat on her.

When she walked into the dining room with a shit-smeared sleeve and her face red from weeping, her mother shook her head softly.

Ayesha jaan, don't cry. It's a sign of good luck.

When your father is home, is what the general had said. The strange resonance of those words. How could her father come home to a place that did not feel like it belonged to him? The switch of energy during his visits, the house worked into a dark frenzy. It could only work in small bursts, the spikes of energy of reordered lives.

There was no space for him in the larger sweep of their days—how long could Ash keep wearing her dupatta over one shoulder and pinning back the tufts of her hair that escaped from their short nest. How many nights could Leila hold her tongue at the dinner table and bite it against her usual chatter of boys and money and pretty things. In her father's presence she was washed out, a paler version of herself, hands folded in her lap and her voice only murmuring to ask for more roti, a glass of water. Even Bina was required to modify herself: fewer hours spent volunteering, and no more bringing her stitching into the living room to sit cross-legged on the carpet by her mother's feet, listening to her stories with the soft brush of her hand against her hair. The sitting room would become a man's world, where the Captain always saw his visitors, where he finished endless cups of tea with people they had never met before—tea that Bina served in china cups, her hands rattling with her fear of strangers.

And waiting for news made Maria morbid. She began talking about her husband as if he was already dead, the past tense without the vehicle of mourning.

We didn't even have kids, she said to Ash. Can you believe it? Amira told me not to wait, you should have them while you're still young, and I just didn't listen.

Stop that.

I wish I was pregnant. I wish I was full and fat and ready to pop one out into the world.

You're still young. You have time, Ayesha said distractedly, her head still tucked into her Fitzgerald. She was not good at dispensing advice, it was Maria everyone else brought their problems to.

What I don't have is a husband. He doesn't even have a family you know, so if he's gone, it's just like that— she snapped her fingers—no trace of him left in the world but a gaggle of schoolboys and a wife who didn't even give him a baby. Not that I even want a baby. But we never got around to doing any of those things. The things people do. And he didn't have anyone, the least I could have done is give him this. One person.

Amir thinks you hung the moon. He doesn't give a damn if you have babies.

Maybe. Now we'll never know.

When the news of the prison camps began to trickle through, the house grew tighter and quieter. All day long the only voices that rose and fell were those of people who visited with news of the Captain, tirades against the East, and tirades against India. I will makes the rivers run with blood, Bhutto had said, and this was what happened, this was the war that had swallowed Maria's husband, eaten his name and lost it.

The quietness in her only grew colder when her father came home. The harsh winter light of that morning, the surprise: Captain Malik carried home in a hammock, the women of the house running out to the driveway where three young men set him grandly on the ground as if lowering a king from a throne. He came home with only one leg, the other wrecked through with shrapnel. They'd had no warning. In the last year, the Captain had become content to let Amir send missives home—he'd stopped writing entirely. Did no one else think to write ahead? To warn his family? These were crazy times, and at least they'd sent him home alive. Three-fourths of his ship's crew had drowned, taken down on the coast of old East Pakistan.

When his wife saw him, she only put a hand to her cheek, the gasp muted in her mouth. Later, she would say, you send a man to war enough times you stop expecting him to come back whole.

Her daughters followed her silent surprise, four stricken faces behind her own, four pairs of hands that reached to bring him into the house.

I'll make some tea, Bina said, trailing out of the room as her sisters fussed him on to the sofa.

The shock did not lessen as he settled into the house. There was a comedy to how he moved, the big man slowed down by his stump, and his booming voice muffling pain when he stumbled into things. Before, the very chairs and tables, the rooms of the house, had all seemed too small for him—now he seemed to splatter into them, the floral patterns of wallpaper and tablecloth scrambled around his new unwieldiness.

Do you want me to tell you about the last time I saw Amir, he asked his daughter. The cough and wheeze of his voice. He had aged a thousand years since his last visit, loud, rusting hinges in his vocal chords, the whole machinery of his mouth working slower.

She moved her head just a little to the right. They were at the dining table and she was ironing Leila's school clothes with the table as a board. She kept pushing back her hair as it came down around her face. The breeze was blowing the white net curtains into the room.

Not really, she said.

No?

Not unless it's something you want to talk about. And not if this is your way of trying to tell me that my husband is dead.

He watched her fold down the corners of the polyester uniform.

Sometimes it helps to talk, he said. That's all I was trying to do. If I knew he was dead, I would have told you.

III.

Eid in London, his first one yet, coincided nicely with Munir's visit. Seeing him in the lobby of his building when he got back from class, waiting by the potted plants with his trench coat and funny flat cap—he was dressed in some approximation of how he felt Englishmen must dress but his socks didn't match and even the buttons of his shirt were not done up properly—felt strange and unreal. They hugged, the way he didn't think men here did, not a pat on the back but a proper one packed with warmth, and Munir, whom he never liked very much back in Karachi was the dearest person in the world to him just then.

They bought a bottle of whiskey the first bar they
stepped into, shouted Eid Mubarak as they clinked
glasses. People looked at them wherever they went. They
were tall and loud, and the hug, and the broken English
as they spoke and mixed their tongues.

So what's this about Lyari then? he asked.

Munir shook his head. Khabar tumhe yahan bhi mil
gaye.

I have my ways, you know.

He snorted. The Malik girls—that's the only
connection you've ever had.

Jimmy shrugged, took some of his drink. They're the
only ones I've ever needed.

Oh come on, khoobsurat toh hain, but everyone
needs boys.

They laughed and drank then to the boys, to all the
St Pats boys scattered all over now, none left in Karachi
but Munir really. Some shipped out to war and more who
had gone back to their estates in wartime. There were
young men missing, between Chittagong and Karachi,
more than anyone would ever count. Men the same age as
them, some who probably even went to the same school.
Across the continent, there were new borders being built,
politicians switching faces and they watched it all out
of the corner of their eyes. A glance over a newspaper,
a letter from home detailing the very basics. There was
a heady disconnect with that world, slowly every tinge
of horror muting—when he first heard about Amir, he
had not been able to sleep for weeks. Eventually, every

headline and every name became just that, lists stacked up in the backs of his notebooks, an indifferent menu of humans who had nothing to do with Jimmy.

So they drank till their legs were loose beneath them and they felt bold enough to go to the kind of bars with dancing, places Jimmy's classmates went on weekends.

With Munir Jimmy possessed an unimaginable boldness, more than alcohol or anything could bolster in him. The surprising lightness of Munir's feet, how he managed to charm people wherever he went. Picking a girl out of the crowd and holding her by the hips with both hands, the white cuffs of his sleeves rolled back. He peeled off his jacket, still dancing, and tossed it to Jimmy in the corner.

This, he shouted in Jimmy's ear when he came back to their table, the girl still clinging to his arm, is what I came to London for.

Everything worked for Munir. He was exactly the same person in London that he'd been back at home, captain of the cricket team, poker champion Munir. The Lyari girl his almost-fiancé forgotten, his mother who called drink the devil's drug forgotten. He slipped so easily from one world to the next.

Under the streetlamp outside, his hand on the girl's neck, his mouth smearing hers.

Jimmy watched them shimmy as if they were still dancing, Munir backing her up against the brick wall. How she broke away to giggle and swat him on the shoulder before smoothing her hands along the lines of his jacket and then turning up her pretty chin to offer her throat.

Even here, nothing had changed. Love was a glass box he couldn't get into. Munir and his anonymous girl were colours through the prism; he on the outside, looking, always, in.

There were days when he considered writing to Ayesha, of course there were. His oldest friend, in some ways, and in some moments his only friend. Maybe it would make him feel better. The last few weeks before he left, everything had gone faster and, at the same time, slower—the days crammed up with packing, with him sorting through his things to pick out what he needed most. Trips to tailors to be fitted for suits. Lectures on investments abroad delivered to him by his grandfather's friends and various other relatives, even a phone call from his uncle in Lahore whom he had not seen in almost two years. There had been no time to make things up with Ash, to say goodbye with any resolution.

History offered no refuge. People in his family did not fall out of love easily. His uncle waited twelve years for his bride. In that time, she married another man, lost two children and escaped a country in wartime. She came to him a different woman. When asked why he stayed so long without marrying, he said: I could not have been happy with anyone else.

Twelve years seemed impossibly long to Jimmy. He did not want to think about that kind of time. The thought that something could change between now and then was tempting—to imagine some kind of resolve cracking along Ash's spine, loosening the taut, unbending mile of her will. In the distance between them, she separated from her sisters. He thought of her twice; first in the thought of home, which was almost always of the Malik women. Of the four of them crowded in the soft light of their living room.

The second was Ash alone. Here she could appear anywhere. Across the street, he saw a flash of black hair being untucked from a collar and the quick movement of another's wrists would put him in mind of her, even though she no longer wore her hair that way. The spines of old books made him think of her fingers, the tips of them running over a library shelf. He saw her in shadows, shapes of grey cut out from the darkness of his hallway, slinking along the carpet like a cat. The strain of jasmine brought up the hollow of her throat, the waxy smear of perfume along her collarbone in the summertime. Trees bent the way her knees did, folded into his armchair, listening to him play.

He flattened his fingers on the keys in the lonely flat. She would sing with him sometimes. Her voice came to him now as if from a deep well.

IV.

They found Amir's body scrambled up on the shore, a blessed wreckage of limbs. These were the days when any unaccounted men became cells of desperate hope in the hearts of their loved ones, imagined alive or stranded in some forgotten part of the world or, worse, strapped into prison camps a country away. Maria was lucky to have a husband definitively dead.

Beyond the first three days she did not wear black. Usually houses would fill up during mourning. Death brought with it relatives carrying plates of food and setting down mattresses in the night. Instead, there was only the lingering burn, not of death but of mourning, circling through the house in ghostly rounds. Something that could not be removed or emptied out, something that stayed in the walls even when the body was washed and wrapped in white and carried out on the shoulders of strangers. Maybe she'd felt it before in other houses but then it had only been a brush in the air. Here it was heavy, a hand to the heart pushing it lower into the rib cage. In other lives, her husband's family might have gathered to share her grief but Amir never had any.

She was with her sisters and her mother when the news of his death came to her door. They were all she had. They were all she would ever have.

Three days of black. She observed the mourning period only as long as scripture dictated, though society expected more of widows. Maria refusing to behave the way other women might, seen a week later in the market, picking out lace to match her dresses or picking up Leila's paints, and even, once, out to dinner with a man

Amir knew before the war. An old school friend who said he wanted to pay his respects.

When her father questioned the wisdom of this, she only put up her chin and said she wanted to meet someone who knew her husband when he was little, was she not allowed that at least—no family to mourn with, no throng of loved ones, how could they deny her this?

Afterwards, taking off her clothes in the bedroom she shared with her sister, she watched herself in the mirror. Ash was still typing furiously downstairs.

She'd forgotten what it was to be looked at. She needed to remember what it was to be touched. It surprised her, what caught in her and what didn't. There was a coldness she was discovering in herself. A space where her husband was only a small part of what she missed.

She missed the privilege of her own house, those benefits that went with being a married woman. Hers was not the love of Ayesha's books. It shifted with its context, she was married once and now she was a woman without a husband. The flux and switch of it, her body a halfway house. Unwritten letters rattled about in her head. She plucked through the motions of what to do, folding up his clothes and sending them to the poor. She packed up their house, locked the door and waited for it to be sold. She did this, unmaking what they'd lived together, and she did it alone.

Now her days were filled with questions of what would come next. A widow was not afforded the same luxury as a woman waiting for her husband to return. She was expected to pick up and go on.

Her days spent by the window, she and her father and the harsh February sun glowing out on the green lawns. She hadn't even really thought about him since he'd been back, his vital shrunken self beside her, every day. Her husband came back in a box, but her father returned without a leg. Home for good now, fixed into the living room the way sofas and cushions and cat were. Before, when he'd come home for visits, the girls would shift around him, making room. Here was something they'd never thought to be prepared for: a permanent father.

His leg ended in a stump just below his left knee. They didn't talk about it much, the sinking of him back into their lives. He told her stories about the women he knew, the ones who raised her, Ma and Khalajaan and others, and how strong they were, how they would never sit around and wait for a man—this was not how she was raised.

He would talk about her arsenal of talents, her education and all the chances she had left in her. Most of the time when lectures of this nature came from other people they were easy to tune out, but her father's voice was not as familiar to her ear as her mother's or sisters', there was a greyness to its persistence that she found catching in her ears. He was still enough a stranger that she had to learn to ignore him, as she did everyone else.

He folded newspapers on his lap which he never read all the way through, the headlines strong enough to make him angry. He waited for his wife before he bit out his anger, the erratic gunshots of vitriol. Maria brought down her embroidery and it sat in her hands, the still needle poised over swatches of cloth and the balls of thread swinging down to Kiran, who snatched them up in her paws and ruined the stitch. She picked them out one by one, tuning in and out of the tirade against the government and the enemy and the broken world, these rants that rolled from topic to the other seamlessly till it was time for dinner. This was Maria's life, the trapped stitch in her sister's blouse.

(And here, the still uglier truth: that there were days when she found herself wandering through a world in which her husband came back with one leg, and her father didn't come back at all.)

Amir's knee bound up, and him with the black cane tapping the floor as he walked. His drawn face and emptier eyes and stilted smile. Even their lovemaking would change, the movements restricted in how their bodies would fit together now. Fumbling where once they were fluid and in the dark room, she pushed him down till he was flat on his back and she above him. She above him, healing him softly back. Undoing his pain and playing down his body, plucking the bad memories out of his pulse points. She pictured filling their cottage with babies, sunlight falling through the kitchen to halo their heads. She would rock them in the late afternoon, packing them into the backseat of the car to pick up Amir from school. She would tell his sons stories when they cried, about their grandfather the war hero, and the bravery of their line. Trace a finger on their plump arms and remind them that courage sang in their veins.

Cricket with the children in the evenings, books read out loud over bedtime. He liked to sing, she remembers— would he have learned nursery rhymes, channelled all of the gentleness of his large bearish frame into this new role? His wide strong hands lifting them up in the air.

It was a strange place to live, this other world. She could never stay too long, lingering there in the afternoons across from her father—his breath drawing her home.)

And there across the oceans, a telegram to tell Jimmy of his teacher's death; it got to him at the end of the week, a Friday-night piece of news hitting him squarely in the middle of his chest. The small whoosh of a life blowing out somewhere distant. Deaths back home were already branded into him. In the classroom on Monday morning, he could still feel it growing inside him, a dark and oily secret. There were people and newspapers and coffee cups milling about him as usual, the machinery of the university swooping out past the columns into the square, and here he was.

In the time they had both been gone, Jimmy had never written to him once.

V.

Khalajaan visited them every week now, every Sunday for tea. Usually the Maliks only saw her on special occasions, Eids or dinner parties in the company of visiting relations. She bore the heat badly. This is a godforsaken country, she would say, fanning herself with a pinched together wedding invitation. They sat out on the verandah usually, the girls lined up on chairs, and over the course of her visits, Khalajaan would go down each of their lives and measure their worth. This was her idea of offering the family support in their hard times.

You must find husbands for these girls, she said inevitably, turning to their mother with a stern look.

Mehrunissa sipped her tea. And where do you propose I look, she asked.

Khalajaan rapped her cane against the verandah floor, the dust ticking off the cement as she lifted her head. You want them to stay here forever?

Oh Khalajaan, all mothers want their children to stay with them forever.

Well they're growing wilder every day. There is no virtue in wasting their youth this way, she said. Ayesha especially—how could you allow her to cut her hair so short?

I wasn't consulted in the decision. And anyway it's grown on me, she looks rather nice I think.

She looks more like her father than any girl ought to.

The girls stifled a collective giggle, which rippled its way through them as if they were a single person.

Anyway, she continued, I can take her off your hands this summer if you want. I can't spend another July melting away in this city.

And so the long-forgotten trip to Europe reared its head again and shuddered through Ash, an alarm bell of hope.

Her travels in all her unwandering life: three trips to the north to visit her mother's family, all before she was old enough to keep much of them. She had memories of snowy mountaintops and log cabins but these were too easy to blur with received knowledge, postcards and books. What she remembered best was warm parathas for breakfast, Kashmiri chai ladled into cups and the sky black and cloudless at night, every star showing without the city smog. The way every one of her aunts pinched the flesh on either side of her nose and told her mother to put some meat on her bones. The air hostess who gave her hot towels to wipe her face and how it made her skin prick, and the wonder of peeling back foil from dinner spooned into a small tray, her elbow digging into the rotting carcass of the window seat and, under the dank, clinical smell of the airport, cheap perfume and sandwiches wrapped in plastic.

Still she was hungry for all of it and for the flux of muscle in her stomach when the plane took off, whooshing through her. Now that it was near, she could not picture the cities on the other side, only the airport, the narrow seats, the boxed-in restlessness of her legs. She lay awake at night with these thoughts flickering in and out, passing through her with nightmarish fuzziness.

Among other wonders, she pictured meeting Jimmy in his rainy city. The strangeness of being with him in another place, the new world between them of everything that happened since he left. Would they even be able to look at each other any more and would she even recognize him, this different boy, not the one who said goodbye to her at Jinnah Terminal—the one who let her drive his car up and down Sunset Boulevard for the first time, who had shared her first cigarette, the only person in the world who could ever keep up with her. The boy she'd thrown away, Khalajaan often said, though she didn't know the truth of it.

You should have locked down an engagement before he left, she often said. A boy like that doesn't come around every day—the money of course, but good-looking, respectable. Now who knows what will happen, probably he'll make off like his father did and bring home a gori mem.

Ayesha ground her teeth and reminded herself that the plane tickets were almost booked, the itinerary sorted and she could say goodbye to this city soon, to its sticky heat and the endless drum of its days and this woman could lift her out of it all—how could she hate her then?

VI.

It was harder for Jimmy to be alone, with Amir gone. He woke up in the nights with his mouth dry and his body shaking and it was months now but he was wrecked through, a half man walking the streets. He'd never known anybody who was dead before. His parents were only distant memories, but Amir was still the voice in his head, telling him to finish his papers, picking him up when he couldn't get out of bed.

It turned something in him—Amir always could. He found himself straightening his spine in the mirror every morning, doing laundry more often. He went to the pub a few times, tailing classmates. A boy from his economics class invited him out; they'd once shared a smoke, and it was the closest he'd gotten to a friend. Sometimes he just ran out of excuses not to leave the house, and it was lonely without Munir even if he didn't want to say.

After a time, he even met a girl. He first spoke to her in one of the usual places. John had asked him to meet them in the pub and when he got there, Sophie was alone at a table with other people's coats littered around the booth. She didn't really look like she was waiting on anybody, sucking cider through a straw. Her chin tilted up when he walked over.

Why are you still wearing sunglasses, he asked, after she stuck out her hand and gave him her name.

She lifted a hand as if to take them off, but smoothed down the top of her hair instead. She picked up her glass.

It goes better with the drink, she said.

John showed up then, slapped Jimmy on the back.

It's good to see you out for once, he said. You should have been at that party last week.

I'm sure, he replied.

Sophie did not take her eyes off him.

There were lights everywhere, bright holiday lights strung out through the pub, and it was the first evening in a long time he hadn't been at home unspooling spaghetti and listening to old jazz records, propping up mystery novels against his lukewarm bowl.

Along the bar there was a small crowd of bodies twisting by the jukebox and Sophie asked him if he wanted to dance. Really, he said, feeling his mouth dry out.

She arched an impatient eyebrow. The look smudged some of the sweetness from her face. She looked at him in a manner he had yet to recognize, something almost sly in the wide-eyed swing of it.

I don't really dance, he said

Don't or won't?

Can't.

Her fingers on his elbow and she stood up so her hips were level with his chin. The shape of her waist in pink dress, tied up in a bow. She looked like a present.

Later, in the cab, she told him she'd been watching him for a while and he remembered then that he'd seen her before too. They'd shared the lift at university a few times and once, on a hot day, it had been out of order. She was wearing a skirt with large red flowers on it, and he'd watched it shift as she climbed the stairs before him, her calves flexing with each step and the flowers disappearing temporarily in its folds, putting him in mind of bougainvillea on the white walls of his grandfather's house. At the top, her flushed skin, the heat smearing over her collarbone, had snagged in his head and stayed there for a while.

Her small, ambiguous laugh. We already know each other, she said, when he introduced himself.

I remember, he said.

You've always been so quiet, she said, and he told her that maybe he was shy.

Never tell a woman that, she instructed. They like to think you've got some secret pain—women love a mystery. You could be strong and silent instead.

Only in the movies, he said and they both laughed even though nothing was funny and the sound of her voice stood the hairs up on his arms, a warm bell chiming in the hollow of his ear. His mouth was paper, now. He wished he'd watched more of those movies, paid closer attention.

In his room the fear gave way to awe. Not a clue what to do with his hands when she pressed her gloves to his chest and pushed him to the bed. She undid the bun on the top of her head and let it fall to her shoulder, the many different browns separating in the lamplight.

She took off her coat in the middle of the room and kicked off her heels, and waited for him. Just there with her hands on her hips and the pink dress rumpled from where his hands had been and this put everything else outside of his head.

Snow battered his window, sugaring the pane, and he had never seen snow before or a naked girl. Her dress had complicated buttons all the way down her back. More laughter when he took his time undoing them, but he did undo them. Her narrow, birdlike shoulders worked their way out of the dress. He turned her over in his hands the way he might a song. Needing less guiding than he expected. She arched up into him, and from there his body followed hers. Her sighing pitched upwards, as he moved into her.

After he felt a certain numbness and the dumb wonder of it worked his way through him.

It was funny to be with her. Courtship as he knew it progressed slowly. He had seen people fall in love over months of lingering glances, their voices halting in their throats like trapped birds. He had only ever been part of other people's romances, with almost-friends from school who wrote notes to girls with a knife-like precision. Nobody moved in and out of love with any ease.

Things with Sophie were not like that—there was no need for preamble. It was as if she'd picked him from a line-up and that's all there was to it. Sometimes she would watch him, her head tilted to one side and he saw there the same look in her eyes as when she stood by the bar, scanning through the glittering bottles and pointing at what she wanted with a gloved finger.

And nothing about this was familiar to him, no pattern for them to fall into. They didn't stroll along the parks or eat at nice restaurants the way he'd seen people do in the city. Nor did they go to the pub after classes with the rest of the people they studied with. There was no special affection in public, nothing passing between them that might mean anything. They never went out. Jimmy did not share her love of the theatre, disliking the dark, cavernous trap of it and when he was on his own all he did was walk through the city searching for buskers to standby, seeing movies and walking through bars just to steal other people's words. But he had her now. He saw no reason to seek anything else. Most of the time they spent in his flat, lazy on the sofa with her records playing in the back and Sophie picking through his things with fascination, at first, and resignation, later. She always picked female singers with broken voices who crooned about ugly lovers. Her fingers brushing through his hair to swoop it up in a quiff and he'd groan, swat her away.

Still he felt something for her. There were mornings in his flat where she wore his clothes, jumpers and trousers that fit her badly, but she'd roll up the sleeves and make him breakfast. He was surprised she knew how. Back home, rich girls like her couldn't turn on a stove.

Morning light on her bare leg and the times they would wake and find each other in the sheets, coming together without asking. He'd watch her take off and put on her make-up, cold cream smeared medically on to her cheeks and the careful pout of her mouth, bearing her hipbones against the sink. Softening cold cream on to her cheekbones and smearing her neck and collarbone with sweet-smelling oils. The stroke of light hairs down her back, feline when she stretched at the end of the bed, to pull on her stockings and how she'd step into her heels, these dizzying displays of womanhood. She poured into his apartment on the nights she stayed over, the crosshatches of her bobby pins and tubes of lipsticks on his bathroom counter, everything gone when she left the next day.

More than this even, there was something about sleeping beside another person. He had spent so many sleepless nights with only ghosts for company, the Malik girls walking in and out as they pleased. The cocktail of loneliness and insomnia weighing his bones. Now there was someone warm and alive and there, a firebrand, someone who touched her fingertips to his chin and laughed at his jokes. It was more than he'd ever pictured having here, new enough that he could paste over the gaps in their world, the many things they'd never know about each other. His was the sleep of kings.

Things within him shifted, a moving of cogs and wheels. At sixteen, he'd grown four inches in a summer and felt growing pains up and then down his legs. This was not dissimilar, only turned in. Dada's letters grew less frequent, less full of advice and soon he was less lost. The city which had seemed so big and imposing was now coordinated to his needs what streets got him to which place. The world twitched into place. Sophie even dressed him a little, picking out shirts sometimes that he wore only for her, but it made him squarer. There was less nervousness now when he talked to people, and it dulled his awareness of not being one of them.

Now, he could play for her. There was something dead about playing to any empty room but now Sophie was there to tuck her feet up on the sofa and listen to him. She told him she liked to see his fingers move across the keys, and lifted his hands to her. If she found it boring to watch him go over the motions, she never said, only rubbed his shoulders when he finished and said, You sound wonderful, darling.

It was months before he realized that she never called him anything but darling or my love. And then, once, she asked him to help her say his name. Trying to make the shape of it in her mouth. Jamal sat flat on her tongue, so he waited for her to switch to Jimmy instead, like so many others, but it never happened. Names got lost in this mix of theirs. Nothing said that they would remember too well or hold on to later.

People together must make a business of knitting their lives he assumed but this never came up for them.

He never talked about his parents beyond the fact of their death, wouldn't know where to begin if she asked him about his home though she never did. These memories belonged to somebody else now.

When she asked once about his grandfather, after a rare phone call, he found himself unable to find the words to describe him. He was tall, he said and he never used a cane and was always up at six, and he took his tea without milk. The silver hair and the imposing cut of his shoulders, the bark of his voice that still made something inside Jimmy bolt to attention—how could he put these in words.

Dada was one of those people who must be met to be understood. He could never live in whatever flimsy photograph Jimmy might conjure up. He lived in his body, the high-backed armchair, knees sharp as knives and in the stories that he himself told—of the old country, of the vast miles he travelled to build his home and of all the people who populated his life, all their ancestors. Dada could tell stories four or five generations back. The history of India through the lens of their family, the stories thickest and most brightly coloured on the days Ayesha visited and Dada took to Ayesha more quickly than anyone could have predicted, could have spoken for hours when she was there.

In fact, most of the stories Jimmy still remembered were told to them both. Sat cross-legged on the floor in the study—a place he hardly ever ventured alone—Ash asked questions he would never dare to. The stories as heavy as stones. The year the country split apart and his grandfather, the first of his family had come over, waited at the train station for the rest of them. The train pulling into the station with the smell of rot and drying blood, carrying carriages of corpses. He could not imagine his grandfather ever giving him this history without Ash as the smokescreen.

Even less could he have imagined telling them now to someone else, this girl curled in his bed, sleepy and soft. The stories he gave her were something else—weakened versions of himself. Difficult to explain to someone how his childhood was shaped, the long years of only him and his grandfather and how he slipped into a different family like a changeling child.

He kept his stories, and she kept hers. Sometimes things would slip through the cracks and he would learn that she loved horses, or how she hated carrots, and these were the things that would build his image of her.

My mum never thought she'd get me out of the stables, she admitted, I think she was glad when I decided to go to university. It was better to spend all my time around books than around horses.

He could maybe picture her then in trousers and high boots, pink-cheeked and grinning. The colour of her face after a long walk through the cold, or after racing him up the stairs.

I was always meeting the wrong kind of boy then too—farmer's boys, travelling musicians. So she sent me to London, hoping I might meet the right kind.

Well, he said, drumming fingers up her hip. That was the wrong call.

Maybe.

He told her about his cousin in Lahore who played polo, suggested she might like him better.

I don't know about that, she said. Her knee slipped in between his.

It was as close as either of them would ever come to declaring themselves and in the end he would forget about this too. Words cast out between them catching nothing by the grace of their distance. Their lives set to different tracks, futures mapped out to part.

Later he would think back on his time with her as a blip on each of their lives. It had felt life-changing at the time to hold her. As if he couldn't believe he had all of these privileges—to be allowed to touch the inside of someone's thighs, to press his mouth to the silky top of her head and smell lemons on her skin. He knew it wasn't quite the same for her. She told him once about the men who came before him. It was near the end only they didn't know it.

I don't regret any of them you know, she said, as if maybe she thought she might. My mother always said men are proud of their conquests and women just want to forget but I don't know, I still think of them sometimes.

She glanced up at him and flipped open a lighter, putting it to one of the candles she left in his flat. Everything smelled better with Sophie there.

Oh, he said.

Not like that, she said. Not to miss them exactly, only I wonder sometimes where they are, what they're doing. Sometimes I'll think I've seen one in the street and I wonder if he's going home to his wife or children or— she broke off. It's not as romantic as you think.

No, I think I see that.

You do? She smiled as if unsure of him. She was dressing as she spoke, pulling a woollen dress over her shoulders. You know sometimes I like to think about what they must think of when or if I guess they ever think about me. Where I fit into their lists you know because everyone has one—am I the girl their mother never liked or the one they thought they might marry— oh I don't know. It's silly.

He watched her hook in earrings, lift her chain off his nightstand. It was only just light and he knew she would not believe him if he said that he liked her best this way but it was true.

You're sweet, she said, and leant over to kiss him. He could taste the morning on her mouth, coffee and toothpaste.

After it passed, the world seemed to shift onwards smoothly. London, slowly thawing from the winter of their meeting, slid into the hottest summer he had known in his few years there. He pulled off jumpers and socks, suppressed the urge to dive into the river. Classes ticked on slowly and somehow he never saw Sophie at school as much as he'd thought he might. They smiled and pass on, their small talk winding down as the year went on.

In the streets on his way, the long evenings were for lovers. He watched men take off their hats and women in short neon frocks stand outside wine bars and walk along the river. Over the next few months, and later, when the years were spread before him, he would think of Sophie that way: a head of brown hair shot through a window, a man holding up a drink.

VII.

It was October and outside, all the streets were patched through with large squares of yellow and brown, leaves damped into the pavement, sticking to his shoes and trudging back into the apartment. He learned the seasons from pictures in schoolbooks that looked nothing like the city he grew up in, the city where all months burned on a long, slow flame only easing off in December, where the weather was governed by the sea and the hot sun. Here in London, the picture book played itself out—an autumn of fallen leaves, afternoons fading early from gold to black.

For a brief time he lost sight of the girls.

There were days when there was no hint of them hanging about him, their spirit-like darkness gone altogether. He found himself leaving all the letters unopened, punishing Maria for writing to him when he could no longer see her step into his living room and pour herself a cup of tea.

There were days, in these empty rooms, when he could hear the family next door. Because he was lonely and because no one ever taught him better, he learned how to best catch their voices through the maze of walls and floorboards. He learned that if he leaned back in the bathtub this was where their sound rang through clearest. Some days, he would come home from classes in the middle of the day to crawl, still clothed, into the empty tub.

The children were being sat down for dinner. He learned to recognize the shapes of their voices. He knew they hated mushy peas, that they loved pudding, he knew that one—Isabella, he thought, was a name he heard often—was growing round and plump. Her mother dragging her to the scales after meal times.

Cake, she said flatly, Will give you spots.

The girl's pinched wails when her hair was braided or her shoes were laced up, or when her mother suggested tennis for her constitution.

The father was never home before nine or ten, he must be going somewhere between work and home. The pub or a lover's apartment. He never saw them in the hallways but he had such a clear picture of how they must look. Her hair up in curlers, green dressing gown, cigarette in one hand. And him with his low glass filled halfway, sleeves rolled up to his elbows. Mostly he heard them arguing or long, cold silences. They must have loved each other once.

Sometimes, he could just about make out their words, the soft humming sound of their laughter through the wall. Other days the sounds were less vague. Broken glasses, fights, shouting numbed through pillows. Silences stretched like Arctic nights.

He sat still and silent in the tub, clothes rumpled, his knees against the cold ceramic tiles. The clink of ice in a glass and then the woman, her voice strained as if lifting weights—my god, she said, Do girls do nothing but giggle. The arch of tiredness in her mouth travelled. Jimmy could feel it too.

There were days when he heard them together, the telltale squeal of mattress springs and the headboard rocking into the wall. The thrum of it against his own wall. Jimmy waited for the sounds he associated sex with: sighs and giggles and gooey moans. Instead, there was only a panting that faded and quickened, a staggering groan (him), then her, finally asking for a glass of water or for the lights to be put out. She always sounded so tired after, tired how she was after a day full of little girls.

They never took each other's names. Jimmy could not imagine anything worse; he missed his name in the mouths of other people. His name said right would sound like home.

What would happen if he knocked on their door? If he took wine or biscuits and belatedly introduced himself? Their faces in the dim hallway. He could talk to them. He could touch the inside of their house, feel the soft soles of their palms. There was nothing in the drama of what he heard that suggested they often entertained visitors—foreign voices were contained to deliveries. (They got Chinese food once a week.)

Maybe they would be glad of him. Maybe they would invite him in—he could watch the children while they went out to dinner. Help them with their homework. He could step into their lives and walk with them awhile. After all he'd done it before.

VIII.

It was difficult to be sure about what it was that took him out of the city. The last few months of university, a restlessness began to grow in him. People had finally stopped speaking to him slowly, as if he wouldn't understand, and he was even sure he would finish his degree without a hitch, so all that was left was the last stretch of the summer. And home glittering dark at the end of it.

There were days now when he got home and fell straight asleep, the hours between class and unconsciousness cut out—none of the fugue he was used to living in. His brain dimmed to blank walls, nothing left of the people who used to walk in it. He found himself boning up on his reading on the bus, his head filling up with economic theory as he walked. How natural restlessness was when all that he lived for was the time he felt outside of his body, when the sun was down and there was wine in him and others' voices swishing in his skull, none of the boring work that clamoured it up now. Then it would have been simple to explain why his bones felt uneasy, why every muscle in his body twitched as if someone had plugged him in and was running electricity through his skin.

He found himself in bars on his own on the weekends, picking fights in pubs where no one knew his name—seeking them out. Learning to hunt the men who would hit him the hardest, to tell from the way one might hold his pint how keen he was for a punch, and how well he would throw it. It was the kind of game men who chased women must play, to find someone who would give it up.

He was never one for fists before. At school, he stayed clean away from them that even his grandfather—forever expectant of pristine behaviour—was baffled. The one time he came home with a scrape, everyone believed it was a sports injury, and so it was.

One of the boys in his poker circle had brought a boxer to the house once. He's only here to play, he assured Jimmy, Not fight. Though if you're lucky, maybe he'll take you for a dance in the garage later.

The man—Hasan—could not have been more than a few years older than they were, but the boys tuned up around him, wary as they might be of a god. Weeks later, Jimmy would find remnants of him in the way the boys held their cards or leaned their right elbow forward to take a drag up to their mouth. Even Jimmy found himself in front of the mirror, trying to smooth his hair back the same way—though without the broken nose, without the swagger or broad body of the boxer, it looked all wrong. Just a kid in his bathroom mirror trying it up.

He was the first to respect Jimmy's policy of no smoking in the basement. Not wanting to go out the front, he hauled himself into the garden from one of the ground floor windows instead. The singular ease with which he accomplished it—no one had the nerve to follow, and so Jimmy, under the thin excuse of fetching more samosas from the dining room, had gone through the house and found him out there. Leaning against the brick wall as if it were his own. He looked more comfortable than he had downstairs. I need some air, he'd said, twisting a finger under the collar of shirt slowly, but maybe men who fought for a living instead of fun were always like this; calmer on their own, wired in company.

I've seen you fight, Jimmy wanted to say, even though it was only half true. He'd been thirteen the first time Munir had suggested it. The sight of the first pounding made him half-sick. Always such a girlish kid.

He'd screwed up his eyes the whole way through, the crunched bone when it finished—Hasan grinding the other man to the floor. Another man might have been able to compliment his technique now, slap him on the back, be easy with him.

How long have you been fighting, Jimmy asked.

Probably not much younger than you when I started, he admitted, Though many think it's younger. He pointed back down at the basement with his thumb. Don't tell them—I'm not having too many people mess with my myth.

The thrill of it—the rest of the night would feel like a private club only they belonged to.

I bet your parents are proud, he managed but it came out wrong, more bite than he'd intended.

Hasan shrugged. Baba was a boxer, he said. So I grew up with the whole thing. When I was very little I swore I'd do anything but this, but these things, they have a way of finding you. I like the rush of it, but it's not forever.

The rush?

You know what I mean. It's the same as fighting with someone over a bad word thrown—you feel all the blood pound to your head and you want the kill. Then after it is over, you let the aftershocks of that rush numb the soreness.

Mmmm.

Anyway, I don't plan to do it for much longer. I want a life outside of it, you know.

What do you think you'll do?

Hasan closed his eyes. Who knows? Allah will show the way.

There was nothing Jimmy could say to that, so he shuffled awkwardly until Hasan finished.

See you down there hero, he said. Crushing his cigarette in a flower pot and shimmying back down the open window.

Now that rush was in Jimmy and no place for it to go, he was coming into some latter-day version of what his teenage self could have been. Was he growing taller? No, only the voice sometimes breaking now if a fist caught him in the throat, going to sleep sometimes with patches of dried blood on his sheet. All this adolescence mixed up and thrown back at him at the wrong times. Licks of pain finding him in the middle of sleepless nights, almost pleasant as they moved over his legs, jumped through his groin, ribs, lungs.

There were days now that he even felt sorry for himself, something he'd eluded outright before—he was a man without much. A country empty of friendly faces, a man without a girl or even somebody to talk to. He was lonely as hell and maybe this is what chased him to the continent. There was nobody between here and Karachi he could talk to, other than maybe Munir. Munir who might pour him a whiskey and slap him on the back and tell him that the world was made for fighting and fucking, and well if he was quite done with fucking for now, then he better fight.

He sent letters to his grandfather, to Maria and even left a note for Sophie.

He'd only thought of Paris a week or so before booking the train, off a phone call from Munir on a Monday night. He was almost falling asleep in the bathtub, holding a pack of ice to his wrist—all he did was fight these days, or play the voyeur.

Munir was loud in the way some happy people can be, and drunk. It's amazing, he assured him. Nothing like London—there was always something dull about London, you know—

Well thanks.

Don't be like that, idiot. I had a good time with you, of course, but Paris is something else. And the women Jimmy—

I don't need details. He shut his eyes.

Not like that! There's just—so many beautiful women everywhere. I've even met—you'll laugh at me.

Go on.

But Munir had already angled past this.

You should come, he said. I can hear something bad in you.

Something bad in me? Jimmy laughed. Have I been possessed?

Munir was serious then. You don't sound yourself. You sound half-dead.

For the first time, Jimmy felt that way. Half-dead. The tub bearing on to his shoulders as a coffin might, and the ice pack slipping to lie heavy on his chest. His breath slowing to a harsh, guttural stretch.

Maybe I will, he said.

For the next few nights he took the phone into the bathroom with him in case Munir called again. He fell asleep that way. His ankles sticking out at the foot of the tub. There was something pathetic about it at all waiting on a phone call from Munir of all people the way one might a lover. He missed talking. With Sophie the quiet had seemed comfortable and this had floated him along for a while but what he really wanted back was the sort of clanging conversation that ran on for hours. Something to take him outside of his head.

His distance from the girls made his head spin. Hollowed out, thoughts muffled as if clouds had been stuffed into his skull to stop his brain from bouncing around. He lost the energy to fight, even.

By the time the week was out, he was at a travel agent's buying tickets. Something he'd never done before. He'd not been back to Karachi once in the whole time he'd been away and never thought to go anywhere else, not even out of the city. Maybe there had been a lack of curiosity in him, some hunger that most people his age have that Jimmy was missing—something vital, something that keeps him from being young the proper way, the way Munir was. He was always circling the same pubs and squares and tower blocks. He was always waiting for things to find him.

IX.

On the ferry over he thought of Ayesha and her worn copy of *A Moveable Feast*, the spine wrecked from being folded open. It was dark when the cab took him through the city, nothing really to see outside the windows but the fuzzy lights. He put his hands in his pockets and leaned against the window of the car, eyes blurring shut. Already he felt a little better, less like he was going to peel the skin off his face. There were messages for him at the hotel, the first from Munir congratulating him for leaving London at all, and the second from his grandfather. He told Jimmy he'd earned the holiday, and the sound of his voice through that message that told him that at last, here was something he understood, made him feel as if he could sleep for the first time in months.

The last message was from Maria, letting him know that if he was going to be in Paris he might as well look up Leila. Her little sister was in town.

Of all the things he expected to find in Paris, Leila Malik was not one of them. All those unopened letters meant he'd never even heard she was in Europe. And now they were even staying in the same hotel; he remembered this was the one Khalajaan had mentioned on her last trip to Europe. Ash had kept their soap in the bathroom, still wrapped in cream paper.

Jimmy almost did not recognize her. He had grown so used to seeing versions or snatches of the Malik sisters in other women that real, live Leila Malik was a shock to his senses. Here she sat in the hard-backed chair of the breakfast room, hair brushed back, tall neck, pinched eyebrows. There was the spell of a second where she looked like all her sisters wrapped in one person—it only passed when she lifted her eyes.

Jimmy, she smiled, just like that, as if they had both run into each other on the street where they lived, and not here in a city flung far from home and everything they knew.

Beneath everything else he felt when he saw her there was an uncomplicated joy. He remembered Munir's face in the lobby that first day and how its quiet familiarity knifed through him, cutting cords of loneliness in his body. This was the same but bigger. He was happy the way small children could be, completely falling into it without any thought of the world working around them. He bent to kiss her face and held on to her paint-splattered fingers, until laughing, she shoved him off.

She was not alone, a gaggle of young girls flitting around her. They pricked up around her when he walked towards them.

I'm embarrassing you, he said, low in her ear.

Not yet, she said. These are my friends.

Of course Leila, only on the continent two weeks, would have friends, where he'd gathered none in his three years at university.

She told him she was taking some painting classes at the school of fine arts. Khalajaan thought it was a good idea, she said.

Sounds fancy. He put down her hands. How on earth did you get here?

She screwed up her eyes. Maria didn't tell you?

I've been travelling a little. I must have missed her letters.

We meant to come to London next to see you, she said. But you came to us.

That would have been a nice surprise.

Yes, Leila said. Khalajaan says she's got her life force back whatever that means—I swear she has more energy than I do these days.

You're a lucky girl.

Well, she put up her face, I like to make the most of things.

I should take the two of you out to dinner and then you can catch me up on your stories.

Around her the circle of girls began to drift and he looked down at Leila's clothes, the long white skirt and the panels of lace in her blouse. She'd fit in so quickly. In London he never knew any Pakistani girls but when he saw them from time to time on the bus or buying fruit at the markets, they were still wearing their kurtas and their hair braided over one shoulder, bangles glittering on their wrists. He'd liked to watch the twist and sparkle of them, how they pulled baskets to their hips and grinned. Once, in the corner store, he had tried the Urdu rusty on his tongue—Aap kahan se aaye hain?—but the girl had blushed and pushed his bottle of milk at him over the counter. In them, he saw his own self, unfitting. Leila was put down on this soil a new girl.

Of course you should. When?

Tonight?

She laughed. The bend of her mouth, the fluttering down of her eyes. The intricate dance of Leila's new smiles, played for mirrors and big stages. Her coyness now full blown.

You can't just waltz in and take me to dinner tonight Jimmy, she said. Maybe some other time.

He walked back to the room and remembered at his door that she never even asked how long he was in town. In any other woman he might have taken that as a putdown, but with Leila he knew not to look too far. Later, in the lobby, he asked for the number of her room and thought maybe to send up flowers or a note. Instead, his feet found him there at seven.

She answered the door as if she was maybe expecting him, even though she wasn't ready yet. Standing in the frame with a dressing gown on and a single roll pulling up the front of her hair.

I told you I was busy. There was no impatience in her voice, none of the old strain of someone having trod up her nerves (her nerves even when she was twelve, thirteen, fourteen).

I'm here to see Khalajaan.

She's in the one next door. We stopped sharing rooms as soon as we got out of Karachi. She says she's been alone for too long to have someone pottering around her now.

Giving Leila her own room seemed sort of risky, extravagant. A hundred different things he could imagine her mother disapproving of. And yet, somehow it made sense. He did not know this girl, not the same person he had last seen at fourteen and that thought shuttered through his brain. Passing and then gone just like that. There was something that had settled in him from when he saw her, a homecoming that couldn't be explained away.

Maybe you should get dressed and take me to her, he said.

Jimmy. She dragged out his name between her teeth, holding the two halves of her dressing gown together now. I told I don't have the time.

I'll walk you out.

I'm not going with Khalajaan, I have dinner plans.

Oh yes? With your new friends?

This was a new smile now. Turning up the corners of her mouth, somehow real and secret at the same time.

Jimmy, she said, I am very happy to see you.

What's that supposed to mean?

It means I will have dinner with you tomorrow, and the night after that if you like, but it also means that I am late and if you do not leave very soon, I will be even later. I have to go.

There was no other explanation as he left. He half expected her to follow him down the hall with a changed mind, but nothing unfurled from that firm, adult act. He could not recognize her in that hotel room—more than just time that worked into her. She moved like a different person. Maybe he had expected her to grow into her sisters, or into her mother, in their distinct femaleness; instead, Leila was some blend of the girls he had known since, girls about town, girls who looked down their lashes.

He didn't sleep that night, but there was something comforting about even that. He was waiting only for the morning, the seep of sun from under his windows, for its warmth to pull him out from under the covers: simple things, things any man might wait for. Meanwhile, he lingered in the drowsy spell of the dark.

The next morning he waited in the lobby till she came down. He caught her before she came fully into view. Even as a little girl Leila had walked just that way, the same arching stride.

He would have liked to say she was surprised to see him.

You're stalking me, she said. I don't mind though, you can buy me breakfast. She put a hand on his arm and leaned forward. I drink coffee now. Don't tell Ma.

Mehrunissa thought coffee was bad for young girls and it was the one thing she and Khalajaan always agreed on. They both hated for Ash to drink it, Khalajaan leaning forward at teatime and pinching her cheek. It'll make your skin dark, she said.

All writers drink coffee, Ash had argued. Coffee or whiskey Ma, you can choose. Which ended the argument promptly.

Over breakfast now, he found it difficult to stop himself from looking at her. The world crashed and built itself up again every time he looked up from his food and she was still miraculously there.

So, he said, brushing his crumbs off the side of his plate to help keep his eyes down. Are you going to tell me what you're doing here?

She wrinkled her nose in her old fashion. That Leila look for keeping out of trouble, the cat-swallowed-the-canary look; like Kiran, who would slink up to the sofa and look at you with the blinking eyes that suggested she could climb into your lap or you could come and get her.

I thought I already said. I'm here accompanying Khalajaan—you know she's wanted to travel. She's been sitting on her husband's money for years and well, with everything going on in Karachi at the moment, she rather wanted some time away. I can't say I blame her. And I told you yesterday about the classes—Leila, he warned.

You know very well what I mean. For years it was Ayesha who was meant to come on this trip, wasn't she?

Well nothing was decided.

He spluttered coffee, knocking it down his wrists. The darkening stains spread on his white shirt. He thought instantly of Ayesha in her father's shirts, ink marking out similar beasts on the cuffs. He had not thought of that in months. A year.

She'd been talking about it for years Leila. She was organizing that woman's bookshelves and reading to her every weekend since she was fifteen.

Don't look at me as if I've somehow sabotaged this. I'm not some kind of witch Jimmy. I think I know well what my sister's been planning and what she wants.

Well then? What changed?

You're charming, you know that. Buy a girl breakfast and then bully her to death before she can finish. She found him through her eyelashes, mouth tightening to a low pout. Anyway, if you must know, it isn't my fault.

I never said it was.

My darling sister—oh you know what she's like. She's got a mouth the size of a cannon on her. She was forever getting into arguments with Khalajaan over something or the other—oh don't grill me on what they were about please. Everything. Politics and books and whether or not Maria should go back to work, and how women should behave, for god's sake. Absolutely pointless if you ask me, it's not as if she or Khalajaan are in charge of anything.

So she just changed her mind? Just like that?

Well after Amir died, Maria went back to Pats and Khalajaan thought it was a shame. And I suppose she had a point—it did look bad, you know. He'd only been dead a few weeks really, and there was Maria back in the school. In pink, no less.

Leila raised up her eyes as if to say, *my sisters*. And people had been talking about us anyway.

What people?

Oh Jimmy. Have you forgotten how things work back there? You know it's all gossip. Well I guess people were wondering why Amir's family didn't come to us.

What family? He didn't have any at the wedding.

There were his cousins, she reminded him. No immediate family but still people he knew—none of them came to the house or to the masjid or anything.

I don't see what this has to do with it.

Khalajaan was saying that the people said it was Maria's fault. That she had sent him to war to protect Papa, and that's why he died. And that there was something about the way she was after that which was—

What?

I don't want to get into it. Her voice flattened, the pout smoothing. Anyway Ayesha got into a big argument with her over it, and at the last minute Khalajaan picked me instead. She wasn't going to take Maria, who was obviously wandering around sullying our family name, and Bina's got no interest in leaving home so—so here I am.

He studied her face, how carefully she was holding herself off from a smile.

You're pleased, aren't you?

Well why shouldn't I be? All my life I've played second fiddle to my sisters—oh and I know Ayesha wanted to come and I feel for her, I really do, but Jimmy I've wanted it too. And I'm here now. She grinned and squeezed his wrist across the table. With you. Why shouldn't I enjoy it?

He shook his head. I can't even imagine how furious your sister must be.

Leila swung her eyes upwards. She almost killed me. Not that it would have made any difference—she just can't see her own fault in it.

In not wanting to be Khalajaan's pet?

Whose fault is it then? I didn't ask Khalajaan to bring me here Jimmy. I know you think I'm selfish, but I wouldn't do that to her.

I never said you did.

She shook her head. We're not going to be very good friends if you keep insinuating things.

He reached across, tapped the side of her cheek.

We're friends whether you like it or not, child. I'm certainly not leaving you here on your own.

It made a certain dirty sense for Leila to be here instead of Ash. A guilty thought but it stuck. There was nothing about Paris or London or any of the other cities on

Khalajaan's tour that Ash wouldn't have loved; she would have loved them better than Leila. Ash was the one with the maps, the plotted-out histories, the girl with the world all drawn up in her head. Only waiting for it to come to flesh. And yet he couldn't quite picture her here. Not on this kind of trip, buttering Khalajaan's toast as Leila did; pressing her pink mouth tightly closed to swallow yawns when Khalajaan insisted they have breakfast at seven in the morning and told them about the trips she'd taken with her husband.

Ayesha's yawns unhinged her jaw, lion-like and loud. They sucked breath from the room and ended on a grin.

Leila flirted and fluttered, and put whole rooms at ease. Men tipped their hats to her and girls clung to her elbows. She had a way of making admirers out of people. People wanted to make her happy. It was something he couldn't explain, but the world sometimes worked this way. She flickered up under attention, a roman candle, a parade. She was one of those women who had only ever been on the periphery of Jimmy's knowledge before.

From what he'd heard, his mother had been one of them. Snared his father at only eighteen, he remembered them saying. Not that he would know anything about it.

This was it, he remembered, the city where his parents met and married and conceived him, and this was a lifetime ago; stories he would never truly know but they shifted in him nevertheless. Though still, there were things about his mother and about women he would never know. What he did know was that the men toppled in Leila's wake the way dominoes did.

And, for the first time in years, something switched in him, in how he thought of Ayesha. Always in his mind she was trapped as the same person she was when she left. The same but waiting. When he thought of her in a way that was abstract rather than person—thought of her and not his feelings for her—she was her passport photograph. The teeth and short hair, waiting to run away.

Now he rearranged her in his head. No longer poised for something but trapped instead. She paced the corridors, a panther in green trousers. She used to bite her nails when she was angry. She used to roll her hair over her index finger and pull until the tangle ripped off her head. Did it without thinking or even noticing much. She'd wind it around her knuckles till the blood stopped.

He wondered if her hair had grown out.

It was a week before he even thought of contacting Munir. The number of his hotel and the address were scrawled on the notepad in his room. He glanced at them every day, shaving in the morning or reaching for water in the middle of the night. It wasn't that he wasn't eager to see him, it was the inertia he felt when around Leila. The rest of the world just seemed further away. He caught her in the mornings for breakfast, and while she painted and went to class, he wandered the city. Munir would be asleep during those hours, he reasoned.

In London he only went to places he needed to be.

Here, he expanded the circle. Every day of that first week there was rain but the city was new enough to him that it didn't grey out in the rain the way London did. He dripped over the floors of the galleries, catching up on things Leila had already done. He would do them with her again anyway, when her classes were over, so they were in step. He would take her to Montmartre on the weekend and they would walk back down the hill together and drink hot chocolate outside those cafes. She would explain things to him as Ash once had. The Leila he knew had never been much of a reader but here, he found guidebooks in her bags and notes on the city scribbled into them, the trappings of a professional tourist.

After his touring, the light thickened over the streets and led him winding back to tea with Khalajaan and Leila. He never took tea in London, which they couldn't imagine. Leila loved it and he liked to watch her eat.

Khalajaan's narrative of her first trip to Paris softened. This was how people lived, these were their stories. In all those years she had never before spoken to Jimmy or Leila about her husband, now on every street she shared the little snippets of their life together. Khalajaan, with her loud voice and her slow manner of speaking, whom Jimmy could never even have imagined being married, sparkled here. She had been the first person in her family to ever travel abroad. She had kept everything: the names of the restaurants where she and her husband had their first meal, the ticket stubs from their first train journey, the museum guides, receipts from the small shop where her husband bought a razor with his name engraved into the handle—souvenirs of a life fully lived. How could someone who had seemed so stuffy in their drawing room in Karachi, always dragging her eyes upward and telling Leila her kurtas were too short, be so different here: her laugh as warm as butter, telling them about the time a man tried to chat her up in one of the cafes and her husband, returning in a fury, had upended his coffee on the man's lap.

Here Jimmy became conscious of the moveable history of the world. His parents had met in this city, he had been conceived in this city and half of him still belonged to it, a birthright even though his mother's family had never came forward. The absences dotted in the stories, Khalajaan's dead husband, his deceased parents and Leila glowing in a space empty of sisters.

He and Leila played chess after dinner, or some approximation of it. The girls owned a set since before he knew them. The Captain brought it back from Egypt, a set of ivory pieces. When Jimmy arrived on the scene, they'd asked him to teach them. Having no knowledge of the game himself, he'd made up all the rules. He couldn't keep up with them all at first, but over the course of a few rounds and some of Maria's Oh I sees, he thought he might have actually come up with a workable alternative. This was what they played now. His knowledge of it was a rusty creaking thing. Leila frowned across from him. It was a miracle that none of them had yet unearthed the deception.

Then there were the evenings when she would plead off for dinner, and visit her new friends. Back in Karachi he would have known all her friends. He'd have gone to school with their brothers and maybe dropped Leila off at the restaurant, and almost certainly brought her home. He offered now, but she brushed him off.

We're only going to a place across the road Jimmy, she said. Khalajaan doesn't mind if I go on my own, why should you?

He didn't mind having dinner with just Khalajaan instead. It was the sort of thing that surprised him; back in Karachi, he could barely stand to be in the same room as his own grandfather for more than a few minutes. He was not the sort to be able to converse easily with grown-ups. And yet now he did it voluntarily. Even spent some time after dinner reading to her on the balcony that connected her and Leila's rooms, from a copy of *The Woman in White* he'd bought at Shakespeare and Company; he'd found it by accident one afternoon. He had the front page stamped with some thought of giving it to Ash someday. Khalajaan didn't quite have a taste for Wilkie Collins, and dozed off during longer passages.

Ayesha used to read her Austen, he remembered, making a note to find something she might enjoy more next time.

In the meantime, he kept his ears pricked to catch Leila's footsteps and the telltale clang of her door when she returned, humming under her breath. There were nights when Khalajaan went to bed early and he considered waiting in the lobby till Leila returned, but he stopped himself. He was not her father, not even really her brother.

Maybe I could come for dinner with you sometime, he asked the next morning. They were walking to her drawing class, the morning dark and damp.

Why would you want to do that?

It might be nice for me to know your friends a little.

And give up your lovely evening with Khalajaan? You'd break her heart.

What's wrong? You used to love for me to meet your friends. You begged me to come places with you.

She huffed and blew hair off her face. I was a lot younger then. I thought it made me look grown up to have a boy around.

Have I not grown up in a way you like then? Are you ashamed of me?

Don't be silly, she said. You look very well. She stopped outside the doors and put up her chin to look at him. She would still be the smallest of her sisters.

You look better than I thought, she said. You always used to be so messy when you were a boy. Not that it didn't suit you, but there's something almost dapper about you now. It's even a little strange, if you ask me.

Well then?

You really want to come? You won't be bored with our youthful silliness?

I'm not ancient yet, child.

Very well. I'll think about it.

He put a suit on that evening. Leila dressed for these dinners with great care. She preened and fussed twice as long in the evenings as she did in the mornings.

He stood outside the lobby with a couple of Italian men in dark suits. Cigars disappeared under the black forest of their moustaches. He had very little Italian. He had very little French when it came to that.

When he saw Munir, it was English that came first to his mouth.

What the hell are you doing here? Munir asked.

The shock yanked him up in his skin. Jimmy moved forward to hug him but it didn't land the way he intended, the whole motion stiff and awkward.

You told me to come here, he said. You said it was the best holiday of your life—you might have had some wine because you even said it was better than Murree. Jimmy winked here, but even this old joke between them hung stale. What are you doing at this hotel?

He knew the answer before Munir could find the words. There were many beautiful women here. He tried not to think about the odds. Leila appeared in the lobby, all in white. She looked like a painting, one of the Venuses. Then she put up her eyebrows and looked just like her mother.

When I said you might join us some time, she said, I didn't mean tonight.

Theoretically, there was no reason for the three of them not to get on. In every other permutation, there was nothing but fondness between them. The other people at the table were not unpleasant, and it wasn't just Leila and Munir. Nothing so improper as that.

Her artist friends from the other day, pretty French girls with long hair and floaty dresses, blurred behind Leila, a charming backdrop to her performance and then, a few men they all knew from back home. They spun stories about their summers abroad, the sort of group he was not surprised to see Leila with. The men seem plucked from the same poker games he and Munir had run just working out of a different part of the world.

Jimmy sat by Munir, and kept his glass full.

When you said, he hissed, That you were meeting beautiful women in Paris I didn't think you meant Leila Malik. You didn't think to tell me she was here?

Munir turned to him. I thought you must have known.

That you were going around with Leila Malik?

That she was in Paris at least.

Well I didn't. You might have mentioned you were seeing her.

He shrugged. My mother asked me if I would take her aunt out to tea.

What about Nighat?

Nighat, Munir grinned, is in Karachi, and has no aunts bringing her to Paris. Her family are going to Lahore this summer.

Well how long are you here?

I don't know.

What's that meant to mean?

Nothing. He put up his hands as if in a fight. I'm just not so sure of my plans yet.

By the end of the evening, Jimmy missed his bathroom in London, even the weird family on the other side of his tiled walls. He stayed up for another hour after they all returned to their homes and rooms. He tried to read but the words sloshed together on the page. Lying down, he could feel the sludge of wine and food still moving in his gut. This was real misery, not that old numbness he had fallen into in London.

It was the most miserable evening he had endured. He resolved to join them every night for as long as they stayed here.

X.

He was in a city he never thought he would see again. Always he'd told Ayesha that he had no memory of Paris, but here it came back to him somehow, either real or imagined. His parents were in the street corners. They were at the bar; they floated over the love-lock bridges. He wished he remembered more of their lore. The stories of their wild short lives. He could not imagine them alive, or taking him to school, or growing old. His pictures were of a young couple going out to a party, and there they remained.

He got up at six the next day, when even the light seemed to still. Downstairs, he ordered coffee and a plate of eggs that would grow cold before he touched them. He finally wrote to Maria. It came difficult and slow. He forgot what he meant to say by the afternoon and wasted much of the hotel's paper.

He wondered why she kept writing to him. He was not a very good correspondent, his letter after Amir's death was not so long or so heartfelt as it should have been. He wondered what Ayesha would say if she had to put how he felt in a letter.

He was joined by Leila.

No art class today?

I thought I might sit here for a while and practise with you. The light is extraordinary.

The tall windows and blue curtains—she fit very well against them. Her black hair swept up simply, and he liked her this way.

Are you going to draw me?

She tilted her head to the side. I might. It's been so long since I've done so.

Have I changed much?

It was a question he regretted right away. She considered him, longer than on that street corner. The moment stretched and arched he felt the way a corpse might, being picked apart with a scalpel. Women have always made him seem anxious but to feel out of his skin with a girl he had known since she was thirteen was too much.

You look older, she said.

A brilliant observation, he remarked.

Don't be snide. I didn't mean older than you were—older than you are.

Is that right.

Maybe it's the beard.

You don't like it?

I haven't made up my mind about it.

No?

Well I have not seen you now without it. She smiled. That's the only way I could make a fair assessment.

You're a harsh mistress.

Still he was glad there was nothing in her expression to suggest that he had changed for the worse. For all her manners she was easy to read. She was still Leila.

Go back to your letter, she instructed. Just try not to twitch so much.

He held himself still, pen static over the page.

I was going to surprise you, she said.

What?

That's why I didn't call you in London—I was going to come there and surprise you. Your dada gave me the address. She drew her lower lip between her teeth, the way a woman on the stage might.

You might have killed me.

She laughed. So finding me in Paris is fine, but me at your doorstep would kill you?

Yes. I'm not sure why—there's something about travelling you know. It makes anything seem possible, don't you think? When you're abroad, you're a different person.

So London is home now.

I didn't say that.

It was implied.

Well it isn't what I meant.

Oh Jimmy. She looked up. Are you ever going back?

Of course. I'm going back at the end of the summer, lovely. He touched her nose, Don't worry about it. Are you?

Sometimes I think maybe not. But I don't have the same kind of choices you do. Khalajaan will take me back at some point, I guess. Unless other opportunities arise, I don't have any other options.

What other opportunities?

Don't sound so disbelieving. Now pick that pen back up. Your hands look better when they're holding something.

They had come a long way from the days when he had taught her maths at the dining table. She took him on walks—she only had a week's privilege over him but her sense of direction was tricked out more fully than he might have expected. She was more self-sufficient than she let on.

When I first did this with Khalajaan it took forever, she said, taking his elbow and leading him down the street. First I was slow with my maps and then she was slow with walking and by the time we got there we were both so flustered we just sat ourselves down in the coffee shop and stuffed ourselves with pastries.

That doesn't sound so bad.

She narrowed her eyes.

He was not accustomed to being led around. The past week in her company and with Khalajaan had been a strange kind of homecoming. It felt as though the warmth of Karachi has been wrapped around his shoulders. Still he was not the same person he was back then. For so long he had been on his own. There were breaks of other people—the months Munir had raised hell in London and passed out on his sofa and the quieter times with the girl. It was different. No one else had felt like home

Here with Leila he was unpeeling the last few years from his skin, years spent cocooned in his own head. He'd lost what it meant to be outside of himself and to have talks that would last for days, conversations that wheeled from breakfast to galleries and lunches all the way forward to dinner. Often, at the end of the day, he would lie back on his bed with his eyes shut and try to remember all that happened, all that was said. It had been so easy when it was only him. With Leila, his head was fireworks, full as a bottle frothing over.

Her new wisdom came out only in flashes. Once, she said to him, You never knew me as well as I knew you.

It was said lightly, an argument over who it was that had stolen Khalajaan's prayer beads. Still, the words hit hard.

And it was true. Leila had only ever been in his peripheral vision. Those years flickered back, memories and images shuffled and bound together. He remembered her coming home from school and begging her mother to let her pierce her nose. He remembered the drawings she did of him, and her in her school uniform and socks sitting at the table, feeding the cat to distract herself from homework. But she unravelled now, in the face of those stills.

There was an imperiousness that she wore that was wholly her own. He could not imagine this Leila going to bed at nine and dressing in only the clothes her mother sent with her and not drinking coffee or having dinners with strange men. She held her neck the way opera singers do—the swan shape of it, in the candlelight. She spooled her hair up and knotted it at her nape. Something of her teenage self bending at the fingers. She slipped between the two—worldly and petulant at once.

They took coffee in the hotel after dinner. He noticed silver bangles on her wrist.

Where are those from, he asked, tapping a finger against her wrist.

Munir, she said, not looking up from her cup.

What's Munir to you that he bring you gifts like that?

I must have forgotten what this has to do with you, she said.

Some would say we're practically family.

Leila twisted her nose.

You're not my brother Jimmy.

I'm enough your family to know that your mother wouldn't want you accepting gifts from someone like Munir.

And what, in your opinion, is wrong with Munir?

He's not the marrying kind Leila.

Here he felt the space between them grow taut. History walking on a string between them.

Like Ayesha.

Don't.

Maybe I'm not the marrying kind either.

Leila.

My sisters aren't the marrying kind why should I be? And anyway. Who says I want to marry Munir of all people? And who—she slowed down, laid her fork alongside her plate—Says I couldn't get him if I wanted?

Is this some kind of challenge for you then?

Maybe. That girl from Lyari's not going to be the next Mrs Baloch, is she? I may as well take a stab at it myself, she continued, poking at her cake till it collapsed.

He was reminded here of how Leila had always been in a race. Even at thirteen or fourteen she had never lost at anything, steely-eyed and clearheaded even as she simpered.

He ordered a drink.

You want one?

I don't drink, she said.

Oh that's fine, he said and then, I'm not baiting you here.

She sighed the sound through her throat of silk being released to the wind.

Then leave it alone Jimmy.

You really don't care if I tell your mother?

She picked up his silver cigarette case and unclasped it. You really think you're not baiting me?

I show a healthy level of concern.

In the moment that followed, he could see her pause, that bomb of a word—jealousy—fizzing on her tongue. She did know him better, he thought—his open nerves were all laid out for her fingers.

She pressed her lips around the filter instead.

That's kind of you, but unnecessary.

Well I feel a kind of responsibility towards you.

You are not in any way responsible for me. In any way.

Really Leila—

Save it for my sisters, she said.

Mmmm.

Have you, she continued smoothly, Heard from Maria?

Not since ... you know.

Her husband came home in a box.

His throat worked up, the muscles tightened. Yes, he said. That.

Leila's eyes, wide and flat.

Sometimes, she said to him—an unexpected rawness between them—It feels like we're the only people left in the world.

You seem to fit in here, she said, lifting her shoulders as if maybe this was what she expected.

I miss things about Karachi, he said, I miss—the noise sometimes.

The noise?

And you and your sisters and everyone at home. Of course.

That's not the same as wanting to come home.

Well what do you miss?

I miss Kiran, she sighed

More than your sisters?

Maybe. Is that so bad? She's naturally more affectionate you know, Leila said, She started sleeping on my bed after Maria left.

I miss pani pouri.

She sighed and dropped her chin on to one curled fist. So do I. And kebab rolls and even Bina's awful daal.

Every Sunday.

See you must miss things. Things I mean not people.

I guess. I think about it sometimes when I can't sleep. Nothing good though—just small things. I'll trace out the way from your house to St Pats.

You're very strange, she told him caught between laughter and impatience. He was not even really sure she meant it but somehow it stayed in him, worked its way up and down his gut when he was alone the way a piece of music might do.

He missed things he never thought he would—even arguments with Ash were fond memories now, the brief spells of time when they didn't speak and glared at each other over dinner. Being angry with her would be a boon at this point. He'd take the bitter jabs at each other's lives, the way she'd call him lazy—even spoilt—thinking nothing of it because in two days, maybe three, they'd be friends again. On these days it was their friendship that was a harder loss than any imaginings he may have had of the two of them together.

Had Leila always been a woman in some way? The secret way she would slip about the house. How she had avoided him for days after he walked in on her in the downstairs bathroom with her hips up against the sink, plucking her eyebrows. She was only thirteen then, but the furious silence ate away between them for a whole week, just as it coloured her pout when she was sent up from tea after dinner while he and Ash were allowed to stay.

They never really discussed things the way he might have with Maria or Ash or even Bina. Arguments never reached resolutions; the bones of contention simply slipped through the cracks. They padded over all the sore spots. She didn't ask about the letters he wrote. And he didn't say anything when Munir was missing from dinner one night, or the next night when it was just the two of them.

They picked a different restaurant. She wore her mother's pearls, and the waiter called her his wife. She kissed his cheek at the end of the night, her lips cold and too quick to register on his skin.

His hotel room, afterwards, alone on the balcony. A cigarette that burnt out without touching his lips, as the clouds scrolled past him. A foreign nervousness crawled into him. Made its way up and down his bones.

Say something, she said, It doesn't have to be clever, when he only picked at his toast next morning.

I don't want to ruin the moment.

What, of me watching you eat toast for forty minutes? If you're not going to talk to me we may as well get out of here, Munir got me a new guidebook last week.

And go where? I don't know that I feel like doing anything.

Leila leaned back in her seat. She plucked a rose off the arrangement at the centre of the lace tablecloth, smashing it experimentally between her palms like a restless child.

Because it's in Munir's guidebook or because something's wrong?

There's nothing wrong with me.

You're not a very good liar, she said. She opened her fist and the crushed flower emptied itself on to the table, the petals dirty along the lace.

He had been quiet all morning. A sort of dumbness that he remembered experiencing on his first days in the Malik house. He was quiet in other company, with the boys and his grandfather's friends, but that was out of a comfortable, male kind of nothing to say. With the girls, he had felt trapped in his own silence. They were so clever and bright. Their voices volleying back and forth in the little room; a collection of shared jokes, a small world he was being let into. It seemed that anything he might say would only break the spell. That he must be careful of his words and pluck them into a string that might mean something. Anything he could think of seemed to fit wrongly in his mouth.

They walked through the Luxembourg Gardens without really looking at each other. He thought of the aunty parks near Khalajaan's house in KDA, and the women who wore their dupattas tied to one side of their waist as they strode through them. There was one near Munir's house; if Leila married him she might join the other wives. She would wear pearls in her ears. Munir would call her—as he did all his women—raat ki rani, in a low whisper.

When he tried to kiss her she looped away from him, a ducking so expert that he thought maybe she'd done this before or maybe she'd just seen it coming. They slipped around each other till he was holding her only by her fingers, and she was arched away from him still.

I didn't mean to scare you, he said.

I know, she told him, I know you didn't.

I want to marry you, he said. He hadn't meant to say it just then. He wasn't sure even if he wanted to say it at all but it happened there with the trees bending away from them and the path narrowing as they walked.

Leila stopped walking. Because I won't kiss you?

He stopped two steps ahead from her, angling himself around till they were face to face again though he talked to her shoulder now and not her face.

No, he said. Because I want to.

It still doesn't sound like a question, she said.

Leila.

I can't marry you just because you can't kiss me or because you're in love with the idea of my family or because someone else wouldn't.

That's not why, he said. That's not what it's like.

I don't believe you, she said.

Well if you've already made your mind up, he said, feeling the heat rush into his voice.

You push Munir away because you say he's no good for me, but neither are you. I don't know what you want from me Jimmy, but we're not the solution to any of your problems.

Her spine snapped to attention. When she started walking away from him he sat down and waited for some reason to move. She had taken her map; he was lost, in the dim dark.

XI.

Though it would never fit into his version of history, Leila claimed to have loved him since she was thirteen She said she saw him one afternoon, doing up the laces of his shoes by the door, and she just knew. It was as though she had put everything he knew of her back then in a jar and shaken it.

There was the time they went crabbing in Hawke's Bay, she reminded him. Bina and Maria decided that the little boats were not for them, that they'd watch from the shore as they floated out trailing nets. Ash was in some kind of fight with Leila that week—they were forever at each other's throats. She had not wanted Leila in the boat with her.

But in Leila climbed, folding herself between them, Jimmy's knee tucked into her side. He'd not really wanted her in the boat either; he was hardly ever alone with Ash by then.

I wanted to be close to you, she said when they spoke now, lifting a strand of her hair off the side of her face.

He remembered: little Leila leaning over the edge of the boat to watch the lights on the shore fade to blurs behind them.

You'll fall over if you keep that up, Ayesha said.

I wouldn't have to if you'd just move over.

I told you to take the next boat.

There is no next boat. Leila's face scrunched up with frustration.

You really are the most impossible child, her sister said, putting the lamp down between their legs. From below, it lit up their faces, ghostly and half-dark.

Leila told him she was calculating the colours she would need to make a painting like that—the disappearing scape of the docks. She edged around her sister, leaning on one knee out the boat. It was dark enough now with the lamp down that neither of them noticed she was doing this—and just like that she was overboard.

All that nonsense about your life flashing before you—I was drowning Jimmy and all I could think of was to be saved. Nothing quite as romantic or philosophical as people say. I was just scrambling to get out. And then you dragged me up, like something you'd caught out of the ocean. I must have been filthy—it was only a minute or so, but I'd taken a good dunk. You gathered me up to you and didn't let go.

I don't remember that.

You did. You held me all the way back to the shore. I was so scared, so cold that I was wriggling like an eel— even though hours before I'd have died, absolutely died, to have you hold me like that.

Leila grinned. Her whole mouth went up, one of her more natural smiles, not so considered.

It was very lovely of you, she continued more softly. When we got back, all anyone could say was how foolish

I was. You were the only person that whole evening that didn't shout at me. You complimented me on not having screamed at all. You said I was a good egg.

He tapped the side of her knee with his fingers. You *are* a good egg.

Jimmy remembered, too: Ash's face in the hallway.

Oh J, it's all my fault.

Don't be ridiculous, it was an accident. It could have happened to anybody.

I should have moved, she said. It came out the way a strangled scream might, working its agitated way through the pipes of her throat. I shouldn't have been so angry with her—I can't believe it.

You're working yourself up over nothing. He walked over to her, touched her shoulder. The way one might touch a sleeping lion. It's happened to grown men. Munir's cousin fell out of a boat crabbing once—he was thirty-six. There must have been half-a-dozen people in the last year I've heard of.

He didn't mention what happened to Munir's cousin. How he had sunk below the ink-black surface and how he had never come back up. They never found him. They never did find any of them.

She switched around so they were face to face. Her hands gripped each of his elbows.

He remembered: the way her face changed when she tried to thank him. Her whitened mouth, knuckles pale from clenching. Jaw loosened and slack. The first time he saw her without words. The first time something about him had undone her.

He saw in the nakedness of her gratitude the same thing he felt every day. Every time he looked at Ash how he wanted to thank her: for the tall lines of her personality, her live-wired life. For knowing him.

XII.

They were married there in Paris, just the two of them with Khalajaan and witnesses gathered from the local mosque. It was not the wedding he remembered her having talked about as a girl; she'd wanted a grand reception at the Metropole and large golden-yellow tents. She'd wanted white silk tablecloths and rose petals down the middle of the aisle. I want a palanquin, she'd insisted, even when Maria had pointed out they had no male relatives to lift it.

There's Papa and Jimmy, Leila said.

That's only two.

I'm sure you'll all be married by then, she'd sniffed. Your husbands can help.

And there she was in the small clerk's office, dropping her head with the anachronistic coyness of brides. At dinner, Khalajaan told them to be good to each other and asked no questions about anything: not the rush, not the secrecy, not the dumb fact of it here in a city that did not belong to them. Her hands folded on the tabletop, the glow of her rings in the candlelight. She looked at them with an indulgence he hadn't expected, a flash of warmth in her smile like butter in a pan. She was fond of Leila, he knew. She was the only one of the girls who had followed, in some way, in her image.

Marriage is hard, she said, and she pointed at the space between them with her fork. You will have to work hard. You will have to compromise.

She had never been in his room before. He realized then, as she stood by the windowsill with her hips angled against it, that they had never really been alone together. Only in parks and restaurants, never in the deafening silence of a hotel room. She shifted in the window till she was the whole room, all he could see. He sat down, held on to his bed.

Did you mean what you said about loving me? she asked.

Her question small, and nearly swallowed up in the space between them.

They came together as lonely travellers will do. The ugliness of his proposal was buried under the language of their bodies. This time when he reached out to hold her there was a sureness to it that seemed separate from the wreckage of his nerves. He felt disconnected from his body, as if he is watching them from a great distance: the two of them in the empty room. Her body shivered, his hands shook.

Leila curved into him, fit a hand along his waist. The boldness of her touch pushed him back into the room. Here it was cold and she was near enough for his mouth to catch her breath if he opened it.

She seemed to fold inwards as she undressed, her shoulders narrowing together and the slow dissolution of her nakedness giving him a chance to come up for air. Brides wore red so she bought a dress that Khalajaan disapproved of, even though it went past her knees. She wore someone else's earrings, gold-flecked. They were glossy with hairspray and stuck to his fingers when he lifted them from her ears. She smiled at him with her eyes closed.

After she said, I didn't want you to think I'm one of those women.

One of which women?

She rolled her eyes. Jimmy, don't pretend.

Alright, he said. He held her. Alright.

The walls of his room were blue and he was happy to have her, he was.

The next week they went to London. He settled Khalajaan in a nearby hotel, and took Leila back to his flat. Everything about the city and his flat looked different through her eyes. The blackened windowpanes, the bookshelves gathering dust, early evening light filtered through the curtains in streams of dirty gold. He put his coat up and sat, said Well here we are, in what seemed a very British way.

The stack of mail by the door was caked in mud from where he stomped in. He unstuck the envelopes from the mat and peeled them apart while Leila undid the laces of her shoes and rubbed her feet through the soles of her stockings. She sat cross-legged on his sofa, small and strange, as if she had stolen in through the window and made her home here. He thought maybe he would try and make a fire later. It was not very cold, but he liked the idea of her cracking her knuckles by the fireplace he had never used much.

There were bills in his hands, a few pieces of mail from the office, some letters from Karachi.

He was ripping open the latest envelope with his teeth when the phone rang. It was the kind of deadening sound that he recognized. His heart was in his throat before he even picked it up.

BOOK THREE

I.

We got out of the airport and only Dada and the driver were there. Outside the glass doors the heat wrapped itself around us, a sticky second skin: the physical fact of being back in Karachi. Everybody else disappeared into throngs of family with garlands of flowers and mithai. Maybe if things were different, this might have been what we'd have got, banners and one of Bina's terrible cakes with pink frosting.

Dada and I shook hands without speaking. He softened when he hugged Leila, a one-armed tug of her into his side, and then he walked her to the car.

How's Bina? I asked.

Better, he said.

It was good news but he didn't look pleased. He turned his head away from us to get the driver's attention. When the game of fitting all our bags in the car was over, he got into the front and we stayed quiet the whole way to the house.

I had told Dada we'd got married two hours before we left for the airport, back in London. The silence at the other end of the line was in the car with us now. Ash would have taken me through our journey with a rolling commentary on every shifted brick, but here there was only the wheezing of the air conditioner, Leila's shallow breath as she twisted her too-big ring around her finger, and my own fingers drumming along the door.

You can smell death in a house. Leila would call me morbid for thinking that but it's true, the cloying smell sticks in your lungs and slows everything down. Grinds the minutes to hours. I caught it when we stepped in, even though Bina was better and though Dada had grabbed my shoulder as we left the car and told me that things would be fine.

I don't see why they wouldn't be, I'd said, and in a moment of brilliant calmness I squeezed his fingers. I was thinking of something else I guess—of the city or of my marriage, and there was a kind of weakness in his eyes when I let go.

Leila got to the living room first. She put down her bags and they all jumped. Bina lifted herself off the sofa, moving closer in small steps, and the sisters walled around her. I never heard anybody say it, but I knew.

Mehrunissa died two days ago, in the time it took us to book a flight and pack our bags and make our way here.

They buried the body without her. It's the way things were done around here. We didn't leave our dead lying around.

Dada told me that her husband never made it to the masjid. They tried to pull him out of his chair, but he thundered and rumbled so they left him there, and a group of young men with little or no connection to the family carried the body instead and stood through the prayers. Some of them were soldiers and some were men from my father's family who were used to doing things for my grandfather.

The particulars were still unknown to me: the last time I'd spoken to Dada two days ago, there was no notion that Mehrunissa was sick. Only that Bina was out of the hospital, and being nursed at home. She'd asked to be discharged. The doctors, Dada said, asked her too many questions. For two nights Mehrunissa had stayed up with her daughter. The day we got on the plane, she'd flared up herself.

Leila didn't react to the things the way I thought she might. It was not that she felt less than I expected only that it moved through her differently. She'd been so quiet when we got the telegram. Our departure from London had been cold. She'd kissed Khalajaan's cheek and waited patiently while she blessed her, the litany of prayers folded into her hands. But when we walked away, I watched her narrow, straight back, the spine taut, and she did not turn back once.

We barely spoke at all, each leg of the journey more exhaustingly silent than the last. She played with her sleeves and tried not to look at me. I tried to make her laugh with stories about Munir, impressions of people we knew: Khalajaan, the Captain, her uncle who only ever visited on Eid and always chewed paan in the ball of his cheek.

Before London there had been this sense between us that something was coming alive, our lives were being braided together. On our layover in Dubai we checked into a hotel and when the concierge handed me the keys it was hard to imagine that we weren't playing pretend. It made me think of the earlier days in France where waiters would mistake her for my wife—something I found amusing and Leila appalling.

I wish we didn't have to stay tonight, she said.

She stood in front of the mirror, fussing with the zipper of her skirt. I got the feeling she no longer wanted to be alone with me.

I'm sorry.

I wish I knew what was going on back home.

We could call them, if you like. Do you need help with that? I asked, pointing to the zipper still squeezed between her fingers.

No, she said. She sounded tired though she'd slept all through the flight. The same distracted sleepwalker movement as she dragged her nightgown over her head, pushing the curls on to her shoulder and wrapping them into a bun at the back of her head. She walked over to the bed and lay down without touching me. You can call them if you like.

You don't want to talk to your mother?

I hate talking on the phone. It makes me feel farther away from them.

She turned on to her side.

You think we'll get there by midday, you said?

The flight lands at eleven.

She closed her eyes. I was picturing it with her. The city at noon. Streets unwrapping themselves all the way to the shore. We'd squint as we got out of the glass doors, and hide behind sunglasses till we got home.

Here was where we split off. I was worried too but I could think beyond the slap of the ground. I could think of what it would mean to get home. The sweetness of coming indoors, of peeling off my clothes by the bathtub. I could picture Dada in his chair across from me at the table and I could even think of drinking tea with him, of building something new into the old silence. I had been waiting to go home for two years now. There was more of me than my worry.

But Leila wore her right down to the bone.

Sleep came badly to both of us. The next morning we dressed on either side of the bed like boys in a dormitory. When we got down to the lobby our taxi was late. She looked at me, eyebrows pushed together and I felt for a minute as if the things crashing around us were my fault. I shouldn't have waited to speak to my grandfather before I booked the flights, and I shouldn't have agreed to a layover, and it was even my fault that her sister was sick. It passed, I was outside of everything again.

I touched her hand in the car. Her small, cold fingers curling away from mine. By the time we got back to the house, things between us had already begun the business of unravelling.

Malaria wasn't contagious but Mehrunissa had got it anyway, bad luck visited twice upon the Malik house. She must have been sick for longer than they'd realized. She was a good nurse, I remembered. She must have stayed by Bina's side all night, never sleeping, and her reddened eyes and pallor would have been explained away as a lack of sleep.

I felt only the passage of information through me, as if I were a transistor radio. The room was a flurry of news, Mehrunissa's death slamming into us as soon as we stepped through the door and, as Leila put her head on my chest at last, her sisters noticing the ring on her hand. Maria's mouth dropping open; Leila's hurricane body in the cage of my arms. I felt like I'd been shaken up and put back down.

In some ways, Ash said, as we stood together on the verandah, late into the next afternoon, It's a good thing that Leila wasn't here. She's always been particularly sensitive.

Was it bad? I asked.

A flock of crows overhead cawing their way home, the sun coming down behind us. Ayesha snuck out of the house when she could. Most of the time she would go up to the roof or just sit behind the door with her smokes. I knew she liked to be alone. Even when she was younger, too much time with people wound her up but I followed her anyway, watching the grey crescents smudged under her eyes, the shiver that tripped through her whenever we said her mother's name.

She lifted her shoulders. Ash always had a way of cutting you down with one look.

I don't know about bad. It was quick, I didn't even know what was going on most of the time. But you know how Leila is about things like this.

Did I? Something about Ayesha's face put me in mind of the time Dada had been in hospital two weeks and there were days in that time where the world seemed less certain. Everybody was worried. They'd all developed an affection for Dada that was separate to me. But it was Leila who couldn't sleep all week, Leila who drove to the hospital fitted under Maria's arm. Her pale moon face eating up the room and she looked that way now, her pupils blown up over the turn of her nose.

She's upset, I said, which seemed a weak word for it.

Death isn't this big drama everybody makes it out to be, Ash said, It's—a person being there one minute, and not the next. It's the passing of a second.

Her eyebrows curling together, a not quite frown. She followed the line of my hands, where I spread my fingers on the chair. The wedding ring in the last light of the day.

We meant to write to you, I said.

Yes, she said. Her face was soft and faraway.

There wasn't any time, I said.

There was hardly time now, we were outside in a stolen minute. I had forgotten what it was like to be back in this house, how it was impossible to be alone. Even more so now; the sisters curled around each other, even sleeping in the same room like a litter of kittens. I hadn't shared a bed with Leila since we'd been back, and most of the time we only spoke in rooms full of other people. We used the small voices I usually associated with people who had been married much longer than us.

It felt as strange as it did to be following her sister outside. Ayesha shook her head. I guess it's not as if we were in contact.

No.

You never wrote to me.

Well we weren't exactly speaking when I left.

She laughed. It was the first of its kind I'd heard since I got back.

No, I guess that's one way to put it, she said. She put her hand out. I want to say—

Yes?

It's not fair to blame you, I guess is what I wanted to say. I could have written too.

I took her hand.

Maybe we can learn to be friends again, she said.

I nodded.

Now, she said, Go and bring your wife down to dinner.

She put her cigarette out in a flower pot, and patted me on the shoulder.

II.

Six days after we got back, Dada and I went to speak to the Captain.

This is what people did after a death, they made arrangements. When my parents died, my uncle came down from Lahore and he and Dada met with the lawyer and even more distant relations for the conversation. My uncle had wanted to take me home with him, he and Chachi never had children of their own and he had a kind of fatherly love for me. I was too small to know what was going on, too small to know to hide under the dining table as I did later on when I wanted to know how grown-ups' meetings were going. At any rate, he got on that plane without me and I stayed behind with Dada.

The girls were upstairs; Leila hardly ever got out of bed. She wasn't eating, either. Bina took her cups of hot, milky chai with spoonfuls of sugar swirling at the bottom.

I undid the collar of my shirt, as Dada went over the papers. I'd been waking up and working and living as other people did, but the shock of her absence weighed on me too. It was a dark flash, something you could only see out of the corner of your eye, but it followed me everywhere. She was a dark flash in the corner of my eye, slinking about the edges of every room. The cat, her girls, the moving shadows, all seemed like shades of her, moving slowly through the house.

The Captain was mostly quiet, hadn't even really said very much on the topic of his youngest daughter's wedding. In my day, things didn't happen this way, he told me. People brought rishtas, we all sat down and the families decided. People didn't just get up and get married. He sighed. Well boy, I guess I thought you'd weasel your way into this family somehow.

It was true. I'd always wanted to be a Malik.

He was sitting across from us in yesterday's kurta, black and too big for him now. He'd lost so much weight. I'd expected to see him diminished, but he was shrinking right in front of us.

My daughters, he said, Are very unhappy.

Dada shifted his legs under the table.

It's still so soon. You must give them time.

I think, the Captain continued, That the best thing to do is to give them some space—

Out of the city?

Outside the city, yes. He picked at his teeth with the nail of his little finger, the flat yellow stones biting down on his lip. This place is choking them.

I have to say, I said, I think it's their mother's death—

Jamal, Dada warned.

No, the boy is right—why shouldn't he speak his mind? He's not a child any more, and I respect that.

I shrugged. Well where do you want to take them?

The naval colony in Manora. I think they need some time away from here. He paused and took a breath that hitched and halted through his body. People have not been friendly to us here. They are not part of the community.

I don't necessarily think moving them to an island will help, I said.

The Captain coughed. I won't subject them to the eyes of people any more—you don't know what it means to be a father, son, a father of daughters. They watch my daughters like they're zoo animals, all these men talking and these hissing women. I won't have that. It's still my job to keep them safe.

There was a long silence after he spoke.

It was everybody's job to keep someone safe. There was no stronger impulse on earth. I couldn't see the merit of this plan at all, but Dada seemed to agree. He was the one who'd been here for the last three years without me. He knew better about this as always.

And so we went.

The news rippled through the girls, raising them like an army from the dead. They set to work immediately, with a militaristic dedication. Maria directed the shift, arranging all the boxes and having them loaded into trucks with the precision of puzzle pieces.

They cleared the house while I was out. I went by in the early evening to see Dada before I followed them and couldn't help stepping into the Malik residence on my way. The house always held a certain wonder for me. No matter what was going on, I expected the same energy to fold me past the threshold.

Places look different when they've emptied out. They had left behind only a pile of cards, and letters of condolence. Most of them addressed to the Captain, some for Maria, and maybe one each for the rest of the girls, from school friends or the mothers of school friends. They started in similar fashions—your mother was lovely or we wish we could have been there. Some of these women were army wives or widows calling to some greater kinship with Maria and her mother. They all offered something: prayers, charms to fight the devil, advice for young women beginning their lives over. Advice for unmarried women.

I piled them back in their neat square.

The floors were scuffed and there were pale squares on the wall from where paintings had gathered dust, and still there was no trace of what I was looking for, not even in the collections of marks against the door that measured the girls' heights from six to eighteen. The littlest mark was still Bina's, coming up to my shoulder.

Even this solid trail of their lives bearing into the house seemed small now. It really was all gone: the rooms were empty, their spell was in the girls, and all of it was now across the narrow body of water nearby, settling down someplace else.

I'd never been to Manora before. I'd gone to school with a boy whose father was a naval doctor and he'd once invited our whole class on the ship, which was posted out near Manora, but I never went. When the boys got back the weekend after that trip, all they ever talked about was the ship: the wide white body of it, the leathered sofas, how they'd been taken through the controls, the heavy machinery that kept the beast moving. From then on, Manora had only ever been a blank canvas in my head, a picture propped behind the action. Still it was quieter than I expected, the houses plotted far from each other: a release of air after the crush of the city. The shops were all places that would know my name in less than a week. In the evenings, people came home from work. The anonymity of the city wearing off as the ferry lobbed closer to the shore. Most of them wore wedding rings or carried packages of naan wrapped in newspapers. Even that first evening, I felt as if I was one of them; we all smelled of the city, its smoke and dust. Speaking wearily and abstractly about our days as we scratched at the bites on our legs and arms.

The girls had settled in swiftly and completely, as if landing their old house on an empty Manora plot, with a soft thud. Everything was arranged just as it had been in the city. The Captain's study was plucked into sameness with careful detail. The rooms were all doubles of the old house. Even the cat was pawing at the curtains in the dining room when I got there, just as she had in the old house. Someone had told me that cats took time to adjust to new places but not this one, and certainly not in this house, where only the walls looked different. I expected to turn any corner and find their mother in her rocking chair, prayer beads in her lap, nails painted red and her hair pulled up.

Upstairs everything was as it had been in the last house. The only outlier was the room I was to share with Leila. It was a little away from the others, empty other than our boxes and cases lined against the wall. It stayed that way for a long time. I kept meaning to unpack but there was always something else to do, something pulling me out to the city or weighing on my mind. I thought Leila might do it but by then she was only ever in bed, only ever drifting between the rooms of the house in her nightdress, climbing in and out of beds. In chairs, she leaned back as if almost falling asleep. She moved as if her joints were made of oil, slick and crawling.

I'd never lived with anyone before. Her lipstick glowed on the rims of empty water glasses; I'd always find her hairs on my clothes, caught in button holes or wound in the links of my watch. All the time I could feel them around me, the girls, breathing in the same house.

When we married, I was only thinking of the moments that would follow in the next few days. Of taking her through London and bringing her home. Beyond that, nothing existed and now here we were, in this bedroom in a new house with all her family filling the rooms. It had been weeks since we'd been on our own. I reached for her in the dark but she spun away from me, rolled tightly into the sheets. The long net curtains peeled back and there was the wind rocking over us. Here on the island a current of uncertainty ran through everything. The quiet unsettled me and breathed between us. I was used to the noise of Karachi, of London—of places that ran like clockwork through the night. When I couldn't take the silence any more I said, Well I guess you're tired.

Jimmy, she sighed and turned from me without sleeping. Though in the morning she would be the one to wake me. It wasn't the way it had been between us before. Leila rolled on to me without speaking, the shyness shucked off. Her hands ran up and down my ribs as if she was counting them. I said her name so she would look at me. It was still dark, first light clouding her hair and the small bones of her face. She watched me without really even being in the room. Our bodies lined up next to each other, not moving closer or apart.

I was waiting for the sun to come up, for the boats to start moving to shore: to do anything other than lie where I was.

In the house I was underfoot. People seemed to clam up when I walked into rooms. The most contact I had with the girls was through conversations they didn't always know I was part of. I'd get in from work and sit out on the verandah, undoing my collar and wiping sweat and city grime from my neck. I could hear them in the garden, or in the living room.

You don't mind do you, Leila asked.

About J?

Well what else? Of course about J.

Why should I mind?

I finished off a glass of water and stalked upstairs to undress.

I found myself looking forward to the office. There was such a vast portion of my life that had gone in resisting Dada, and now none of that seemed to matter. The house on the island didn't even have a piano, and I never noticed. My head was full of other things: the brewing storm, the need to be anchored.

Most of the time I took breakfast on my own. The girls never woke up before noon any more, so it was just me at the table and the cook frying my eggs in the kitchen. It felt stupid to be using the dining room for just one person, jam and bread and butter spread out across the long table. In London, I'd got my own breakfast and listened to the radio or read. I thought maybe it was time to arrange for a newspaper to be brought to the house out here—after all, other people on the island must read—but anything beyond the very necessary seemed like too much effort. Besides, I think the rest of the household preferred it this way. Life outside was a distant and fabled thing.

Ayesha would wander the thin strip of beach outside our house where the unmanned sea looked so big. I'd see her walking up and down the dunes, barefoot, her hair swinging up on the wind, a black stripe against the sky.

I wanted to follow her out, but I waited just outside the gate instead, my hands folded into my pockets. I didn't want her to think I was crowding her. She had always been prickly but now it was as if the air around her was resisting approach. Still she gave me a small smile as she walked up to me, meeting my eyes for a second before looking back out at the sea.

If I disappeared in there no one would find me, she said, as if she'd been thinking about it for a while.

It's the same sea, I told her.

Not really. In Karachi, I'd lob up to the top in a mangled mess of garbage.

Ash.

I'm sorry, but it's true.

No it's not. People go missing from the coast all the time.

Well here it feels like nobody is watching, she said. She had her slippers in one hand. She padded forward towards the line of water and dunked her feet in the mud. Standing on her toes as a ballerina might.

I'm watching, I told her.

You don't look very closely, she smiled and I had the sense that the conversation had got away from me as so many of them seemed to.

It took half-an-hour on the ferry and then another forty minutes driving into the city to get to work, but I didn't mind any of that. Even the drudgery of the journey was welcome. In the office, everything was busy around me and everything inside my head went quiet. I'd never realized how filled with roaring it was—in the house I could hear my own thoughts echoed back at me as a lion in a cave.

In Karachi, it seemed that the city was starting to pick itself back up. There was work to be done, gaps in the market where young men had disappeared. I got better at it than anybody predicted. Three years at university where I hardly ever left the house and spent most of my time reading were finally paying off. I'd never had the head for business but I'd picked up more than I'd realized. It was easy also to move in this world. They thought a London education me smarter. They were wrong but I stepped into it anyway, there wasn't much skill in becoming who people already thought you were. You wore the clothes and showed up.

Dada and I spoke more in the few months of my return than we had my whole life. On Fridays, I went for dinner with him. It didn't feel like the same room we'd spent so many silent nights in when I was a boy. The walls warmed by our conversation. He even listened to me play after dinner. We'd sit in that sea-facing room, and Dada would call out for coffee and talk in that rambling way he never had with me. He used to talk to my uncle this way, to Ash—storytelling so that each one was a gateway to the other, the histories of our family rolled out between us. They weren't always old stories; we even retreaded the years of my youth, those badly spent teenage years and all the people I'd kept company with, the ones he'd never approved of.

I drifted in and out of the sound of his voice. The outline of the sea hazy in front of me, colours in a palette. This was the house where I'd dreamed the girls into my life, and this was where I watched them now.

That strip of water outside the window. Miles between me and them.

The canteen at work was always empty in the morning. Getting there early meant I had somewhere to sit and read with my chai. Being on my own in the dining room of our house was different from this; here the offices were already awake, waiting to be filled up. I'd make lists of what needed to be done. It made me think of Mehrunissa with her pens and her legal pads. No one planned better than her. She was quiet about it though. Her daughter's wedding was small but meticulous. These things could be large affairs that went on for days and never started

on time, but Mehrunissa ran a tight ship, without giving
the appearance of it. It was the Captain who paid the
bills and supervised the men mounting marquee. But I
remember his wife who put everything in place as she
had been doing for as long as I'd known them.

I learned things from this family without realizing
it. In the morning, tea bitter in my mouth, I trained my
mind to keep off the past.

There were other people who came early; a girl from
the downstairs office who was there for a few months of
the summer sat across from me most mornings. It was
some time before she came up to me—how strange to
think I was the boss now, that people could be nervous of
me—and said she was Munir's cousin, that she'd seen me
at parties before or getting in and out of his car.

What's Munir doing now then? I asked.

You know Munir, she said. He's always in and out of
some kind of trouble.

Well?

She dropped her voice like there was a scandal
coming. People have always trusted me too easily.

He went to see Nighat when he got back—the girl's
dropped him, you know. She's marrying some oil baron,
and well he was never serious about her in the first place
but you should have seen how he reacted. Almost put his
fist through a wall apparently.

That doesn't sound so bad.

He ran someone over driving back—out of his
mind, I heard, drunk or angry. Some kid on a motorbike.

Mamoo took care of it, of course but he was furious. He'd been thinking of retiring, handing it all over to his son, but now he's thrown the whole idea out. Doesn't think Munir is ready yet.

Poor Munir, I said. What's he doing now?

He's working for my father.

Maybe I should see him.

I'd never known anyone whose mind worked the way Munir's did. No matter what happened, he always seemed to land on his feet. By now, I'd known him longer than almost anyone in my life. When I first got back to Karachi I'd put off seeing him, but he was just the same. He stood up when I got into his office and grabbed me just as he'd done that first time in London. He was the same person he'd been back then even if I no longer was.

So, he said, swinging back into his chair, The prodigal son has returned.

He didn't look particularly shattered about anything—not Nighat, not Leila, not the business he'd almost lost, not the man he'd run over. There was still a boyishness to Munir that most people we'd been to school with had lost. I saw them occasionally when I stepped out to buy cigarettes at lunch. Funny how they all worked in much the same area as me. In the short years that had passed, their faces were worn and aged. Even the facial hair hadn't aged Munir.

We were in his father's office. He got his secretary to bring us cups of tea that would go untouched but Munir liked to float his cigarette butts in.

How are you finding being back? he asked, stretching one arm over the back of the vinyl couch, one leg crossed up at the ankle.

It's not what I expected.

It never is for anybody—I get it every time I come back. My father says you notice how dirty the streets are the first time, and after that you just roll with it. Me, I think it's like going to the movies and never really getting your head out of the story. He laughed. Only worse, you know.

I did know, even though the shock of the city was lower on my list of priorities than Munir seemed to notice.

I guess, I said, It's been choppy since I got back.

Ah of course—all this business with the Maliks. Very sad.

I've had my hands rather full.

With the lovely Leila.

I shifted in my seat.

I was meaning to talk you about that, I began. Everything about my marriage seemed impossible to work into conversations. I almost missed my former loneliness and the weeks in London that would pass without anyone ever seeing me.

Don't be silly. You know how it is with me—there's always something. Are you happy?

I suppose that's one way to put it.

Well good for you. I could never have handled her myself.

No?

You know what they say about the Malik girls—it's a little out there for me.

No, I don't, actually. What do they say?

Munir scratched the side of his nose. He looked suddenly older, grave. Maybe it was just that we'd never really spoken seriously about anything before.

Look Jamal, maybe I shouldn't have brought it up.

What do they say?

Well talk like this was bound to come, he said, putting a cigarette in his mouth, I'm not sure why you're so surprised. If you ask me, I've never understood why the Captain went about things the way he did—leaving a wife and four daughters all alone for so many years, not a man in sight to look after them.

What are you talking about?

I mean, you think Mr Amir would have gone after her like that if she'd had a father at home? Nahin yaar! He'd have kept a proper distance, done things properly.

So why are they talking about this now?

Yaar, what does anyone say when people fall on hard times? People have been saying the Captain's cursed for years—a man with only daughters.

What's that got to do with it?

Well I wasn't here for most of it like you. But Maria's not like other women; she was done so quickly after he died. That sort of thing always makes people suspicious.

So they don't like to mourn publicly. She's a private person, they all are. Suspicious of what, anyway?

You know what people are like.

It was the second time Munir had said that.

Come on yaar, just say what you're on about.

Well they think she's being punished. Her mother—it happened so suddenly, it must be retribution for her husband or something.

That is vile. What kind of jahil people are you hanging out with?

Munir put his hands up.

I don't think we should talk about this any more. You said it yourself—they're not like other people.

You're not going to tell me? You're going to make me ask around after my wife's family?

I didn't say that. I'm saying maybe you should let it lie—people talk, so what. It's human nature. The Maliks have always—what's the saying—marched to the beat of their own funny drummer. It's nothing, let it be. Maybe this time away from the city will do them good.

Maybe.

I left my tea and went back to the office after that. Munir offered to take me out for biryani but all this talk had killed my appetite.

On my way home, I tried to put him out of my mind. In the evenings, the whole world seemed washed in blue, the island cast over by moonless nights. Past the mangrove trees, the swampy edge of the coast, I could see the flat-topped houses. A hum of movement shaking each one as the boat pulled in, the scatter of footsteps up the stairs, children streaming through the hallways. Signs of ordinary life puddling through kitchen doors: sizzling pans, screaming fights. Each window blinking up yellow lights as it grew darker, all but my house. The single glow of a bedroom on the first.

The girls would be huddled together on one bed, curled about each other, a close impenetrable nest I saw it as I drove towards the light. They were limbless on the bed, breathing as one beast. They seemed not to need anything when they were together, no water or food; kept silently alive by the collective groan of their bodies.

Lights darted on, down and across the house, as I walked down the beaten path that led to the house. They would spring apart when they heard my key in the door, my footstep heavy on the marble even if I tried to move quietly. I wished I could leave my body on the doorstep and breathe myself into the house, drift silently into their world.

The light darted down the house as I walked up the beaten path. They were in the living room when I got in. Ayesha was sat in the window. Her face was turned away from the room. It was funny to see her smoke. It made me think of how, in school, she would talk with her pen stuck out the side of her mouth, hands piled up with books. She finished the cigarette and climbed back in, kissing the side of Leila's face as she did so.

You smell like Murtaza Chacha, Leila said.

Well that's reassuring at least, she said. I've always felt I was an old man at heart.

An old man who keeps hides of his kill on the wall and wears an ashtray as cologne.

Ayesha laughed. Do you remember how much you hated going to his house when we were younger? That rug with the tiger's head still on it made you jump every time you went into the room.

I remember. I also remember you locking me in there with the lights switched off for almost twenty minutes once.

It was so disappointing. I thought for sure you'd wet yourself. And anyway you could have got the lights.

I was six! I could barely reach the lights let alone see them.

Maria put a hand to her head. I saw her mother in the way she moved; Mehrunissa had touched her forehead just so when her daughters fought around her, two fingers tipped to the temple. I'd never seen Maria do that before.

Do you have to do this right now? Maria said. You're giving me a headache.

I could bring you some tea, Bina suggested.

Don't be ridiculous. I can get my own tea. Lie down.

Slowly, we'd all begun to forget about Bina's recovery. She was the only one holding the house together. She fed the cat, gave the cook money for the sauda, and even helped him clean up. She seemed a little annoyed that he was there at all, not that she'd ever tell me. There was a sense he was taking over her territory, and that she didn't like it. Maria found her mopping the roof two days ago and was so distressed that she'd taken to hovering around her with a chaddar, hoping to catch her sitting down and swaddle her on to the sofa.

Bina was stillest of them all, quieter than Kiran when entering a room, like a shadow person; she'd hid for hours when we played hide-and-seek or dark room. When she sat with her sewing, only her fingers ever seemed to move. I never really saw her with a book, or lazily dragging a bit of thread in front of Kiran's nose as the other girls did.

The impulse to make herself useful was still in her, even though only weeks ago, people were circled in the living room with prayer beads, counting for her life.

III.

This was the constancy of my days. My hours with the Captain were the longest time I spent with anybody in the house. I brought up coffee and zeera biscuits to his room, though both would remain untouched. I would pick out books in the morning before I left for work. They would anchor me into my evenings, the only thing I knew to expect out of my time in the house.

He liked it when I opened the windows and switched off the ceiling fan so, without the whirring, my voice rose in the clammy room.

Ayesha had read to Khalajaan this way. I felt the Captain's cloudy eyes follow me as I tried to speak to him. There was never the sense that he was listening, though he didn't fall asleep either and the smudged pupils seemed fixed somewhere just above my collar. Sometimes the girls' voices would carry into the room. I couldn't make out what they were saying, but my pulse jumped every time. His eyes on my throat.

I stopped trying to make conversation with him after a while. We would just sit there and let the words of other people move between us.

It became clear after a time that there was a slow method to his silencing. He didn't lose his words altogether, the conversation just began to fall away.

Everybody told me not to marry her, he said, early into the move to Manora. Even Khalajaan—maybe her most of all, actually. These things are meant to work better when the differences aren't so big, your families should come from the same place, you should speak the same languages and pray the same way—you'll have heard all this, I know. They'd even chosen a girl for me. I never told Mehrunissa that. Baat paki se pehle—I saw her. And that was it.

I heard you met in a store?

He nodded.

She was picking out silks with her sisters. It was their first time away from home—she told me later that she'd never spoken to a man she wasn't related to before. I tracked down her family that week and dragged my parents there. They hated the idea but what were they going to do? I was their only son.

They must have come to love her, I said.

Maybe they might have done. They never really had a chance—oh it was a different world then. You kids don't know how easy you have it.

I'd heard Dada say that enough times that it circled straight out of me. More interesting were the times the Captain chose to talk to me at all. Any interactions were scattered across our days without any patterns or regularity. Sometimes he would ask me about the summer in Karachi, if the power breakdowns in the city were bad and if my Dada was well. I would tell him about my week: the hold-up in the bank on Shara e Faisal and how the price of maida was rising again. I was his view into the world—he no longer read the papers or listened to news on the radio as much he used to in Karachi so I kept throwing out information, casting it in front of him on small hooks, waiting carefully for his interest.

I asked Leila if he ever spoke to her about their mother, or about anything at all.

She was brushing her hair out in our bedroom, in front of the mirror. She shook it forward so that it fell over her face.

We don't really talk much Jimmy, she said, from behind the wave of black.

What do you do then?

Well I sit with him in the mornings sometimes when you're at work—I take up my drawing sometimes.

And so I would find smudges of chalk and charcoal in the room, on the lace dollies that Maria had draped over the table by the window. Leila must have sat there where I did in the evenings, and in the same silent way. I never saw those drawings but I'd try to see what she might as I sat there: the scar of the sea blotted through the net curtains, her father drooping in his chair. Every fold in his face reproduced on her notepad, like drawings of pyramids. My books, stacked and unmoving. The rotating arrangement of cups and plates. Still-lifes of the Captain's last days, plucked from life and on to his daughter's pages.

What we never spoke about: how he felt about being on this island.

It would be the last decision the Captain ever made. The girls may have been bound to the house, but he was trapped in that chair. The week we arrived, he took his meals with the rest of us in the dining room. After that, he stopped coming down for breakfast or tea, and only joined us for the main meals of the day. By the time the month was up, he was taking everything in his room.

I'm too tired to come down, he said. It takes too much out of me.

The flesh worn off his face till you could see the bones; even the small muscles of his mouth were softer, folding around his teeth, which, when he moved, I could see rattling like dice. The rest of his days measured out in cups of coffee and meals taken on his lap with the radio on. I was the only one who came every day, though there was no special fondness between us. When Amir married his eldest daughter, the Captain said: I always wanted a son. I never got such a welcome. I would always be that boy from across the road, the boy who spent too much time with his daughters.

He looked straight through me. The Captain and his daughters just let everything else drift away from them. They pulled themselves out and further away.

I waited for it to cave beneath us.

IV.

I began to get used to the way things in the house were working. I'd spent all those years across the road from the Malik girls, and even when I was friends with them, the veil of womanness had separated us always; even Ash who wore trousers and chewed paan and wouldn't have thought twice about punching me had lived apart, in some sense. I'd always wanted to live inside them. A night in their house would have meant miracles.

Here I was, under the same roof as them at last. But there was nothing that felt farther to me. Even Leila was a locked box. I'd stopped offering to take them to dinner on the weekends, or suggesting trips to town carefully tailored to each of their interests, as I had done in the beginning. There was a new exhibition at the Ragoonwala centre I thought Leila might enjoy, or movies I wanted to take Maria to. None of them took the bait.

They had their books and their cat and their secrets. On Sundays, while they walked along the craggy coast together, four identical sweeps of black tangled in the wind, I would wander the island. The roads that were empty on the weekend now filled with families, boys playing cricket in the street or sitting outside the stoop of the one shop on the island. The owner had been forbidden to sell cigarettes to the children, though ones as young as twelve were still trying to bribe him.

There were almost no cars on Manora, and that silence, without the accustomed mechanical buzz of cities, was so curious to me that some days when I was lying on my back on the flat roof of the house and staring at the telephone wires, I could swear I heard the sound of a starting engine.

One weekend on my way to the shop for the paper, I saw a sleek silver Mercedes in the streets. It was so hot, the sun thudding down even though it was barely eight o'clock, sparking off every corner of the car, blinding as a can of bright coins. There was a kid behind the car, maybe fourteen. He reminded me of someone I'd gone to school with, a young pilot who'd died in the war. The car moved jerkily up the road—his first lesson I thought. A moustachioed man who was either his driver or father leant forward in the passenger seat, one ringed hand holding a cigarette out the window. The look on the kid's face—the sheer terror and glee to the point of sickness, his mouth stretched wide over jigsaw teeth—was so raw it made me look away. If I could have snatched that feeling off the kid's face and fed it to the girls I would have.

I raised a hand to wave at the boy. His car swerved around the roundabout, while the man in the passenger seat barked at him to slow down. He gave me a wink and almost ran the car into a pole.

It didn't surprise me when the only one of them who asked to go ashore was Ash. There wasn't an island big enough to hold that girl.

We went out together on a Sunday. She was wearing a long, grey kurta but had left her dupatta at home. Maybe it was what Munir had said the other week, but I felt people turn to look at her this time. I might not have picked up on it before. She walked off the boat without any help, swinging up her legs and grinning at me when she landed on the other side with a thud.

Fondness for how familiar this felt wrestled in my chest with the uneasy new awareness of how strange we seemed to the world: not a lick of make-up, as ever, the two of us matching our strides as we moved through the bazaar's rolling dust and crooked tents. We'd come for books, just as we used to in the old days.

The booksellers were new. They picked out romance novels, pulpy volumes from twenty years ago at least, and shoved them to her. The covers were bodice rippers and lipsticked women. I picked up one or two for Leila—a joke that would fall flat.

I've not had anything decent to read for weeks, she said. I finished the last good novel I had left two weeks ago. Since then it's been Maria's magazines. Tips on how to cook the perfect biryani, that sort of thing.

I watched the frown on her face. A stray hair darted down her forehead and she puffed till it blew away, the heat of her breath brushing my arm.

Why didn't you ask me to bring you sooner? I asked.

Ash didn't look up She pulled at her ear, an old tic.

I didn't know how things were between us, she said. I wasn't sure you'd want me to come.

I cleared my throat. You're the one who said we could be friends, I said.

Ash got down on the floor with a pile and dragged her hair up from her neck, knotting it at the nape.

I flagged down the drinks vendor and bought us a couple of bottles of Pakola. It was the first time I'd had the syrupy green stuff since I'd been back in Karachi—another sickly something I'd had no fondness for before I left the country, but that now glowed with the power of nostalgia. I'd have been too embarrassed to ask the office canteen for any. We slurped them down without talking to each other, sorting through our own separate sections.

Bhabhi reads too much, the bookseller said. It's not good for her. You should take her out more, saab.

She's not my—we're not married.

Ash unfolded herself off the floor and laughed.

He's not my husband, she said. We grew up together

I paid the man and watched him bundle the books into paper bags, while Ash moved her hands over the rest of the dusty covers, checking to see if she'd missed anything she would regret later. They were mostly secondhand, dog-eared and damaged. Ash said she preferred it this way, that the selection was bigger than any proper bookshop she might go to in Karachi. I'd never been sure if this was true or if it was just because she read books so quickly that she could never afford to buy them new. Still, I wished I'd had her with me at Foyles or some such place, that I'd had time enough before I got back to bring her something new. I pictured opening the door and putting glistening new paperbacks in her hand, writers she'd never heard of before. I wanted to be the one bringing her things.

On the way back to Manora, she put her hand in the curve of my elbow and we stood close. The sailors nodded at me as we got into the car, Ash driving and disappeared along the road to the house we shared and I thought about what they must have seen, about the distorted reality we lived in. Everything arranged a little different to how I might have wanted it before I left. At dinner we sat at the table, disordered around the empty spots for Mehrunissa and the Captain as always, uneasy as people who have just sat down during a game of musical chairs.

Did you have a nice time, Leila asked. At this point my trips with Ayesha were a part of the way things worked on the island. Leila made no move to join us, though I told her Dada asked after her often. Sometimes we went out early and met him for halwa puri, before going to the bazaar. It was another thing about my life I could never have predicted, this new strange relationship with Dada, where we could speak to each other for long stretches of time, ribbing each other without tension. He looked almost exactly as he had the year I left for university but there was a stoop to his walk, a thinning of his figure that I only noticed when he stood.

Leila too was much diminished. Her bones made spikes in the folds of her clothes. When she took them off I found each bump in her spine, running a hand lightly down her back. We slept spine to spine, her shoulder blades like broken wings. I ended up eating the sweets I brought her: gulab jamun, chocolates, little blocks of mithai boxed and wrapped in gold. Leila was known for her sweet tooth so I got the cook to make siwayan to tempt her to the table. But she just sat there with her cups of chai and watched me eat, fist tucked under her chin, watching me with a forgotten fondness.

Why don't you come with us tomorrow, I said. My fingers slick with syrup, as I reached over and brushed her cheek.

I can't Jimmy. I have too much to do.

Like what?

Well we haven't even unpacked the bedroom yet.

And it's been fine that way for weeks. Don't you want to see Dada?

To be honest, she said, I don't really understand why you keep going out in the first place. The whole week's not enough? You have to keep making trips on a Sunday?

I saw your friend the other week. Well maybe not your friend, but that girl who always came to your birthday parties. What was her name? Mariam maybe, she looked like a Mariam.

Leila tilted her head. Everybody looks like a Mariam in Karachi.

The one who always stayed too long after the party was over, and ate too much cake but never got fat.

That was Mariam. And she wasn't my friend, she was Bina's.

I heard her husband left her. He told her he was going on a business trip to Lahore and just never came back—this was a year ago now. She keeps calling him up and asking him when he's going to come back for the children. I have to say they weren't the best-looking kids, so I guess it makes sense he's not that keen on them.

I didn't even know she was married, Leila sighed. She was Bina's friend, not mine.

Will you come with me to Dada's or won't you?

She put her head down on the table like a child; the way we used to at school when any of us were sick or had headaches, waiting for the teacher to come and touch our foreheads to check for a fever.

I'm really not up for it Jimmy, she said.

All the solutions I had seemed too simple. The wasted effort of these tricks that came to nothing, time and time again.

You haven't left the house since you got here.

That's not true. Bina and I went for a walk the other night. She's been collecting shells. I mean it's mostly rubble out there, but she's building up quite the collection. I think she wants to make jewellery or something out of it. Anyway you have Ayesha with you, she won't want me there.

She's not sixteen any more Leila. We both want you there. I turned a lighter over in my fingers, clicking it on and off. It would be good for you to see people.

Leila picked herself off the chair, the dupatta floating after her. I watched her get on her tiptoes, and kiss my cheek. As she turned I could the dusty soles, the turn of her ankle. Her head dipped away from me, even that brief contact more than she planned for.

Maybe next time, she said.

V.

It got easier to be around Ash for stretches of time, just the two of us. The familiar running up behind us on our trips, as we walked through the same steps. There was not as much change in the landscape as there had been in us. Some houses on the road to Sunday bazaar were rearranged or painted, a row of pinks and blues looking like cakes in the sand. And maybe the men who brought our tea and sold us trinkets were different, but it still followed in the rhythm of those long days. The car would still heat up while it waited for us to shop, as hot as a small, tin coffin when we piled back into it to drive to the docks.

We ate at those dhabas on Sea View, the kind of place I'd never have taken her when we were teenagers. I couldn't imagine what our families would have said if they'd seen Ash pull up her legs and light a cigarette somewhere as seedy as this, with the truckers and paanwallahs. It was the sort of thing I thought she would prefer. For birthdays we would go for high tea at Metropole, and the other girls looked delighted but Ayesha was bored, with the small sandwiches and round cakes and the families milling about who looked just the way people we saw anywhere might: people from school or Maria's friends or generals' wives who occasionally called on Mehrunissa.

Even outside of her grand travel plans, Ash wanted to be somewhere else. I knew she thought it was strange when we were younger, that I didn't go out with the boys when they asked me. Munir was always inviting me places, once even to take a car along the coast over the winter break. I always ended up staying behind, spending my time with the girls instead, and Ash would look at me when I told her, her mouth curved a little to one side.

Not that she didn't like having me around or that she'd have wanted to go with them—I couldn't see Ash making conversation with any of those idiots for longer than maybe three minutes. But because I could and she couldn't; the freedom I never took advantage of was a closed door to her.

Now we were older and things were different. There was no one to look over us. I thought of my grandfather, alone in his big house, and of the Captain locked to his armchair. We were the caretakers now.

Leila was on the long wooden swing when I got home, sleeping only a few feet away from our bed. In the old house, the swing had been in Mehrunissa's room. She kept letters in its slats, the frantic hand lettering framed by the wooden carvings along the seat's edges. If you lay straight on your stomach, all you could see through its wooden frame were the trees outside the window. Here, we'd wedged it between our dresser and the balcony. Kiran would come and curl up in a corner in the afternoons.

She looked better than before, even asleep. Her hair, wet from the bath, swamped over the cushions; she smelled like talcum powder and roses. When I leaned in to her, I could see the kajal lining her eyes.

The swing rocked as I touched her and there was the sound of something rolling on to the floor—I realized that we'd split open a string of prayer beads. They drained out of her hands and on to the floor as I sat down next to her.

What's happened, she asked, shooting up.

It's fine, I said. I plucked one off the edge of the swing, and dropped it in her palm. I'll get you another one on Monday.

Oh Jimmy, she said, pressing her face into my chest. That was my mother's.

I put one of the amber beads in my pocket. I'll take one with me, I said. I'll make sure I bring back one that looks just like it.

It doesn't matter about that. It won't be the same one. You couldn't understand.

Leila, I laughed. You don't even use them. The last time I saw you praying was when you were fifteen and you'd burned one of Ash's short stories. You begged me not to tell her and prayed it would be—what was it you called it—unburned in the morning.

She drew away from me.

You're not taking this seriously, she said.

Because you're being silly. I know it had some sentimental value for you but I'll get you a new one this week and it'll—

I can't use a different one, it doesn't work like that.

Use it for what?

She rolled herself off the swing. I could tell she was angry and trying to peel away from me, but the movement of our bodies on the flat cushion rocked her closer.

I don't want to talk about this any more, she said. Why don't you go down for dinner and I'll see you in a little while.

We sat around the table, the rest of her sisters and myself. Half an hour later we stopped waiting, though Bina still wouldn't eat until Leila came down.

There's no point in waiting, I told her. It isn't like she eats any more, anyway.

That's not why I'm waiting. I don't like to think of her on her own up there, Bina said, moving to get up.

Food's getting cold, I called after her, but she was already halfway up the stairs.

Maria shook her head at me. She was ripping at the roti with her fingers and her mouth flicked up at one corner.

Oh Jimmy, she said. I thought you knew better than to try and control us.

I'm not trying to control anything. I just don't understand why we can't all sit down and have one nice meal as a family.

Her eyebrows went up. We're not a family though. Not really. You can't just put us all in a house and fix a cook in the kitchen to make us a family.

That's not what I'm trying to do.

Look, I know it's hard for you, but you're not going to get anywhere by putting her back up this way. You just need to give everyone time to adjust. None of this what we expected.

I drank some water, trying to splice out my thoughts before I said anything. What is that supposed to mean? I said. I didn't plan any of this either.

She reached across the table and put a hand on my wrist, her fingers smearing grease over the strap of my watch.

I wasn't trying to say it was your fault exactly, she said. I just think you have this idea that you can fix everything, and you can't. It's not the same for you as it is for us. You can't make our problems disappear with money or connections. And if you don't give Leila her space she will just keep pushing you away.

I couldn't remember the last time Maria and I had spoken this way. Her thumb went over my wrist and I was seventeen again, in a too hot classroom, embarrassed because I'd failed a test or been caught flying paper planes out the window.

What do you think I should do, I asked.

Ash put down her book and flipped it over the corner of her plate. Without her parents to stop her, she read at the table all the time now, turning pages with one hand and eating with the other.

I don't think you should do anything. Leave him alone Maria. It's their marriage.

I'm only trying to provide some advice.

I think it's probably best if we all stay out of it, Ash replied. It must be hard enough to be—well to be here at all. Imagine if you and Amir had to move in with us just after you were married.

What's that got to do with anything, Maria said half standing out of her chair. She looked as if she might put her hands on her hips and send the two of us to bed without our dinner.

I'm only saying that perhaps the two of them need some time away from the rest of us, Ayesha said. Just some time to work things out without everyone else involved.

Maria lifted her eyebrows. If it's space we're talking about, I don't think your involvement is exactly helping.

What's that supposed to mean?

You don't think Leila might prefer to have her husband with her on the weekends rather than jetting off to the city with you?

Ash put her book back up and switched through the pages. Well, she said, If she would, then she's given no indication of it so far.

I didn't mean it was a bad thing Ayesha. Only maybe it doesn't need to be every weekend.

It doesn't have to be, she said, without looking back up. And at any rate he doesn't need to come with me if he doesn't want to.

I pushed back my chair and stood up. Look I don't want to cause any arguments here.

Well you're not Jimmy. Finish your dinner I'm leaving.

I knew Ayesha would go out into the courtyard. I walked over there and stood by the tall windows to see if I could make her out. There were sheets of mesh knotted over the frames to keep the mosquitos out in the summer, and through them I could smell the coming of rain. It was too dark to see anything but the line of her leaning against a column. That and the bright tip of her cigarette.

At the top of the stairs Bina was leaving our room, with a tray of tea gone cold and a plate of untouched biscuits.

You shouldn't fight, she told me. I don't like it.

I'm sorry.

It just upsets everything. Why can't we all just get along with each other?

I smiled. She'd changed so little since I'd left. Bina was still a picture of what it was to be seventeen.

No one's really angry with each other, I explained. We just want to help Leila.

Bina shook out her head. Her bird shoulders moved so the dupatta fell off them, and without it she was even smaller than I'd realized. The disease had sapped her through. I thought Leila was thinner than before but Bina's body was a different beast entirely. You could see where the sickness had ravaged her, clothes catching on her bones the way a scarf catches on branches.

Everything is so different, she said. And you don't even understand at all.

You can talk to me if you like, I said. I tried to beat out my voice the way her mother would, talking slowly so the words slipped out of her mouth like butter.

It's okay Jimmy, she said, twitching her shoulders up. I'll be fine. She walked away, and I heard her close the door to her bedroom as I went into mine.

In the house in Karachi, Bina had shared a room with Leila. I saw it once, on my way to Mehrunissa's room to help carry down her dresser when she gave it to Maria as part of her dowry. There were twin beds, Bina's by the window. All those years she'd slept with the sound of Leila in the same room, her small snores colouring the air. I didn't like to think of her in the lonely dark now. I knew she slept badly, lately. The other girls would have read before bed or come down to watch television. But Bina was the kind of girl who must lie there with the lights off, waiting for sunrise.

In the morning it was dark and grey. I went outside because Leila hated for me to smoke in bed. She was still asleep. Everything was still and the sky overcast with giant clouds, melting the beach to a single storm of grey. At school we used to wait for the monsoon. If the rain came down heavily enough we might get a day off from school or at least a free period to stomp around in the mud. Now it just made me gloomy.

Three years in England taught me how to appreciate light. We took the sun for granted in our cities, never noticing the way light could fill a room. Only in the months without it did I realize that there was something to love in the way summer would stretch out the days. At the end of rain-battered months in London, even I was looking forward to the sun. In the parks and squares, couples curled into trees with their kisses and people licking ice cream and men down to their shirtsleeves even if it was still cold really—just the sun glowing out at us. When it got hot I had to open my windows and soon the inside was filled with bugs and moths and butterflies. I drank cider and my pores remembered how to sweat. Newspapers called it an Indian summer which was funny, very funny and even though I left the house every morning with a jacket tucked under one arm and an umbrella under the other, I was the only one. London in the summer was optimism. It swept over the city like a madness, and every year I waited for the rain and every year I grew to like it a little bit more. The wind stopping in the streets as if it were waiting for something.

Standing at the start of a monsoon season on Manora Island with Leila still asleep in our bed, I felt the aching distance for the fresh clipped grass squares, the summers that pricked only lightly beneath the armpits.

On the island the skies were bigger than they'd ever been in the city, stretching out overhead. Looking out at the coast from Karachi at this time of year, I'd felt as if the storm was always coming, gathering somewhere in the middle distance and making its way to our shores. It never seemed to get closer or drift farther apart. Now, the churn of clouds was smoke-less, alive with heat. They hummed like burning telephone wires, stretching shadows across the empty streets. I could feel it in my bones as old women did, the creak of changing weather. In Karachi, we drank falsa juice to stave off the summer, the women lay on thakhats with damp washcloths draped over their foreheads. Even the heat had a festival quality, a shared groan. The storms were the same. Children danced in the downpour and the rest of us left the windows of the office open, so the smell could drift in. The cool relief from the sun.

I stood on my own in the middle of a deserted town: the dark sky pressing down on me, heavy enough to grind me into the gravel and smudge me along the coast. I was a dot on the blank canvas of Manora and it stretched out around me, the quiet streets and decaying temples, forest groves and swamps. I could walk for days in solitude.

VI.

The rains came and it was too rough for me to go into work. I called to let them know and it was gratifying to hear them sigh at the end of the line. Someone wanted me at least.

This was August and our skins were oil. I went back to bed and crawled into damp sheets to find Leila just waking. We undressed lazily as if our bodies were too hot to do the work. I dipped my thumbs in the bend of her hip and pulled her under me, happy when she slid over to me. Even the unspeaking between us did not seem so distant or grim. I seized these moments with her. We were only ever together in the mornings, and never at night and never during the day; sometimes I'd be home for hours before she even noticed.

When we peeled apart, she rolled back into the nest of sheets, twisting them back over her body despite the heat; the electricity was out again, no overhead fan or air conditioning.

I drifted in and out of sleep till noon. My hazy dreams chased me through the house: I looked for the girls in every room and when I got to the Captain's bedroom, he was gone. Four young Mehrunissas were sitting on his bed, matching hair and matching grins.

This is a nice surprise, Ayesha said, when she saw me come down the stairs. Has the office finally realized how to function without their London-returned graduate?

Don't be ridiculous, I said. Is there any toast?

Let me guess. They found sheet music in your desk. Proper businessmen don't play instruments, do they?

It's the rain. It was madness a few hours ago, I said, looking out into the courtyard, Looks like it might have calmed down a bit now.

Really? I saw boats leaving the shore this morning anyway.

I shook my head.

Some people like to play fast and loose with their life I guess. I've never understood that.

Ayesha laughed. Some people don't have the luxury of days off when there's a little rain J. They didn't inherit companies from their grandfather. And anyway, she said, leaning forward to pass me the butter, This life is—well fate or luck or whatever. It's all out of our hands.

I scratched butter on to my toast and eyed her. You're very philosophical for nine in the morning.

Unlike you I've been up for hours, she said. She was cradling a small apple in one hand and rolling it down to the curve of her wrist, like it was a cricket ball.

Oh?

She narrowed her eyes as if she were trying to determine whether or not I could be trusted. She uncrossed her ankles, and put down the apple.

I've been writing again. But I don't want you to tell anybody. She flushed and lowered her neck. There's a publisher in Delhi who might be interested in my manuscript. I met some editors when I was working in Lahore last summer. One of them must have referred my work.

What are you going to send them? Anything I've read?

She snorted, Don't be ridiculous J. I dropped all those stories years ago. I started working on a novel while you were away, she said.

A novel. I'd never even known she'd been to Lahore. We'd never talked about our time apart. Most of our conversations seemed picked up instead of begun anew— people and books and stories retold till they shone with the lick of our tongues, alive in the well of the past. When that was exhausted momentarily, we slipped into our comfortable silences. On some of our trips back over the water, Ash would bend her elbows on the rail and wordlessly watch the receding shore. I trained my eyes to follow the water and not the bump of her nose.

I don't really want to talk about it, she said, shaking her head. I'd rather wait and see if anything happens first.

Another shut door. I poured out the tea. I told Ash I thought I'd go see the Captain.

When I got upstairs he was asleep, but I stayed in the room. The bed shook with his snoring and I watched the whirring rain, drank two cups of tea and read ahead in our collection of short stories. Up in his room I felt as if I was hiding the way children in books do, in a fort or treehouse.

By the time the weekend rolled around, it was mild enough to venture out. Leila was encouraging that Ayesha and I should visit the mainland again. Even Maria thought it was a good idea. Having me at home for a few days had disrupted the rhythm of their lives. I was always underfoot, in the wrong place at the wrong time; distracting Leila from her prayers or scaring Maria on my way to the kitchen at night.

The cook packed sandwiches and we unwrapped them almost as soon as the house was out of sight. I wolfed mine down, wiping egg from my chin with a handkerchief. There was a stillness to the air when we disembarked.

I should have checked the forecast, I said, looking up the rearing grey.

The radio said it wasn't going to rain.

Ash squinted up. It was still only freckled with clouds overhead, but the heaviness of my lungs was a warning.

People were packing up their stalls when we got there. It's going to rain, the bookseller told us, You see how the crows are flying low in the sky? They only do that when rain is expected.

There were others who still insisted it would be fine, that going home was the waste of a day. They continued to call out even when it began dripping and then pouring down. I still had the lone amber bead in my pocket, from the string I'd promised to replace, but Ash's sodden hair was hanging down in her face and her shoulders were scrunched up. She had a feeling hatred of the rain. I could picture her hissing if we stayed out long enough.

I packed her into the car and took her to Dada's for dinner. In the house we could still feel the storm. Chandeliers were shaking as we ate our dinner, white curtains blowing out as if there were ghosts charging out behind them.

Dada was glad to see us, insisted we stay the night.

It's only a little rain, Ash said. We're big kids now, we'll be fine.

I'm not having the two of you out in that weather, he maintained. You'll stay here till morning, and we'll see what the weather is like then. He went to bed early and then it was just the two of us. I couldn't remember the last time we'd been alone this way, not since we'd first met in that dark study.

We put some records on and sat cross-legged on the carpet in the drawing room. As children we had never really been allowed in here, only during parties or when I practised the piano in the afternoons. It was a mysterious, adult world, kitted out with scratchy sofas and cushions you couldn't lean against.

I poured out Dada's scotch, and Ash asked for one though I'd never known her to drink before.

Play me something, Ash said, slipping backwards till she was lying on the floor.

This isn't good enough for you, I asked, nodding my head at the crooner on the sleeve I was holding. He wore his hair slicked to one side, a style Leila tried to get me to try when we were still in Paris but it never stuck.

I've missed you playing.

I'm not that good any more, I fell out of practice. It would take longer to tune me up than it would the baby grand.

I thought it was meant to be one of those things you never forget. Muscle memory or something like that. A reflex. Like riding a bicycle.

You don't know anything about music, I said, putting the sleeve away and joining her on the floor.

I stretched my toes out beside her.

Maybe not, she said. Maybe I'll take it up. You and Leila can't be the only arty types in the family.

Your writing doesn't count? If you publish you'll have had more success at it than both of us put together. You know I only play on the weekends now. Leila hasn't finished anything since we got back from Paris.

That's true I suppose, she said. She was not the kind of person who felt the need to tell me that I was doing fine myself.

Why do you suppose Leila doesn't paint any more? I asked.

Hasn't got the energy for it I think, she said. You know what she's like.

I don't think I know what Leila's like any more.

Ash got up, leaning halfway up, on her crooked elbows. She reached over and grabbed my hand.

Look Jimmy, she said, I don't know what it's about but I don't like it. I didn't want to talk about it in the house but there's something strange happening and I wish you could see it.

Something strange? Like what?

She snapped her hand away as if I was made of fire.

Never mind. Forget it I mentioned it.

I dropped my head to the floor and breathed out slowly. If you ask me, I said, though no one had. There's something strange in just about all of this.

What do you mean?

I almost laughed then. Her hair was long again, and I could feel it move when she stirred to look at me. Not quite snaking down her back in the same way but enough to feel the way it had before: a dark creature whipped around her face in the wind, moving when she lay down of its own accord.

Nothing ended up how I thought it would is what I mean I guess.

What do you mean? Ash asked.

I meant that I wore a suit to work every day, and I lived in the same house as Ash, but still two doors away—but I couldn't say any of that.

She sat up and crossed her legs so we were face to face. Maybe you have too many expectations of things being a certain way J, she said.

Well now you don't even want to tell me about your book, I said.

She smoothed a hand over my forehead, and smiled down at me. Oh J. You're so sensitive.

Don't call me that, I said shutting my eyes. People always tell me I'm sensitive.

It was very nice with her fingers brushing through my hair.

Look at all the things that haven't changed, she said, You and I are still the same.

She leaned over me and her hair fell over my face. The long dark curtain. Through it the world was blurry and her whiskeyed mouth was near mine. I felt as I used to that Ayesha was only an extension of myself. We were close enough once for it to almost be true. And despite what she said this was the first time it felt as though things were the same between us. Not all of that feeling was good for me.

I wish you'd stop leaving me, I said.

You're the one that goes away.

Not like that, I told her, Only sometimes you feel very far away.

I watched her bend towards me. Her palm flat on the buttons of my shirt and they strummed up against her, shook by my nerves and we caught on each other. Her hair and the strap of my watch, my buttons on her bracelets till we rolled to the floor. She shifted her hands to my wrists and held me beneath her.

We went up the stairs with our shoes in our hands to be quiet, matching each other's footsteps in the dark. I'd only been in my bedroom once, since I'd returned to the country. There were dust covers on my dresser and trunk.

Here, among my comic books and faded blue sheets, with the window still open and the storm still coming through, we took off our clothes. It was dark so I only saw her in flashes of lightning. The slip of skin under her breasts lit up, her leg crossing the sheets to move closer to my own.

I moved into her, our bodies sinking together with the weight of our years.

Don't say anything, she asked me, when we shut the door behind us. Don't ruin it.

My tongue in sailor's knots, throat squeezed tight—I don't know what I would have said if I could. Finally, I could feel the slip-tide of her.

The crumbling of our history in the light from the hall.

I want you to tell me something Jimmy, she said, after a long time. I want you to tell me something right now because if we don't talk about this now we never will. She sighed up at me. Tell me what you love most in the world.

What?

I'm not fishing for anything, kid, don't worry. I just want to know—if you lose one thing right now what would really—*really*—break you?

I don't know, I said.

There was a dumb dryness in my throat, an emptying out of thoughts.

Think then, she said with little patience.

You—I stumbled with that. All of you. You're my family.

She snorted at that, and I guess the irony of this while we were both in my bed must have got to me too, so I laughed with her.

Think harder, she said, serious again. Pick one thing. You—you don't even have to tell me what it is. Just pick one thing that could ruin you if it left and hold it there.

Is this some kind of game?

Are you doing it Jimmy?

Okay. Okay I've got it.

Now tell me, she said. She propped herself up on one arm and looked straight at me. If you lost it, what would you do?

What do you mean what would I do? It would ruin me, we just said that.

I mean what would you do to get it back?

To get it back?

Don't be so slow, yes, to get it back.

Anything, I guess.

You guess or you know?

I pulled the breath right out of my lungs, and sat up. I know, then.

Ayesha looked pleased with that. Well then, J. There's the answer to your question.

What question?

You asked me what was wrong with us—remember? My sisters and I. You wanted to know what was happening. Well we're the same. We'd do anything.

The way she said it took my legs out from under me.

She shifted her head to my shoulder, the weight of her hair settling my chest. Beyond her sparred fireworks of lightning, thunder warbled still. There was a thudding in my rib cage, unnatural and high. I would wait till morning to trace all of it back to a single moment.

The next day we did not go back to the island together. We did not braid our fingers together on the boat watching the city disappear behind us, pretending maybe we were the husband and wife everybody thought us. Instead, I put her in Dada's car and sent her off to the docks on her own with his driver, while I went to work in one of Dada's ties and shirt. It was too snug around the shoulders.

She'd snuck into my room as I was dressing and knotted the green silk at my throat.

Don't start worrying about this, she said, eyes fixed at a point between my collarbone, It's not going to change anything.

With us?

With anybody. It's all still the same as before, J. I told you. You and I are the constant.

I put my hands around her shoulders. This was the time to speak.

Something's changing, isn't it Ash? You said it yourself last night, it's all falling apart. Well it isn't gone yet—maybe we can fix it.

Oh J, she said. She reached up and kissed my cheek. Promise you'll leave it alone, she said, Us and everything else.

How can I?

She was tying the secrets of a hundred other people at my neck and pulling.

Everything will turn out fine. Don't pay attention to anything I might have said last night. The whiskey . . . and you know I always get funny about the rain.

She took a step back to look at me, shifted the knot so it was slightly askew, said, Well I suppose I was a little funny about you too.

VII.

At the office, I rolled the small amber prayer bead along my desk. When one of the boys was sent out to pick up lunch I gave it to him, instructed him to bring back an identical string.

My secretary came in at about three with a phone call.

It's your wife on the phone.

Everything alright? I said, picking up the receiver. No one ever called me at the office.

J?

It was Ash.

Something's happened, she said.

What's wrong?

I can't talk about it here.

Her voice was low. I hadn't thought there were many forces on earth which could shake Ash. Before her chemistry finals, she'd asked me to pull over on the side of the road so she could lean out of the car and puke into the rotting pavement, but otherwise, she was always likelier to respond to things with anger than with worry.

Can I come meet you in the city? she asked.

Of course. But how will you get here?

I've spoken to the boatman and he says he can get me out there around six. Is there anywhere near you I can wait?

I met her at Maxwell's at fifteen past six, and there was a plate of French fries next to her and an already full ashtray next to her Salinger.

What's going on then, I asked, dropping into the booth across from her. I slipped off my jacket and spread it out on the seat next to me.

Hello to you too, she said. That's some greeting.

You scared me earlier.

She shook out a couple of cigarettes on the vinyl tabletop.

Goddamnit J, I think I'm losing my mind.

Would you just tell me what's wrong? I asked, moving forward in my seat.

She lit a cigarette and leaned an elbow against the table.

Leila's been seeing Ma. She's been seeing Ma in the house she says—

Your mother?

Yes, my mother. Keep up J. My god. So I went home and she told me she woke up this morning and Ma was on the swing in your bedroom and she was telling her the rains would stop in two days.

I ordered a cup of coffee.

I don't see why you're getting so worked, I said, She's half asleep most of the time anyway. I don't think she's even stepped out of the front door in weeks.

J, she said hands shaking as she smoked. You're not listening. You don't know the full story—she's been seeing Ma in her dreams for weeks now. This is different.

What?

I understood then that the dreams must be what Ash had tried to tell me about the other night: Leila talking to her mother from beyond the grave as easily as she spoke to anybody

You know Leila's always said she has the second sight, Ash said. Well she told us a few weeks ago that Ma came to her in a dream and that she was sorry she was gone. And that there was a way back.

A way back?

A way back to us. I've never seen my sisters like this before.

Your sisters? Maria and Bina know about this?

Ash gulped down some of my coffee, flicking some of her cigarette on my cuffs.

Yes. Yes, they've been with her from the start. She's almost here now.

With her how?

They believe in Leila. They believe she can bring Ma back to us.

And how do they think she can do that?

She closed her eyes and pressed her fingertips to them for a minute, then looked down at her plate.

Leila thinks—she thinks Ma died instead of Bina. In place of her.

What do you mean? It wasn't some sort of sacrifice Ayesha. Your mother had malaria.

I know that, she said. Don't just repeat the fact back to me Jimmy, I'm trying to tell you what they think. She thinks it must stand to reason that if Ma could sacrifice herself for them, it would work the other way around you know. We would be able to exchange her life for someone else's.

I raised an eyebrow. And whose life would you be sacrificing? I asked.

Oh J don't ask me that. It's too awful.

Her hands cupped her face. The place was starting to fill up. People from the financial district came here after work to cut deals and share war stories. They sat at tables near us and the cigar smoke rose in the room, and there were plates of greasy food coming out of the kitchen. I could see again how Ash caught attention, her unbrushed hair, the sloppy collar of her shirt.

I finished my coffee and left some money on the table. On our way out, I caught Ash's arm in one hand.

Why are you telling me this? I asked. Do you really believe her?

We were sandwiched between the traffic and the alleyway. Ayesha unlocked herself and hailed a taxi. My car was still at the office but I insisted on riding with her out to the docks. Her hands were shaking as we climbed on to the moth-eaten seats.

I don't know what I believe J, but I wouldn't have come to you with this if it wasn't important.

You can't expect me to tell you everything, she continued. They're still my sisters. But you need to keep your eyes open.

Leila was asleep by the time we got home. I uncurled my fist and found that, at some point, between the taxis and the boat, I'd got a hold of those beads I'd said I would get her. I dropped them on to the nightstand, not caring for the way they clanged against the glass top.

In sleep she was smoothed out, the silent rhythm of her chest and gentle turn of her mouth. I got into bed beside her. My hand brushed the jut of her hip, ran down the arch of her leg, but she didn't move. Her shoulder was still even when I leaned in to drop my mouth against the curve of her neck. When I woke up a few hours later, light shifting over my eyes and plucking me awake, there was an empty spot beside me. I slid on to the still warm patch of her sheets and tried to steal the thoughts from her pillow.

In Paris, it had seemed she cared for me. We'd not been married long but I'd imagined it would be easier for us than for other people. Most of the people I knew married without really knowing each other, after a few arranged meetings in their family's drawing rooms. Even Maria and Amir, the closest couple I'd ever known, had only known each other a few months before they married. Compared to that, the years Leila and I had spent in each other's lives should have made this easier. But the edges of our days kept getting harder and sharper.

It was true that I didn't understand what Ash had been talking about this morning, but it scared me all the same. If I couldn't count on my wife's affection, on the ease I had with any of these women, I must be the sacrifice.

I lay on my back and stared at the window, curtains blowing out at the foot of our bed. A world without me, as it had been before we'd met at that party: my body cold in the sheets and Leila waking beside me, reaching for her slippers to go find her sisters; Mehrunissa raised from the dead, opening the door of her bedroom.

I had never been without counsel before though I was never any good at taking it. In a pinch I would turn to Maria or her mother and this connection set tiny quakes down my spine. Dada would have been impossible to approach. I could see him picking his glasses off his nose and telling me this was normal.

Young girls are always caught by the thought of the unnatural, he'd told me once. In a moment of frankness he even admitted that when my parents were married, he was advised to turn curses against my mother. People told him she must have charmed Abba, a spell of love veiling his judgement. It was the only way they could explain such reckless behaviour. Not love or any other kind of connection, the type that may emerge between any two people drawn to each other as my parents were. The theory made me sorry for these people, people so distant from humanity.

Dada put no stock in that kind of thing and would be embarrassed I'd even brought it up. And so I was left to riddle over it on my own, writing down what I knew or what I thought to try and make sense of it. I turned over what I knew in my head with the concentration of a mathematician trying to unlock a puzzle. There was some secret code hidden in this mix of perceptions that was currently beyond me. I became nervous for Leila to find it in my pockets or books so I would burn the pages when I had stared at them long enough, crushing them into the ashtray in a pagan ritual of my own. I knew there were people who believed that prayer could bend worlds and people who thought the same of love or black magic or curses.

Ash grew noticeably absent from the house. She took her meals in her room, claimed to be working on her book. She avoided being on her own with me, always leaving when I entered the room because something had just come to mind that she simply had to put down, or shadowing Maria as she did the gardening or finished unpacking the crystal from polystyrene boxes.

When the weekend came around, she begged off our usual plans with the same excuse. I went on my own, if only to get away from the house. They seemed as if they could only take my company in small doses.

I called up Dada before I left, asked him to tell the cook not to prepare anything, I was taking him out. We had gone for biryani sometimes when my uncle was in town, and there was a place I remembered liking that was still open though it was different now, with a big cooler where the outdoor stove was meant to be. They didn't cook meat on a spit any more, the whole kitchen shoved in the back and the waiters wearing grey shirts with the restaurant's name embroidered on the pockets in red. I bit into a chilli and stared at my plate.

He must have noticed, because he asked about Leila just then.

We've not been doing so well, I admitted. I was shifting rice around my plate with my fingers. It's been so different between us lately.

Well that's marriage, Dada went on. You were married for a few weeks maybe before you came home? That feeling wears off eventually. Poor child. She must be suffering so much.

They all are. I don't know how to help them.

If you want my advice, Dada said, You'll stop trying. You can't fix everything in their world, Jamal.

But the Captain—he's not himself.

Maybe you should come back to the city for a while and stay with me, hmm?

I sat up straighter in my seat. What do you mean? Why would I do that?

Dada sighed, and leaned back. He rested his palms together.

You're not going to want to hear this but I think your being there—maybe it isn't the best thing for them right now. I know you've always been very close, but they've just experienced a huge tragedy. Maybe the greatest tragedy in their lives. They need some time to heal as a family. Much as they love you, and much as you love them, you'll never quite be family in that way. Now you've helped them settle in and that's very good of you, but maybe you should come back home for a little while and let them have their space. You could still visit. And Leila could come see you—I'd like to have my family under my roof as well you know.

I ran a hand through my hair. It wasn't something I'd really even thought of before but he had a point. Getting away from the island, from the cloying atmosphere of that house where I always felt unwanted, always watched—it might be the thing I needed to give me new eyes.

I think maybe we could all use the space, I said.

He smiled, a rare treat, the full curve of his mouth under the whitening bristle.

Good, he said. I think this will maybe be good for you and good for your marriage as well. You could have your own space in the house you know. It wouldn't be the same as a real holiday but that's not really appropriate right now, is it? This way you can spend some time together and you wouldn't have to take her away from her family.

The news did not yield the results I might have hoped for from the Malik household. When I told the Captain, he gave no indication of understanding what I was saying. Our conversations went this way, by now: I would talk to him and his grunts would fill in the spaces between my words. He looked up at me and maybe I imagined in his eyes the flicker of fear that animals have when they are abandoned. That summer in Lahore when my uncle took me out for the sacrifice I had put my hand on the goat's neck the evening before the slaughter; it turned its wide eyes up at me with a well of impenetrable sadness. It struck me somewhere between my ribs, putting me off the meat that was served in charred and steaming piles for the rest of the week. I left him with new books, and closed the door behind me.

Maria just nodded her head and said maybe it was a good idea, but Bina and Ash didn't look at me. Leila, in a lightning bolt, kissed the side of my face in full view of her sisters, told me in her molasses voice that she would miss me and would I come home to her soon.

I packed my bags on the Sunday. All the girls were reading or sewing in the garden. I could see them from our window, laid out on wicker chairs with a low table holding up their ankles and loaded with teacups and glossy magazines.

I folded away my favourite shirts, a tie Leila had once said she loved.

Can I come in?

Ash was in the doorway. I hadn't seen her leave the group. She was wearing trousers again, a pair of her father's, belted high on her waist.

It's your house, I said.

She sat cross-legged on the bed.

You're really leaving then?

It would appear so, I said.

I wrapped my shoes in tissue and shoved them at the bottom of my suitcases. I didn't need to take so many

things. My old things were still at Dada's, still cloaked
in old blankets. The museum of my teenaged years, net
curtains strung up over the bed like a shroud.

Is that wise?

I don't know what you're talking about.

Look J, I told you I can't be on your side.

I dropped my suitcase to the floor. The clasp unclicked
and spilled all my things about the room: shirts and
shaving cream and razors. Ash untucked her feet from
under her and slunk across the room to help me.

What side? I don't even know what you mean when
you say that? Whose side am I on?

Nobody. Nobody. That isn't what I meant—it's just
very complicated.

I don't feel like we're getting very far with this line of
conversation.

She bit her lip and handed me a bottle of shaving
cream that had rolled under the bed.

It isn't quite the same as when we last spoke. You
know how I said she came in to talk to Leila? Things
have changed. She spoke to Maria yesterday.

I had to sit down.

What are you talking about?

I was reading in the bath and well I must have
fallen asleep or something, but I woke up and Bina was
banging on the door. She said Ma was in the living room
and would I come down and so I went just like that in a
towel. They told me she'd been with them on the thakhat,
picking out the stitches in Bina's needlework.

My god.

Bina's been seeing her for days but that's different you know. Bina's always been so impressionable. She was always so quick to follow us into anything but Maria isn't like that—

I could see how it was different now. I knew. Maria held more sway, and not simply because she was the eldest. She was the worldly ideal the girls had followed their whole lives—the first to leave home, the first to dance at a wedding, the only one to marry. The only friend Ash had ever had. Unlike the girls, Ayesha never had even the most distant smattering of women friendships. Her whole life outside the home was concentrated on Khalajaan and myself. It was Maria she confided in, Maria whose sleep she shared.

What do you want me to do?

Ash had taken hold of my hands as we talked, her fingers folded over my own, and we were standing by the bed together. She dropped them now and took a step away from me. Outside, Leila reached out a leg and rubbed the cat with her bare foot.

I'm not asking you to do anything J. I only thought you might want to know that's all, she said, with her back turned to me.

There was no fixing it now. The car was ready and waiting, I had to catch the last boat out and Dada was waiting for me for dinner.

You should come and see me, I told her.

And what purpose, she smiled, Would that serve?

We could talk maybe. I'd like to see you, I said.

She shook her head.

I don't think that's such a good idea.

It might do you some good to get away from all this. Some time to think.

A thin strand of hair across her face, bright in the sun. I wanted to reach out to her, her skin pinking from the strain of our conversation, but I kept my hands in my pockets, the teeth of my keys biting into one palm.

My place is here, she said slowly, explaining it to both of us at once. I have to stay.

They're my family too you know.

And she shook her head again as if I didn't understand, but I did. It wasn't the same. It never would be.

VIII.

By October I was ready for winter, and so was the rest of the drenched city. The rains lasted longer than any year of my life. The times in between were quiet awe, the world washed new in the early morning and threads of sun through the shuttered office blinds. I was still living in the city. I didn't take down the posters of cricketers, I wore socks with the heels worn off them every day and the curtains lay to one side, but that didn't stop it all from feeling more permanent than I'd expected.

I'd been back just the once since the move. I had taken the boat out on a Saturday morning, hoping to surprise the girls, with bags of halwa puri packed into one of those plastic coolers Maria used for picnics.

Salaam saab, the cook said, when he opened the gate. It's good to see you back.

Have you been looking after the begums?

They're doing very well, he said. He leaned forward as he unloaded my things from the car and whispered, They seem much better to me. Leila bibi is eating again. They've even had visitors; their aunt has been coming over for tea every evening.

I knew Khalajaan never visited and that Mehrunissa's sisters hadn't come south even for weddings or funerals. It must be some woman from Manora. Maybe the shopkeeper's wife who ordered in the kind of newspapers Ash and I liked to read, or one of the Captain's old comrades had finally moved to the island and his wife had come over to pay her respects. It was hard to imagine the girls making a new friend, bringing someone into their fold.

I handed him the bags of food and headed upstairs. The curtains were still drawn, Leila and Bina were in our bed. They scrunched up their eyes when I opened the door and turned their head to me.

Jimmy! I didn't know you were coming home.

Leila swung her feet out of the bed and walked over to me. She was wearing one of her mother's nightgowns, the wide flap of cotton swirling around me as she got on her toes and shifted her hands to my neck.

You should have told us, she drawled, I'm not even dressed yet.

It was eleven. I brought breakfast, I told her. Halwa puri. The two of them screeched like schoolgirls and went barefoot down the marble stairs, shouting for their sisters as they went.

We gathered around the table, unwrapping the food from greasy newspapers. Each of them tucked in, with an appetite I'd not expected or seen for a long time. Soon they were all slick-fingered and smiling, voices jumping over each other in competing bids. The cat was sick, the guardsman on holiday, and the cook had learned two new dishes from recipes Maria cut out of her magazines, Leila was painting again.

I caught a fleck of green on her cheek, smudged from where she must have rubbed it into the pillow.

You're all very animated, I said. Bright-eyed and bushy-tailed.

But none of them looked directly at me, their firefly gazes flickered around the room. The room lit up electric with new storms still brewing, batting against the wires of the windowed courtyard. I lit a cigarette and concentrated on my wife. Her grin was lantern yellow, oily mouthed and sticky-toothed. Under the table, I felt her foot brush my calf. It was the most physical intimacy I'd been given in more than a month, and I had to stop my leg from kicking out.

We've missed you, she said. She removed the cigarette from my mouth without looking at me, and took a long drag. It was one of those funny cigarettes that businessmen always brought Dada from abroad—Sobranies, black with gold tips and a creamy ash, lasting for days.

Leila, who I'd never seen with a cigarette before, drew on it twice before passing it on to Maria and then even Bina, who coughed and screwed up her eyes.

Ash blinked at me over her own cigarette; she'd plucked one up first, even before me. She pulled down the sides of her mouth and looked straight between my eyebrows.

I found the Captain worse than before. There was a thick smell in the room, of old tea leaves and clothes left wet from where the rain had fought through the windows and soaked them. He hadn't been shaved in a while, the sides of his face grizzly and unfamiliar. He could have been anybody in that chair, greyed and hollowed out at his cheekbones and knuckles, lost under the swathe of his kurta.

I sat across from him and took his hand, bending my head to it.

Salaam, I said, and his milky eyes moved past me.

I tried again. How have you been?

There was a shift in the corridor behind me, the stir of a small cat entering a room, and then Bina. He's tired Jimmy. You should let him rest.

I dropped his hand and left the room. The Manto was still folded where I'd left it, not a page back or forth.

She came to me after lunch, straight from the bathtub, shiny-eyed and pulling the wet weight of her hair around our faces so I was lost in the dark. I half expected to find scales under Leila's clothes.

I'd been sitting on the swing in our room, going over the household accounts for the week before. It was still light enough that I only had the fan on, my papers were propped up by the window. These stormy days stretched out in one colour, the sun smudged constant through the clouds; clockless, we were without time.

She led me to the bed and I stopped thinking for the first time in months. The trapped static between our sheets and skins sent shocks through me every time we reached for each other. The electricity blew out again in the rain, and the palms of heat pressed on to our backs till there was sweat licking my spine. I felt an unimaginable grief. Those long hours of that afternoon, they seemed to go on for years, spilling into each other in a long grey line. Scrambling rationality to the jumble of other things, the flesh and bone of what things make us feel.

Leila dressed and walked over to her paints and with her fingers she brought the storm into our bedroom. Before she would paint mainly people but I saw now it was the trees outside our window that she was forming on the paper. The trees arching and bending to the rain and the sliver of the sea through their branches. I couldn't move. I'd heard of people going feverish in the summers, paralysed and breathless. I could have lived on that bed, sheets tangled south of my feet, for the rest of my life and it did not seem the heaviness would ever dissolve. The rains would keep me there overnight. I would be late to work the next morning, going in with a clean shirt that would get soaked before I reached the city. It was still coming down the next afternoon when the phone rang in my office. In the blackened-out windows between me and the rest of the workplace, I could see I still looked like Lazarus, raised from the dead.

IX.

I wasn't the only man at the office who got phone calls from his wife at work and maybe not even the only one no longer living with her. None of the girls ever picked up the phone when I rang. The last time I'd been at the house, we'd gotten into an argument about it and so Leila had taken to calling me instead, at strange and uncertain hours—early in the morning when I was not even yet up for work or else the early afternoon when the day at the office was finally kicking off.

She told me she'd been swimming in the sea. The month almost eaten up and no sign in hell of the rains letting up but when we spoke, she dropped it into the conversation as if it were nothing.

Bina and I have just been for a swim, she said. There was an odd lightness to her voice at the moment, clouds caught in her throat.

You're not serious? I asked. Leila you can't possibly be swimming in this weather.

It's harmless darling. Remember we would swim in the summer at your cousin's beach house? You were always so impressed by how good we were. We can handle a little rain.

A little rain? It's breaking down the city. There are parts of town that haven't had electricity in almost a month because every time they go to fix the cables, the storms bring down another part of them.

I didn't call you for a lecture, she said.

I want you to be safe. Promise me you won't go swimming till this has all stopped.

She sighed and I could hear the rest of the house in that noise. It had a grumbling music to it. Everything I said to them at this point seemed to go through some sort of filter, so they could keep what they wanted to hear and discard the rest. All of a sudden I understood how parents felt, how my grandfather must have spent so much of my childhood.

Maybe we can go in the winter, I went on. We could even go back to the beach house. I don't think anybody's used it since Maria and Amir. We could do it after Eid, and take a few days there.

That sounds lovely, she said. I should really go now— we're making puris. It's the cook's day off.

I put the receiver down and the pulsing ache behind my eyes started up again.

Grief was a strange and wild thing. When my parents died I was too small for it to fit in my head. There was no room for anything, even memories that might carry me out. Death could bring down worlds, start wars and upturn lives. Back at Dada's house, I stood by the big living room windows and though outside there was nothing but the storm breaking and waters rising, I thought I could see them.

It was early November when I went back next. The Captain was even slighter than before. The hum of his grunting and the comfortable noise of his breathing were replaced with the wheeze and gasp of a sick man. But his eyes darted around the room with a black restless energy. Maybe we should take him to the doctor, I suggested at last, when Maria came in with a tray of tea and biscuits. It was what no one was saying.

Grieving could stop talking, it could stop appetites and these were things I understood. But the Captain was a man unmade and I couldn't reconcile in my head what was being done to him. Here was a man being eaten alive. If I'd found a finger missing, gone to join his missing legs, or part of his throat rotted away it would not have surprised me.

Maria shook her head. Her hair was twisted over one shoulder in a single knot and it came undone with the motion, scattering over the embroidered flowers on her kurta.

He'll be fine Jimmy. He just needs time. These things take a long time to heal.

You cannot think it's grief, I said. Maria, he's sick.

Jimmy. Her tone was a warning. This was her teacher's voice: I thought we discussed this. You can't just take everything over.

Look, I said, I can bring a doctor over here. It doesn't have to be a big thing, we wouldn't have to take him anywhere. He'll just come to the house and have a look at him. And if there's nothing wrong then what's the harm?

It's sweet that you're so worried. You've always been so kind to us. But I just don't think it's necessary.

Silent by day, the Captain was a banshee in his sleep. He cried out all night, and either the words were in languages I didn't know, or his words were too garbled for me to piece them together.

Leila slept through it. I couldn't even keep my eyes shut. His screams howled through the house and its thick, solid walls, rising over the rain.

I got out of bed and went down for a glass of milk. I saw something shift in the windows.

The courtyard at midnight. Ash was hiding behind the pillars but I followed the smell of her, the patter of rain hiding my footsteps. I touched her shoulder and she shrieked, dropping the cigarette straight through her fingers.

What are you doing up? she asked, when we'd both dripped back into the house.

I shook the water out of my hair.

I don't know how any of you can sleep. He's obviously in pain.

Mmm. Want some tea?

I think I'm okay, I said, but she busied herself anyway, keeping her back to me.

I ran a hand over the arc of her shoulder and felt the wave of her muscles under my hand, her body going stiff and then soft. The cat slipped in between us, rubbing up against our ankles and I dropped my head to her instead, petting her neck.

Tell me what's happening.

Why do you always drag me into these things, J? Ask your wife.

You're the only person I know how to talk to any more Ash.

She tipped her head to the side, and her eyebrows went up as they always did.

I worry about all of you, I said. Is that so wrong?

Ash twisted around to face me, so she was leaning back against the marble counter. She laughed, a little. It's a little funny under the circumstances.

I spent the next few days out of my mind. I was calling up doctors by the hour and relaying the Captain's symptoms. When I offered to have them brought to the island, the girls bristled. They slipped around the idea until it disappeared. I went to homeopaths and talked to them about the loss of voice, about laryngitis and possible blindness, and what breaks a man. I sent over teas brewed in honey and talked to the cook over the phone, about home remedies for strength, for jaan. I even spoke to shrinks and head-doctor's because people could go mad with grief, it was known.

I called them from the office so Dada wouldn't hear me. My wife thinks she is bringing people back from the dead, I wanted to say, She is praying her mother back to life. But I didn't.

I couldn't bring myself to go over. I'd pack an overnight bag and drive out to the docks, and there were evenings and mornings where the rain would stop and the sun held me in its eye, but I just sat in my car.

I'd go back into the house from the backdoor to avoid seeing Dada, explaining to him the next morning why I was still here even though he would have heard the car coming up the driveway, would have seen the light on in my hallway.

There were days when he'd come and sit at the end of my bed. We never talked but I remembered then that he used to do this all the time after my parents died, on their birthdays or on the anniversary of their death—the softest comfort he knew how to give.

The way it worked now was that everything came without warning, in any case, and what could I do to stave off any of it. Ayesha came to the office one afternoon, without a phone call or message. I stepped out at lunch and saw her in the reception area. She was cross-legged, and there were chocolate wrappers spread around her, a styrofoam coffee cup by her book.

My secretary apologized. I wanted to tell you she was here, but madam told me it was a surprise.

Surprise, Ash said, pushing her Faulkner into my chest and tapping me on the cheek. Let's go. You're taking me to lunch.

The shadows under her eyes hidden behind the sunglasses, talking her usual mile a minute, she was more like herself again. We didn't talk about her sisters until after lunch, when Ash flipped up her glasses and asked if I would take her home.

I told her I had to check back in at the office. But yes, I could go back tonight. I'd never said no to her before.

It was hot again, the streets burning slowly back to life. Roads were still waterlogged and people pushed their cars to work and children walked to school with water up to their waists, but the sun was out. The sun was out and at no other time in my history had the people of Karachi been so glad of it.

No, she said, I don't want to go back to our house for a bit. I paused, and slid over, letting her drive instead.

I let her take us to their house. I'd always liked the way she looked behind the wheel, the long lines of her arms taut, how she pushed her sunglasses farther up on her nose, even how liberal she was with the horn. She drove as if she were going into war; rolled down the windows and shouted kutta at anyone she thought was trying to cut her off.

I'd not been prepared for this visit. There were no real plans to sell this place. Dada had suggested it to me a few months ago but I'd thought then that everything was still too fresh for the girls.

You look different you know, she said, as she stepped towards me in the empty front room. I never told you when you came back but my god you're a different person.

Am I?

She ran a hand over my belly, slipped her hands up under my shirt. Well for one thing there's so much more of you now.

I smiled and pulled her hands away, catching her wrists together.

That's not very nice.

It's not the only thing, though. Everything about you is a little different.

Not that different, I hope. Not different in a bad way.

Don't do that. Don't pretend you haven't noticed, I hate that. You know the problem with people who go away is that they spend so much time thinking of all that's gone differently in their lives, and no time at all thinking of how other people might have changed. You come back and you expect us all to be here, just waiting for you in our places. I expect you thought we'd all be at the table in our same seats as always with a candle lit for you. Just pining and waiting.

She moved to where the dining table had been, marking its oval shape, standing at the head of that phantom table.

I didn't think that at all, I said.

Of course you did. People always do. It's why my parents stopped talking. He obviously thought he'd come home to the same wife every time. Never even moving from her chair while he was gone.

I thought your parents were always sort of happy myself, I replied. As happy as anyone is I guess.

You would think that. You've always managed to rose tint everything about our lives. And maybe it is romantic in a way—a love marriage and all that. But if you don't even live together for more than fifteen years, how well can you even know each other? By the time he came home from the war, Ma had got so used to being on her own she could barely stand to live with him. He was always around, with his leg he hardly ever left the house. She said it was like having her freedom taken away.

Okay, I said. Who knew where this was going?

Ahead of me in the disappearing light of the dining room, Ash spun around. It was a stranger's and even a dancer's movement, a half pirouette, and she stood at the other end of the room from me and grinned.

Well I guess you don't like to think of that, she said. It works better in your head if we're all perfect. You just smooth over the rockier truths.

What I wanted was to crack the veneer the girls were building. To tell Ash that her father was dying, her sisters were lost to the world. None of them had seen or spoken to a person outside the island in months. These were the rockier truths to me but it had never been easy to argue with Ash. When we were younger I was always aware of how much cleverer she was than me but that hadn't got easier. It was impossible to separate anything I said from how I felt, so I kept quiet. I was only glad she was here, that we were alone together again.

Behind us was the garden where all those years ago I'd made a fool of myself. The light filtered through the windows like dust, time shifted in my head. Ash came back towards me, boneless and lighter than air. Nothing else moved this way. She put her hands in mine and led me through the rest of the rooms. The heat of her words was gone, and we moved through the house as quiet as churches.

Why are we here, I asked, when we'd made our way up to the roof.

She folded down to the floor. Maybe, she said, crossing her legs, I wanted to see how much you remember.

I spread open my arms. Ask me anything.

Ash grinned up at me and held out her hands till I was next to her. I caught her wrists and let gravity drag me down. There was no space in my head to understand anything other than feeling that something was fizzing up inside me, as if someone had cracked open a bottle of beer in my gut, my rib cage all suds. We hid behind the low wall around the roof and lay on our backs.

This was where we'd come up to see the moon on chand raat. Before I knew the girls, I would stand on my own roof just a few feet away and sneak off before they saw me.

You know I don't remember anything about my mother from the day she died. I went out to the shops around noon and didn't come back for another hour or so. I took my time, she said, I wasn't in any real hurry to get back. It had been so depressing in the house—Bina had been sick for weeks at this point and when Ma caught it too, we just lost hope. It was like living in a hospital, all sick rooms and wet cloths. And when I got back she was almost gone. I was so confused I didn't even say anything—not even goodbye.

I'm sorry, I said.

I'm not telling you because I want you to feel sorry for me. I'm just saying, I've always been so distant from everybody. And now, she said, taking a breath, They can all see her but me.

Ash, I said softly. You don't believe that's real.

This isn't a game Jimmy. She stood up and snatched her hand out of mine. Either you take me seriously or you don't.

We drove back to the docks in silence. In the evenings, this late, the shore looked so final that I understood why people used to think the world was flat.

Ash turned to me before she stepped out of the car. The dark shifted and I could see her only in the lamp light. The whole of her face was smudged.

Remember, she said, Resurrection is real. We will all rise up again in the afterlife. If it can happen there it can even happen here. This is all God's soil. She sounded just like Leila then. I couldn't tell if she was smiling or not, the hollow tone of her voice hovering between us.

She shut the door and walked and she looked just like her as well, like Leila when she walked away from me the first time I told her I wanted her, like Maria the night she decided to marry Amir, like Bina when she told me that the war was beginning.

In my sleep, the house on Manora island was crumbling. It collapsed into the sea the way a biscuit is destroyed by the dregs of a cup of tea. I tried to save the girls, tried to wrest them back from the water, but their bodies were, logged with the salt and the sea, too heavy even to hold on to me. Somebody was telling me to let go, perhaps it was many people, perhaps it was the Captain and Amir and my grandfather. Speaking all at once, discordant, the way maulvis call to prayer across Karachi, just seconds out of sync with each other.

I splashed farther into the sea, the water never rising about my waist as I went. Already, I couldn't reach them.

X.

I never forgot: the last time I spoke to Ash how she was struck through with fear.

When we were younger Ash was unscareable. Ghost stories and djinn stories and stories told when the light went out and it was nothing but darkness in the house and the rest of us sweating in the hot night and the stench of fear—these did nothing to her. Her iron will, her scoff, that way she had of raising one eyebrow and saying Don't be ridiculous. How the unseen to her was nothing but a fairy story, only interesting to her if it was well told, a good story.

I never forgot: it was a Sunday, when Dada came in to tell me that there was a call for me. I'd heard the phone ringing, a few hours before. It was just before midnight. I'd come home late. I had sat out by the docks for three hours, something in me calling to the water and the rest of me unable to move.

Who is it? I scrambled up in bed. I hadn't taken phone calls this late since my gambling days and those had been a matter of precision; me waiting by the phone to catch that ringing before it woke Dada.

It was Ayesha. She was thunder.

She didn't sound distant any more. It was seven years' worth of her. Her voice came tunnelled down as if through hills. What was happening to the rest of them was happening to her too, at last.

I know you don't believe, she said. But you were right about Abba at least. He won't live long this way.

It took me some hours to make the journey over. I scrambled, though I didn't know if I even had any time left. There were no boats that went through the night, but Dada knew someone who kept smaller boats of his own, for crabbing. I showed up at the old friend's door at one in the morning, and he came to answer it in his pyjamas, hollering down at me from the top of the stairs in his baritone that it was not for traveling in at this time of the night—but I took it anyway.

It was only three or four hours to light now, but I could not wait for the first boat out, could not wait for Dada to dress, could not wait for the banker to explain to me how to properly dock his boat.

The door was unlocked. I went through the house calling their names. There were lights on in the living room, but nobody there. I tracked through the bedrooms and the baths.

When I saw the Captain, I called for a doctor. He was stiff in the chair and I could not even make myself go into the room.

There was no one on the roof, nobody else in the back garden or the courtyard. I plucked up the cat and cradled her to my chest, her small body alive with a pulsing panic. I took him down and walked out the back.

I followed the footprints to the shore still calling their names, Kiran's nails scraping through my shirt. The cook must have followed me.

I saw the begums go out a few minutes ago sahib, he said. I told them it wasn't the weather to swim, I did. But they didn't listen to me.

Listen sahib should I call the guards? Should I get a boat?

Before us the tide was rising. There was nothing I knew to be done.

Years later, I would not remember turning from the sea to go back into the house and find the Captain without a pulse. I sat by him till a doctor arrived and then a coroner, his hand growing cold in my own. I would forget sleeping that night on the island, alone, Dada begging me to come home. And I knew that when I woke finally to walk the house, that it would empty of their secrets, their smells, the more intimate clues.

Ayesha's manuscripts, tucked up in envelopes, ready to be sent off only weeks earlier, would be nowhere. Leila's paintings, rolled up in our bedroom, would disappear. Nothing real was left.

The weeks and months that would pass without meaning—I would only remember the light on the water, the early gold of it coming through the storm.

Beyond the disappearing trace of footprints, I could see the girls walking into the water.

They would have waded in one after the other. Their legs blued with cold and nervousness, the inky sea sucking them in. I could see them sinking in their winter clothes. Fossilized in the muddy salt beds, tucked into this new world and turning to coral. I know you don't believe, she had said.

I'd never really believed in anything. The future would learn that they did not live as other women. The future would find them breathing underwater, as easy as fish.

Acknowledgements

My parents, Shehla and Owais Hasin, who raised me in a house full of books. The Agha clan who made everything possible, Nasrat, Asim, Shezie, Gurya and Meher. My cousins, Shahmeer and Shahtaj who still don't think I'm clever enough to have written a book.

David Godwin, without whom finishing the novel might never have occurred to me and Rajni George who understood it so well.

Daisy Johnson, Kiran Millwood Hargrave and Tom de Freston sat across the table while I wrote this and made sure my fingers kept moving. Julia Armfield and Isobel Woodger for the most constant, immediate support that made the long days shorter. Iva Bilanovic and Miranda Samuels across the pond. The early readers at Oxford who helped shape this: Alice Jolly, Michael Collins and all of the Unruly Writers, who were generous with their wisdom and support. And all my friends, who lent me their ears, their bookshelves and their time, most especially: Gabby Penfold, Jess(s) Oliver and Widdowson, Sophia House, Olivia Majumdar, Tia Ali and Natalya Din Kariuki.